D1626143

County Council Library

2152382

The Opposite Bastard

SIMON PACKHAM

The Opposite Bastard

Macmillan New Writing

First published 2008 by Macmillan New Writing
an imprint of Pan Macmillan Ltd
Pan Macmillan, 20 New Wharf Road, London N1 9RR
Basingstoke and Oxford
Associated companies throughout the world
www.panmacmillan.com

ISBN 978-0-230-71242-3

Copyright © Simon Packham 2008

The right of Simon Packham to be identified as the
author of this work has been asserted by him in accordance
with the Copyright, Designs and Patents Act 1988.

All rights reserved. No part of this publication may be
reproduced, stored in or introduced into a retrieval system, or
transmitted, in any form, or by any means (electronic, mechanical,
photocopying, recording or otherwise) without the prior written
permission of the publisher. Any person who does any unauthorized
act in relation to this publication may be liable to criminal
prosecution and civil claims for damages.

1 3 5 7 9 8 6 4 2

A CIP catalogue record for this book is available
from the British Library.

Typeset by Intype Libra Ltd
Printed and bound in Great Britain by MPG Books Ltd
Bodmin, Cornwall

This book is sold subject to the condition that it shall not,
by way of trade or otherwise, be lent, re-sold, hired out,
or otherwise circulated without the publisher's prior consent
in any form of binding or cover other than that in which
it is published and without a similar condition including this
condition being imposed on the subsequent purchaser.

Visit www.panmacmillan.com to read more about all our books
and to buy them. You will also find features, author interviews and
news of any author events, and you can sign up for e-newsletters
so that you're always first to hear about our new releases.

For Deborah

When one door closes, they all bloody shut.

Max Miller (attrib.)

Prologue
Autumn 1999

The Actor

My Restart interview seemed to be going swimmingly. She was a middle-aged woman with glasses and Marks & Spencer clothes. I was charming her with 'tales from the green room' when all of a sudden she turned nasty: 'This can't go on, Mr Salt.'

'What do you mean?' I eyed her suspiciously. It was at this point that they usually asked if I'd been in *EastEnders*.

'We've given you more than enough time' (six paltry months) 'to find work in your usual profession. I'm afraid you're going to have to cast your net a little wider.'

Nigh on twenty years in the acting profession had given me a solid grounding in DHSS form filling. Somewhere along the line, however, I had made a crucial error. In a mad fit of affected altruism, which almost brought a tear to my eye, in the box titled 'What other types of work are you looking for?' I had foolishly entered 'Working with the disabled.' Set amidst my customary list of 'impossibles' (television presenter, university lecturer, jingles composer) I felt it represented a lovely touch of humanity in what was perhaps a somewhat media oriented and thrusting character sketch. I little realized that, six months later, it would return to haunt me.

'Actually, there is something that's just come in,' she said, running her tongue along the suspicion of a Ronald Colman tash. 'It might be right up your street.'

I smiled a horrible smile.

'You've got a degree, haven't you?'

'Yees.' (Drama BA Hons – red brick.) 'But I don't see how . . .'

When I first entered the acting profession dole offices were cold uninviting places, with lino floors, that smelt of cigarettes and damp clothes. By the late nineties they were carpet-tiled throughout and in my view they'd started overheating them. I think it must have been the heat, because for the next ten minutes I caught only snatches of what she was saying: 'Very bright . . . profoundly disabled . . . virtually twenty-four-hour care.'

My hands were sweating. All I could do was nod confusedly.

'You see, you did turn down the job at the butcher's and the trainee financial adviser. So I'm afraid, if you don't go along for the interview, we'll have to stop all your benefits.'

Actors get used to futile journeys to far-flung corners of the capital. Tattered *A to Z* in pocket, we brave London Transport for a couple of minutes in a church hall with the director and the seldom-kept promise to 'let you know'. It was in this spirit that I set off for East Croydon, not thinking for one minute there was any danger of a job at the end of it. The sight of an efficient-looking lady, clad in full nursing regalia, coming out of the house just as I arrived merely confirmed this.

I was met at the door by a harassed, bird-like figure in a flannelette tracksuit. With her pale, elfin face, and hair scraped back into a ponytail, she had the look of a fifty-year-old schoolgirl who hadn't had a decent night's kip for about a thousand years.

'Hello, dear, I'm Valerie Owen. I'll be with you in a minute. I've just got to see to Michael.'

She ushered me into a cold sitting room with flowery wallpaper and some Wedgwood Victorian ladies in a mahogany cabinet. At some stage they'd 'knocked through' into the back room and put up some sliding doors. Behind the frosted glass I could just make out the glow of an electric fire, and the sound of the lady who had admitted me offering words of encouragement. 'There we are, Michael, *all* done.'

There was a framed copy of that ghastly religious poem 'Footprints' on the mantelpiece and, lurking in the shadows, a fading photograph of a young family on a beach somewhere. My eyes were drawn immediately to the pretty young mum in a flowery bikini, handing out sandwiches.

'Sorry to keep you waiting, Timothy,' said the flannel-etted lady. 'Now, they said at the jobcentre you've had some experience in this area.'

3

So confident was I that this was but a slight inconvenience on the road to my next giro that I felt quite at liberty to come up with a little white lie. 'Not particularly, but I did do some work with disabled youngsters during my university vacations.'

She seemed strangely unperturbed. 'Experience isn't everything, you know, dear. It's a gift. You've either got it or you haven't.'

It was at this point that I started to panic. If only I'd had the presence of mind to come up with a watertight excuse, things might have worked out very differently.

'Before we go through and meet Michael, let me just tell you a bit about him.'

She was one of those people who find it difficult to keep still; perching for a moment on the edge of an armchair before rising suddenly to brush some imaginary dust from an ornament. 'When he goes up to Oxford, he's going to need a permanent carer. I've offered to do it myself, of course, but Michael thinks it would be too much for me.'

It was a pretty comprehensive job description. The 'successful' applicant would be responsible for keeping him clean, feeding him, dressing and undressing him, administering his medication, putting him to bed and getting him up, as well as accompanying him to tutorials and taking notes where necessary. In fact, it made working at McDonald's sound like a wonderful career opportunity.

'I think it's about time you met Michael, don't you?'

I nodded grimly. She drew open the doors to reveal a shrivelled figure in a wheelchair. His small floppy body, coupled with a huge-looking head, gave him the appearance of a ventriloquist's dummy. With a computer screen in front of him and a Dalek's plunger strapped to his forehead, he continued to make a series of jerky nodding movements.

Mrs Owen looked on proudly. 'It's wonderful, isn't it? He controls the wheelchair by sucking and blowing, and uses the wand – that's the thing attached to his head – to work his computer.'

I only wish now I'd followed my instincts and made a run for it, but I was drawn inexorably towards the edge of the cliff and the rocks below. 'Yes, that's most . . .'

'Now, Michael, I want you to meet Timothy Salt.'

'Hello, Timothy,' he said in a breathy treble. 'I hope you know your way around a colostomy bag.'

When Mrs Owen phoned me that evening with the 'good news', I tried to persuade her that as I was a jobbing actor there was always the danger that some theatre work might crop up. This didn't seem to bother her unduly. 'We'll cross that bridge if we come to it.'

Given my lack of references and a total ignorance of all matters quadriplegic, I couldn't have been more surprised if they'd offered me a year's contract at the National Theatre. Naturally I tried to worm my way out of it, but down at the jobcentre they were adamant. I was faced with what I believe is known in literary circles as a 'catch-22': accept the worst job in the history of the world, or forfeit all my benefits and end up sleeping in the doorway of one of the theatres in which I have sometime performed.

When Sorrows Come

The Virgin

Sod formal hall. Mummy's been texting me again, so I'm gasping for one of my specials. You won't believe this, but I honestly thought that teaching Mummy to use her mobile would be a bit of a giggle. How was I supposed to know she'd only use it to torture me with?

Plus which, this morning I had the shock of my life. Can you blame a girl for wanting a well-balanced meal after all that? I scoop an emergency saucer of 20p coins into the front pocket of my rucksack, slap on another coat of lippy, and hotfoot it through college to the vending machines outside the buttery. I hover while that hideous nympho from the Ents committee makes off with her Mars Bar, and then I pounce. I'm getting good at this. I force-feed the machine thirty pieces of silver and tap in the combination. It helps when you know it off by heart. Two minutes later I'm cantering back across the quad with a bag full of swag slung carelessly over my shoulder.

And that's when I see him: the shock of my life I was talking about. He's sitting by the window with that pointy thing stuck to his forehead, staring into his computer; all lit up like something out of the Chamber of Horrors. He did tell me his name, my new neighbour, but, quite frankly, I was trying so hard not to stare at all his . . . paraphernalia that I hardly caught a word he was saying. Don't get me wrong, I think it's really sweet that there's a guy like that in college. I just wish someone had warned me about him. If I'd been expecting a funny little man in a wheelchair I wouldn't have made such an idiot of myself; which is why I cover my face like a convict as I scurry past his window.

Safe at last; *Quatuor pour la fin du Temps* on the CD player, the door locked, and I'm already feeling calmer. I clear a space on the desk between my Italian Lute tablature and that lovely picture of Tom and Maggie (God, how I miss them), and pour out my contraband.

There are usually about forty-five Jelly Tots in a packet. I sort them into colours (eight green, fifteen purple, ten orange and eight red this time) before opening the Hula Hoops (thirty-four plus one broken one, which I eat) and breaking the KitKat. It has to be symmetrical – my confectionery collage of Mummy – otherwise it doesn't work: Diet Coke for the body, KitKat arms and legs, and Jelly Tots for the fingers, eyes, nose and mouth. Hula Hoops are perfect for her hair. They remind me of when she went blonde for her thirtieth birthday party, just before she and Daddy had their big falling out.

I don't know why it makes me feel better, but it does. And don't go thinking it's one of those fashionable new 'eating disorders', because actually it's quite the opposite – the order is the most important part of all. I start with the hair (savoury first, of course), next the arms and legs, followed by the fingers and three sips of Diet Coke. I leave her eyes until last. It's only after I've swallowed the final Jelly Tot that I feel strong enough to re-read her message: 'If you don't bring home a boyfriend a.s.a.p., will kill myself.'

It might sound like a joke, but I know Mummy better than that. She's absolutely desperate to get me started on a breeding programme; anything to take her mind off her own miserable existence. All summer, she touted me round Hampshire like a best of breed: *'Toby Morton's a terribly decent young man. You'd make such a lovely couple, Anna darling.'* Every weekend, she'd frogmarch me to the Range Rover so Daddy could chauffeur me to another grisly melange of marquees, jazz bands and industrial quantities of champagne, Chablis and al fresco copulation. Every weekend, I'd find the table furthest from the disco and lose myself in the Penguin edition of *Middlemarch*; exchanging George Michael for George Eliot whilst everyone around me exchanged email addresses and bodily fluids. As a general rule, I prefer to get hot and sticky with a melted packet of Opal Fruits.

So I haven't told anyone about tomorrow night. Mummy would put a full-page announcement in *Horse and Hound* if she knew I had an 'appointment' with a young gentleman – especially a young gentleman with such good breeding potential. And I'm certainly not admitting to anyone (not even myself) that I'm actually rather looking forward to it. He's different all right. Daddy always said I was a hopeless romantic.

The Quadriplegic

Oxford sucks; a piss-poor combination of pretty-boys on bicycles, double-barrelled Victorias, and rotting, Gothic follies specially designed to be a total nightmare for a guy in a spaz-chariot.

They've never had a proper crip in college before. Must have been almost as traumatic as when they had to start letting women in. That old git in the porter's lodge nearly shat himself when he saw how they'd desecrated his beloved college with a skateboarder's paradise of concrete ramps, just to accommodate Wheelchairboy.

I didn't want to come here anyway. There's a much better course at Sussex. I mean, who gives a gnat's bollock about *Beowulf*? I picked up enough Anglo-Saxon on the streets of East Croydon. But according to my sponsors (thanks to my abnormally high IQ I'm a pin-up boy for state-of-the-art surgical appliances and kick-arse spaz-chariots) it's essential for product recognition to be seen in all the 'right' places. So that's how I became the first all-non-singing, all-non-dancing, 'high' quadriplegic at Gloucester College Oxford – that and to please Mum, of course.

Mum's been wetting her knickers ever since I got my acceptance letter. At last, she had it in black and white; written proof, on posh notepaper, that all the years of blood, shit and vomit had been worth it. But more than that (much, much more) it meant that – in a 'God moves in a mysterious way' sense – her prayers had been answered.

Every Saturday, she played hostess to the Women's Prayer Group. She'd dump me in front of *The Generation Game* and I could hear them, through the sliding doors, praying for a miracle. I'd sit there sipping drinking chocolate through a stripy straw, wondering if Jim Davidson was truly happy in his work and wishing that Mum would take up something more worthwhile, like bingo. At the end of the evening, one by one, they'd stick their heads in and ask me how my studies were going. The weekend before my Oxbridge interview, Pastor Reg led the whole fellowship in an all-night fast and meditative vigil. How come they call themselves charismatics when they're all so fucking boring?

Put it this way, I owed her one. Mum hadn't had much to cheer about on school sports days, so who was I to deny her her one moment of glory? And to tell you the truth, I couldn't wait to get away from her endless yakking. Mum loves to talk, you see; in tongues when the spirit moves her. Dad claimed he'd had a premonition that he was going to die in a car crash. Mum thought it was dead romantic. Every time they went for a drive, he'd kiss her on the head and whisper, '*I love you*,' and then refuse to speak for the rest of the journey because in the event of an accident he wanted those to be his final words.

Me? I don't talk much. It's called laconic. But I'll tell you something; when I *do* open my mouth, you can bet everyone is listening. It doesn't look good to ignore someone like me – especially if you're out shopping with your girlfriend. Which is why people tend to remember a quadriplegic's name first time. Although in my case, the fact that I'm called Michael Owen probably helps.

You're probably wondering how I ended up with a carer like Billy No Mates. There were five applicants for the McJob, four of them female – two quite horny. But Mum couldn't stand the thought of another woman emptying my colostomy bag, so the gig went to the no-hope bit-player who'd been 'resting' long enough to qualify for the latest government rent-a-slave scheme. If you could see his look of disgust when he's cleaning my teeth, or the way he winces when he's creaming my bedsores, you'd understand why it wasn't exactly love at first sight.

He says he's an actor, but I've never heard of him. Is there anything sadder than a middle-aged man in a baseball cap? A middle-aged man who wears his baseball cap the wrong way round perhaps? That's Timothy Salt all over. With his monastic slaphead and blubbery paunch tumbling out of his easy-fit jeans, he's got 'sad fucking failure' written all over him. But he's always going on about his brilliant career. Unfortunately for me, slitting my wrists is not an option.

The Actor

Have you ever seen *Hamlet*? If you move to the bottom of the cast list – I don't mean Osric, not Fortinbras, not even a Norwegian Captain or one of the English Ambassadors

– then, in a top-of-the-range, uncut, sixty-five-hour *Hamlet*, you will notice the Lords, Ladies, Soldiers, Sailors *and* Attendants. For two years I was one of those attendants. (First cover English Lord. Second cover Osric.) If I ever catch up with the prize cunt who claimed that there are 'no small parts in Shakespeare', I shall have a few choice words for him.

I cannot pretend that the Attendant, or Blandio as my agent (Bunny Michelmore at Bunny Michelmore Management) klepped him for the purposes of my curriculum vitae, is the most rewarding part in the Shakespearean canon, yet it was for this role that I was offered some of my most encouraging criticism. It transpired that during the London run of 'The Happy Prince' we were asked to give a Sunday afternoon matinee in Broadmoor. Some of the younger actors were very excited about it, but I have to be honest and say that having played my Attendant both in Stratford and at the Barbican some hundred times already, the prospect of giving up my Sunday afternoon to entertain a bunch of psychopaths did little to enhance my customary *joie de vivre*.

During the informal gathering for tea and biscuits after the show, a rather shy serial killer sought me out. At first I thought he must have been looking for Rosencrantz. Everyone was always saying how alike we were. You might remember him from those amusing life assurance commercials where he finds out that although he's got cancer, insurance wise, he's well set up for a slow and lingering death. Well, if you think of him you'll get some idea of what

I'm like. Physically, that is – personally, he's a total arse-hole.

But the point is, it *was* me that he'd been searching for. He didn't look me in the eye, just stared at my feet. His voice sounded flat, like a comedian on a chat show trying to prove how dull he is in real life: '*I wanted you to know that as soon as you came on stage I couldn't take my eyes off you. That way you had of being there and yet not being there. It felt like my life – thanks.*'

As an actor that's the sort of thing you live for.

The Quadriplegic

I was born for the first time on 21 January 1980. I don't remember much about that but according to Mum, I was the best-looking baby in the universe. I was born again on 8 August 1989. Not Pastor Reg's kind of born again, but the quadriplegic kind. I dived into the shallow end of Croydon Lido as Superman and – after six months in a metal straitjacket, sharp spikes twisted into my scalp to keep my neck in place – I emerged again as Wheelchairboy: a drooling, *fin de siècle* superhero. What could be more perfect for the ironic nineties?

Now for the science bit: I am a C4 'high' quadriplegic. I have full head and neck movement, but I'm completely paralysed from the neck down. I can breathe without a ventilator, but require assistance to drain my secretions. Despite the assumptions of the average loser in the street, I am more than able to think for myself. The trouble is, it's easy to get the wrong idea about someone who's totally dependent on the kindness of strangers for his bowel management. To put it in layman's terms, my head is in full working order, but the rest of me's totally fucked. I can nod, raise my eyebrows (but not independently like Roger Moore) and even touch my nose with my tongue. I can also talk, but because my lungs are well dodgy, my voice sounds like an effeminate nine-year-old's, so I have a special microphone built into my wheelchair.

Mum thanks God, about once every five minutes, that he's given me the opportunity to study at the 'finest university in the world'. Believe me, it's small consolation for the fact that I can do sod all else.

I wish they'd all leave me alone. The same thing happened when I went back to school. The other kids fussed around me for the first few days, but as soon as they realized I was never going to be up for a kick around, they left me to it. I'm hoping the same thing's going to happen at Oxford, but right now I'm quite the celebrity. Every society in the university wants a piece of the Spackmeister: the Christian Union, the Gilbert and Sullivan Society, the Humanist Group, Gay Soc (a homosexual quadriplegic, what a feather in their camp that would be), the Model Railway Society, the Munchkins (some sort of drinking club) and even the Boat Club have all sent representatives. This really pisses off my thespian jailer. From what he's told me about his so-called 'career', Timothy Salt isn't exactly used to being the centre of attention, but by the way he mutters under his breath when they walk straight past him, you'd have thought he was some kind of superstar.

The Actor

I've spent most of the first week (there's probably some fancy Latin name for it at Oxford) lying in my cell, railing against the injustice of it all. It's my intention to keep all contact with Ironside to the bare minimum. Consequently, I avoid our shared sitting room whenever possible, emerging only to scrutinize the soaps for all the talentless bastards who got the jobs that I should have had.

Although our domestic arrangements might seem palatial to an undergraduate at the University of Littlehampton, for a man accustomed to his own heated towel rail they are indescribably squalid. I've had to settle for the bare essentials: transistor radio, coffee-making machine, electric grinder, a limited selection of pornography, the Purrfect Pussy, a little tome entitled *Be Your Own Psychotherapist in One Weekend*, and some photographs of myself. Mrs Owen insists on enquiring after her son at least twice a day; consequently (horror of horrors) I've been shanghaied into purchasing my first mobile telephone. At least it means I don't have to tell my agent (Bunny Michelmore at Bunny Michelmore Management) that I've moved out of town.

It seems that the world and his wife want Michael to join their clubs. I feel like good old Jeeves. The raspberry ripple isn't exactly a treasure domestically speaking, so I'm forced to play the faithful retainer. Incidentally, I do think, in a couple of years' time, it's quite possible that I may have acquired sufficient *gravitas* to graduate to butler roles. Bunny is always complaining: '*The trouble is, darling,*

you're neither fish nor fowl. You're not quite the typical
young husband, but you're not exactly the vile seducer
either.' I'm not even forty until next month. It's only a
matter of time before I come into my own.

'I need to speak to Michael. Is he around?'

You may have noticed that I can't be arsed with all the
Oxbridge bollocks. Descriptions of ancient limestone buildings, amusing old blokes in bowler hats telling you to keep
off the grass, and willows weeping into rivers that aren't
pronounced the way they're spelt. I can't be arsed because
for one thing Oxford is so beautiful that it makes me
want to vomit (Stendhal's syndrome, I believe) and for
another, it's all summed up for me in the spotty twenty-
year-old standing in the doorway.

'It's Sidney,' he says. 'Philip Sidney as in . . .'

For the most part he looks like any other twenty-year-
old: combat trousers, several layers of slightly too big stuff,
old-fashioned trainers, stupid little beard, and a stud in his
nose. But there's something in his voice, a pimply confi-
dence, call it arrogance if you like, so that even the way he
shuffles his feet has a thin batsqueak of Oxbridge self-
importance about it. Already you can detect the latent
judge, chat-show host, drugs baron or prime minister
inside the adolescent's body. Walk through the corridors of
power – the BBC, the House of Commons, even the sodding National Theatre (if I get really pissed I'll tell you what
that bitch of a casting director said to me) – and it's a voice
you'll hear again and again and again. Call it red-brick

peevishness if you will, but I do know what I'm talking about.

Consequently, I make a point of ignoring the grubby hand that Master Philip Sidney has extended in front of me. 'I'll go and see if he's available.'

The Quadriplegic

I've been having some fun with De Niro. I can see how much he hates it, so I rub in the master/servant thing at every opportunity. 'Would you mind getting us a cup of tea, Tim? I'm parched.'

'No sugar, just a dash of milk,' says the guy with the nose stud, waving imperiously at De Niro as he slopes off to commune with his kettle.

What is it this time? Do the rugger buggers want me to be their mascot? 'I'm Michael by the way. But I expect you knew that.'

'Look, Michael, I'll come straight to the point,' he says, making to shake my hand, but realizing straight away that he's made a terrible faux pas. 'Shit . . . sorry.' One of my few pleasures in life is watching the 'able-bodied' squirm as they attempt to decide the correct way to greet a quadriplegic. In the end he settles for a French-style peck on both cheeks, which I guess is quite cool. 'It's Philip, Philip Sidney, as in . . . I'm at Wuggins.'

'So, Philip, what can I do for you?'

He has the same gleam in his eye as Pastor Reg when he's about to 'lead someone to the Lord' or a timeshare salesman moving in for the kill. 'Actually, it's what I can do for you. I'm from Histrio-Mastix.'

(Who are they when they're at home?) 'Right, yeah . . . great.'

'We're not the biggest dramatic society in Oxford, but I'm pretty damn sure we're the most exciting.'

When I was in year six, Miss Minnings had the happy task of casting me in *The Grumpy Shepherd*. A speaking part was obviously out of the question, so she covered me in an old rug, clipped on a pair of sticky-out donkey's ears and sat me behind the manger. 'Right – OK. I'm just not sure how I can help you, Philip.'

All the time he's been casing the joint; nosing around for things to make him feel superior, like an uncool book or CD. I do it all the time. Suddenly, he drops his voice to a seductive whisper. 'Do you know *Hamlet*, Michael?'

De Niro totters out of his room with three mugs of Earl Grey on a plastic tray; ears pricked priapically, like my non-speaking ass. 'Did someone mention the Bard?'

The Actor

I'm intrigued. The thing about being an actor is that you must always be on your guard. On no account reveal your best credits straight away, just in case the spotty young bloke, who says he's in the business, turns out to be playing the lead in the new Mike Leigh film. (Don't you hate it when English people call them 'movies'?) Of course, eight times out of ten all he'll have done is some German

Expressionist buffoonery in a phone box at the Edinburgh Festival. In which case, you may feel free to destroy them with all the self-effacing name-dropping you can muster. The bearded twerp is only a student, so, clearly, I have nothing to fear.

The Quadriplegic

It's pathetic. Why do actors always piss their pants when someone mentions Shakespeare? 'I did the last *Hamlet* at the Barbican, actually,' says De Niro, looking as if he's expecting a standing ovation.

'Ghastly, wasn't it?' says Philip. 'I took Mother. She was pretty angry, I don't mind telling you.'

Three mugs of Earl Grey almost go flying. 'Well, Michael Billington said that—'

'Do you mind, I'm talking here. Come on, Michael, you haven't answered my question. Do you know *Hamlet*?'

Now it's my turn for a bit of shameless bragging. 'I know it.'

To be fair to the arrogant tosser, it's virtually impossible for anyone other than a child *not* to look down on someone in a wheelchair. 'How do you mean, you *know* it?'

'I mean I know it.'

'What, you mean you've read it a few times, seen Gibson in the movie?'

Out in the quadrangle, I catch a glimpse of that fit bird from the staircase above. I know her name's Anna because she came down to introduce herself at the beginning of the week. She must have been the only person in Oxford who hadn't heard about the cripple in residence, because when she saw me, her face turned the same colour as her baggy red jumper and she could barely string a sentence together. Put it this way, I don't think she'll be making a return visit.

'Come on, Michael. I'm waiting.'

'I mean, I know it by heart. The . . . er, First Folio.'

Like I say, I've got a brilliant memory. But don't be too impressed, it's just a party trick. Or it would be if I ever got invited. What you've got to understand is that spending your life in a spaz-chariot is like being one of those old buggers who keeps banging on about how great it was before television – you have to make your own entertainment. Incredible though it might sound, I've never been in huge demand as a tennis partner, so I've had to amuse myself by doing stuff like memorizing the England football teams since 1900 (including the war-time friendlies) or 1938 railway timetables. Mum's always on at me to have a go at the New Testament, but on the whole, it does have to be something you believe might have some practical use.

Philip Sidney sounds like one of those Old Testament prophets that Pastor Reg is so keen on. 'Michael, that's . . . terrific. I don't like to say this, but it must be fate.'

'Fate, eh?' says De Niro. 'I like the sound of that.'

'You see, Michael, I've thought long and hard about this, and I've come to the unassailable conclusion that there is only one man in Oxford with the requisite skills and experience to play Hamlet.'

F/2152 382

COUNTY LIBRARY

The Actor

Perhaps I've misjudged the young tyro. I'm not one to trumpet my successes abroad, so I don't have a clue how he discovered that I'm an actor; I'm just relieved and delighted for him that he has. He's spot on about one thing, of course: Hamlet is no part for a student. I'd almost reconciled myself to the idea that I might never get to grapple with one of the Shakespearean 'biggies'. As Sidney said, it must be fate. Quite what all this has got to do with Ironside is beyond me. Although my duties, where he is concerned, are never less than onerous, surely, what I do in my spare time is up to me.

The Quadriplegic

Philip Sidney looks like some dickhead maverick cop who's about to announce the murderer. 'I see *Hamlet* very much as a metaphor for our times. Mankind, bereft of his metaphysical crutches, alone in a universe which the more he understands, the greater his feelings of impotence and rage. What better symbol of this than a Hamlet who couldn't kill Claudius even if he decided that that was what he really wanted: a Hamlet in a wheelchair, frozen from the neck down?'

My corpulent carer looks like the gobsmacked butler who thought he was in the clear. 'What about the sword fights?' he protests.

'Oh, God,' snorts Philip Sidney, 'not another refugee from the Peter fucking Hall school of dead theatre.'

'What's wrong with Peter H—?'

'Now, come on, Michael, this is a fantastic opportunity, you know. Ask anyone who saw my *Elephant Man*. We're not talking about some crass West End revival here.'

Every Sunday Mum used to wheel me down the aisle, like a reluctant bridegroom. She'd park me at the front where everyone could have a good gawp and thank God they'd been spared the misery of a spacko child. It was the worst bit of the week; fifteen minutes of fame I could have well done without. And I've lost count of the number of times my mum used me as a visual aid on one of her numerous trawls around the local hospital wards and old people's homes. I was Mum's not very subtle way of pointing out to some miserable octogenarian that when it came to the frailties of the flesh, they had a long way to go before they caught up with the Spackmeister.

So there's no way I'm going to be part of Philip Sidney's nasty little freak show. I'd rather play a grateful cripple in one of the boring bits on *Comic Relief*. And anyway, if you ask me, Shakespeare's pretty overrated.

The trouble is, when I look across at De Niro, it's obvious that the idea of me playing Hamlet is so totally doing his head in, that I can't resist prolonging the agony. 'It's a great idea, Philip – really challenging. I tell you what, though; give me a couple of days to think it over. I'd love to be in it, of course. I'd just hate to let you down. All right if I let you know by the end of next week?'

2

Springes to Catch Woodcocks

The Virgin

'My God,' he says in that weird drawl of his, 'you must be the last virgin in Oxford!' He returns the unused condom to a silver cigarette case, and I can't help wondering if he's right.

'So what if I am?' I say, blinking back the tears. 'It's not a crime, is it?'

'Had we but world enough and time,' he sniggers, 'per-haps not. But it is practically the twenty-first century, you know.'

His rooms reek of sweat and those horrid deodorants that adolescent boys douse themselves in on Friday night. We've been on his bed at least half an hour, underneath a black-and-white photograph of Bertolt Brecht. And he keeps doing that guy thing; you know, where they make out they're really into snogging, but all the time they're brush-ing your bits with their tentacles because they think you'll find it irresistible?

'I want the first time to be special, that's all.' (I defy anyone to feel in the mood with a dead East German playwright staring at them.) 'I'm not ready for this yet.'

'Oh, my Lord, you actually mean it, don't you?'

Philip Sidney (yes, that really is his name) swept up to me in Blackwell's during First Week. 'You have a weakness here and here,' he said, pointing at my chin and the top of my forehead.

Well, I'm a woman, aren't I? When someone's talking about my physical imperfections, I'm listening. Secretly, I was quite pleased he'd only managed to come up with two. 'Have I?'

He nodded and looked me up and down, like a farmer sizing up a prize heifer. 'Would you like me to help you put them right?'

'Not really. But you can do if you like.'

I wasn't sure if he was taking the piss. Oxford is heaving with the finest young piss-takers in the country. 'I'm Philip Sidney, as in . . . Here's my card. Come and see me in my rooms tomorrow night. I have an exciting proposition to put to you.'

So here I am. He's pretty much Mummy's idea of the perfect young gentleman. 'Good breeding will out,' as she never tires of saying, and, quite frankly, it doesn't do any harm that he's the spitting image of a young Daniel Day-Lewis. The question is, how long before I can ask him down to the Old Rectory without looking a complete bunny boiler?

He reaches under the bed for an ashtray. 'I'm going to make you an offer you can't refuse, Anna.'

I thought I just had. But apparently there's more. Maybe he's going to pop the question. He wouldn't be the first bloke to resort to such desperate measures in an attempt to get into my knickers. Half the boys in Hampshire have tried that one. 'What's that then, Philip?'

He takes the first drag of his non-post-coital roll-up. 'I want you to be my Ophelia.'

Now I know he's taking the piss. The only time I've ever been on stage was the sixth-form production of *Grease*. 'You are joking, I suppose?'

'I never joke about my work.'

That I do believe. He won't even tell me what he's reading because he claims he only came to Oxford to further his directing career. 'But why me?'

'Well, you're hopelessly inexperienced, pretty in a gauche sort of way, and I'm always up for a challenge.'

'You certainly know how to flatter a girl.'

'Sorry, Anna, I didn't mean it like that.'

'How did you mean it then?'

'There's something about you that's very special, unique even. No preconceptions, I like that, I like it a lot. All you need is a good director. Ask anyone who saw the first rehearsal of *The Elephant Man*. Piers was absolutely shite until I got my hands on him.'

'I'll have to think about it.'

'That's great,' he says, plunging a hand into his jogging bottoms and readjusting himself. 'I don't like to say this, but it must be fate. And it'll give us some time to get to know each other. I always end up sleeping with my leading ladies, you know.'

I'm not one for short skirts and naked belly buttons; otherwise he couldn't fail to notice that my whole body is turning crimson. 'We'll have to see about that, won't we?'

I'm just promising myself a celebratory Snickers when he comes out with something that throws me completely. 'Oh, Anna, there's just one more thing.'

'I thought you said you understood.'

He has this rather yucky habit of chewing his knuckles. 'It's not that, it's just a little something I think you might be able to help me with.'

I suddenly get this awful feeling that he's a drug dealer or something. Mummy hates (non-prescription) drugs almost as much as car boot sales and political correctness. 'Oh, yes?'

'There's a disabled guy in your college, Michael, Michael Owen.'

I can't tell you what a relief that is. There I was worrying that Philip was some kind of drugs baronet, when all along he's just a big softy who wants to do his bit for those less fortunate than himself. 'I met Michael the other day,' I say, deciding not to mention I'd treated him like the Elephant Man. 'He seemed very . . . nice.' Actually, I think he's probably a bit of a geek, but I decide not to mention that either.

'I wouldn't know,' Philip shrugs.

'Then why did you—?'

'That's my Hamlet,' he whispers.

'You're serious, aren't you?'

'You bet I am. We couldn't even get the local rag to review *Elephant*. But a quadriplegic Hamlet! The broadsheets will be crapping themselves. I mean, yeah OK, I hate all that celebrity casting shit, but this could be so good for me.'

'So what do you want me to—?'

'The kid's playing hard to get. Talk to him. Make him change his mind. I need that man to be my prince.'

This has *got* to be a wind-up. 'Have you actually seen him? I mean, the poor guy can hardly move. He's not going to be much of an actor, is he?'

'I think you'd better leave the artistic decisions to someone who knows what he's talking about.'

'I don't know . . .'

He takes my hand and looks me straight in the eyes. 'Get Michael on board, and we can take things as slowly as you like. I'll even take you to that Lieder concert at Balliol.'

'Yes, but how? If the guy doesn't want to do it, surely that's up to him.'

'Flattery, of course, how do women ever get anything? I doubt if many blokes in wheelchairs have babes like you calling on them.'

'Supposing it doesn't work?'

'Of course it will. I'll pop round to your rooms in the morning to tell you what to say. Don't worry, gorgeous, you'll be fine. I mean, I don't want to be cruel or anything, but I imagine his social life is almost as non-existent as that sad fuck's who wipes his arse for him.'

3

A Pestilent Congregation
of Vapours

The Actor

We're only in the second week of the 'Mickey Mouse' term
but already I'm waking up in the early hours and fretting
over the inevitability of my encounter with the grim reaper.
I've been experiencing these moments of claustrophobic
panic for as long as I can remember. (I suppose for as long
as I've known about death.) They used to surface about
once a year, but here at Gloucester College they're as
regular as my bowel movements. It feels like being buried
alive.

Don't you hate similes? I've never seen the point of
saying that something is like something else. The trouble is,
after two weeks with Ironside, I can't see the point in anything. In *Be Your Own Psychotherapist in One Weekend*,
which I purchased shortly after SOWINS (She of Whom I
Never Speak) gave me my marching orders, you are
instructed to 'meditate daily' on the reality of your own

death. This is supposed to give your life meaning, but for me it does precisely the opposite. I've tried to face up to it by rehearsing the moment of my death; relaxing into it like a classic free kick from outside the box that bends around the wall and leaves the goalkeeper stranded. It doesn't work, though. It's about as futile as one of those fire drills where you amble out to the car park, knowing full well that you'd run like buggery if it was the real thing.

No one could blame me for being a bit down. I'm an artist, for God's sake. The whole business of being here, the tiresome repetition, the sheer bloody shittiness of keeping a cocky quadriplegic on the road, is almost as depressing as children's theatre. There's no need for the ghastly avuncularity, of course, nor scribbling countless autographs on bits of bog paper, but then again, at least you don't have to wash the kids' arses when you're giving your Reverend Timms in *The Adventures of Postman Pat*.

One of the other 'rules for life' in *Be Your Own Psychotherapist in One Weekend* is: 'We are all responsible for our own orgasms.' Perhaps my mental health is better than I thought. I have taken virtually sole responsibility for my orgasms for the last nine years, three months and fourteen days – ever since SOWINS suggested I might like to find alternative accommodation.

I lie in the dark, wondering when it's all going to end, bracing myself for his alarm clock and the start of another God-awful day.

The Quadriplegic

Everyone has their favourite crip joke. I like the one about what to get a quadriplegic for his birthday. It's funny because it's so true – blah blah blah. The punchline, '*Well, I'm not having another fucking hat,*' underlines an authentic modern dilemma: What *do* you get for the gommo who has everything? In Mum's case it's usually a totally unimaginative household item, like the 'useful' digital clock-thermometer that sits by my bedside. Some kids get their first car, but hey, my eighteenth birthday present not only tells me it's 7.23 a.m.; it also reveals that the temperature is an unseasonably chilly 8 degrees C. In seven minutes' time its ear-piercing alarm will traumatize the woodworms and send De Niro stumbling from his bed. Crips and movie stars have a lot in common: they both spend 80 per cent of the time hanging around, and they can't even go for a piss without a chaperon.

All I can hear is the hum of my electronic bed, turning me back and forth like a sausage in a frying pan. (It's to stop me getting bedsores, by the way.) In the old days, Mum used to get up every three hours to do it by hand. Sometimes she'd sleep through her alarm, and I'd be left to rot in the dark until the lazy mare got her act together. They say that carers often end up hating their chronically demanding carees. But you've got to understand, it cuts both ways.

The Actor

'Right, Michael, let's get this show on the road.' It's rather like being in the chorus of *Evita*; you have to switch off and do the whole thing on automatic pilot, otherwise the reality is just too soul-destroying. 'Hands off cocks, on with socks!' I say, throwing open his curtains and glancing down at the bright young things picking their spots in the quadrangle. The small talk helps too. Especially because without his microphone (I don't replace the recharged battery until later) he's in no position to answer back. 'And how is Michael this morning?'

I shouldn't be doing this in my condition (chronically torqued pelvis); it's like humping a sack of potatoes. No man should ever have to cope with this level of humiliation, but somehow I contrive to muddle through. With his electronic bed set to Upright, I wrestle him out of his winceyette pyjamas and into a shirt and jumper. I often wondered how I'd get on with looking after a baby. If this is what it's like, I was definitely right to tell She of Whom I Never Speak that I thought we should wait until my career took off.

There's an art to this next bit which, I have to confess, gives me a bit of a buzz when I get it right. I attach a condom-like device, with a plastic bottle on the end, to his superfluous member, and apply a gentlish karate chop to his lower abdomen. 'Sorree, let's try that again, shall we?' If executed correctly (and, hey presto, I usually get there in the end) it can empty the bladder most successfully. 'For this relief, much thanks, eh, Michael?'

After all that foolishness about *Hamlet* (and the more I think about it, the more I'm inclined to believe that it was just a cruel practical joke) I can't resist the Shakespearean allusion. It's not one of my best quips because, of course, Michael can't actually feel anything. However, his mother assures me that the karate-chop method is infinitely preferable to a catheter, which brings with it a high risk of infection and kidney trouble. 'Winter draws on, eh, Michael?'

His baggy underpants, which have to incorporate a spaghetti junction of plumbing for his surgical devices, remind me of the sort of things my nan used to hang out on washing day. Once I've got those on, the tracksuit trousers are a doddle. But why he insists on these state-of-the-art trainers when old ladies' slippers would make things so much easier, I can't imagine. 'Good, that's phase one out of the way.'

I might as well be talking to myself. I am constantly staggered by the gracelessness of contemporary youth. Michael's dumb ingratitude just about takes the biscuit. He's supposed to be some kind of genius, so why does he just lie there with that blank look on his face? What's going on in that head of his? Not a lot, if you ask me.

The Quadriplegic

In the school holidays I got sent on crip trips – something to do with Mum's church. I'd be packed off with a coachload of random window-lickers to places I didn't want to go.

One time I found myself next to a slap-headed sixteen-year-old called Steve: '*I thought we were going to Disneyland. All I ever wanted was to go to Disneyland, Euro Disney even. All the other sick kids get to go to Disneyland, but oh no, I get fucking terminal cancer and they send me off to Brighton.*'

In those days I didn't have all the gizmos I've got now. It was only when they discovered my IQ that I became attractive to sponsors. Back then, if I wanted to go anywhere, some poor sod had to push me. In the middle of a supremely boring tour of the Royal Pavilion (Britain's sixth most popular tourist attraction) Steve decided it was time for us to hit the town. It's a crap job looking after a coachload of spackers, and the last thing you expect is that one of them's going to make a break for freedom, so it was hardly surprising that Pastor Reg and the happy smilers didn't notice when Steve hijacked my spaz-chariot and started pushing me towards Churchill Square.

We sat outside WHSmith taking the piss out of the Plymouth Brethren. After Steve had helped me sample my first – and last – cigarette, we embarked on a hazardous shoplifting expedition. I say hazardous, because back then it was practically impossible to get anywhere in a wheelchair. These days they let us guys in everywhere. Practically half the spaces in Safeway's car park have pictures of spaz-chariots on them. I expect *you've* noticed how they're always empty.

Steve managed to hump me down the escalator at

British Home Stores where we set about nicking a few light fittings and a couple of hats. Despite the tough-guy exterior I think the baldness bothered him, so he'd commandeered a tartan deerstalker which looked almost as ridiculous as the one he got for me.

The manager (a fat bastard in the first hot flush of male menopause) stopped dead in the middle of his carefully rehearsed 'It is company policy to prosecute on every occasion' speech as, looking up, he found himself face to face with a bald, concentration-camp thin teenager and yours truly, dashing as ever in a white fedora, with a bedside lamp on my lap. How quickly his 'demon headmaster' transformed itself into 'television celebrity giving out presents in the children's ward on Christmas day' as he recognized the potentially fatal PR cock-up on his hands.

'I daresay there's no harm done. Boys will be . . . boys. Don't you think, Miss Anderson? It suits you, by the way – Sherlock.'

Wanker.

The Actor

'Now for the fun part, eh, Mike?' How in God's name did people manage before the advent of the surgical hoist? It's a life saver, I don't mind telling you. Although I was born to act, I've often thought that, if Thespia hadn't beckoned, I would have enjoyed operating one of those giant cranes. The solitude is the main selling point, but the feeling of power runs it a very close second. 'Hang on to your hat.'

35

At the touch of a button, his lifeless body ascends heavenwards. He dangles in mid-air until I fly him across the room like Peter Pan, and lower him into his wheelchair. 'I expect you're too young to remember *It's a Knockout*.'

Twenty years ago, I came to Oxford to visit my old school friend, Simon Butterworth. We spent about an hour with a bearded theologian from Hull, trying to find the swear words on a Rolling Stones LP. What impressed me as unspeakably sophisticated was the way he insisted on filtering our coffee into a large hand-glazed jug. As Damascene conversions go, it was right up there with oral sex and blue cheese. So, once I've strapped Ironside into his wheelchair, we pause for our first caffeine hit. 'I think we deserve a nice cup of coffee, eh, Michael? Don't go away now. I'll be back in a jiffy.'

The Quadriplegic

I call it the Pinocchio Syndrome. In my dreams, I'm a 'real boy'. Sorted for the weekend, I dance the night away in a state of chemically induced euphoria, throw up in the gutter, get depressed, write crap poetry and drive like a madman in my clapped-out Metro.

That's why I got into books. My tutor, Professor Bradshaw, might think it's because I want to waste my life on key questions like: '*How do Sylvia Townsend-Warner's impressions of the East-Anglian nuns of the fourteenth century compare with Chaucerian attitudes to monasticism?*' but the truth is, I started getting serious about reading because I needed to know how things felt. Words are all I have. Words are my last link with my former life; the only way of holding onto feelings that are now no more than distant memories.

I'm not talking about the big stuff. I can do fear and loathing standing on my head. I want to know things like, how does it feel when someone tickles you? What's it like to get kicked in the balls? They say you never forget, but after ten years on four wheels, I really want to remember the thrill of taking my stabilizers off and riding my bike for the first time. And what about walking on warm sand? I've devoured whole libraries looking for the answers to questions like that.

But you know what's doing my head in right now? What about sex? I've been involved in some pretty extensive research on the Internet. It's not fair; there's this internecine struggle of the hormones raging all around me, and I can't even have a wank. I suppose you think that's disgusting.

What is it they say? Love someone in spite of the wheelchair and it makes you a saint; love them *because* of it and it makes you a pervert; which is probably why the kids in the special unit didn't get the birds-and-the-bees lecture. I mean, what was the point? Even the could do's amongst us were (tacitly) adjudged to be far too gross to stand much chance of forming conventional relationships, so they packed us off to the Science Museum as a consolation prize.

De Niro's Brazilian blend is probably the nearest thing to an orgasm I'm ever going to get. Stainless steel rips into high-roasted bean and the sense of expectation is almost unbearable. Anyone who seriously suggests that those mean-looking granules, which fraudulently bear the same name, could be mistaken for the real thing is a total retard.

'Here we are, Michael. It's a little experiment this morning. I've blended in the merest hint of Kenyan.' He holds the delicate china cup to my lips and tilts it gently towards me. I'm sure he doesn't do it for my benefit; he just can't bear to see anyone slurping coffee through a straw. 'So, what do you think?'

Didn't some pop star once say that he preferred a cup of tea to having sex? Sounds like a load of Horlicks to me. If he'd said coffee I might just have been able to believe him.

The Actor

'OK, Michael. Stay right where you are.'

The mark of a good coffee is the speed with which it precipitates the call to stool. This is a very good coffee, and I have to repair almost immediately to the latrines at the end of the corridor.

Don't you hate it when people leave books in the lavatory? I find it particularly depressing when they feature whimsical comic-book animals in baseball caps. It's almost as sickening as actors who 'casually' display their Oscars in the bog to show how modest they are. If I ever live up to that wise old maxim, 'Be here now', it is during this most satisfactory of evacuations. Sadly it's one of the many pleasures in life that Michael will never appreciate.

Having paused to examine my stools for any of the early warning signs of bowel cancer (essentially blood in the faeces, which is rather more difficult to spot than you might think), I meditate for a moment on my career. It's good to keep reminding yourself that, in this business, you never know what's round the corner. And thank God for that, because the next phase of the operation has little to recommend it. 'Righty-ho, let's get on with this.'

I heard a woman on the radio saying that estuarial English is the biggest turn-off in the world. Colostomy bags have got to run it a pretty close second. I swiftly locate the translucent container which protrudes from his lower abdomen, detach it gingerly, and return it with all speed to the fragranced pedal bin provided.

'Did I ever tell you about that tour of *Love on the Dole*?'

An hour later, he's propped up in his wheelchair, fully medicated and looking like one of those Guys that children used to charge a penny for. 'Right, you should be wired for sound. Want to give it a try?'

'Good morning, Oxford!'

His tiresome attempts at humour are the last thing I need. 'Jolly good. Now, you haven't forgotten you've got a tutorial at ten?'

'"Why was the Revenge theme so popular in the early seventeenth century?" Be there or be square – eh, Tim?'

I've no desire for a dressing down from some shaven-headed, politically correct, loud-mouthed lesbian social worker, but surely you're thinking what I'm thinking. I mean, what's the point? Why waste an expensive education on someone who, clearly, has no possible use for it? 'Shall I hitch you up to your computer? I need to call my agent, Bunny Michelmore at Bunny Michelmore Management, before we go.'

Whenever I mention Bunny, an idiotic smile comes over his face. 'Yeah, that's right,' he says, 'you're really an actor, aren't you, Tim? Would I have seen you in anything?'

Like most performers, I'm actually rather a shy person. Talking about myself makes me feel uncomfortable. 'You might have caught me in *The Bill*,' I shrug, 'but I'm essentially a theatre animal, Michael. And I don't suppose you get up to town much, do you? Anyway, toodle-pip.'

'That's someone at the door, isn't it, Tim? Would you mind getting it for me?'

I wish he wouldn't keep calling me Tim. Not even Simon Butterworth calls me Tim. I only let SOWINS get away with it until we'd slept together a few times. 'Oh, good grief, not another one; who could it be this time, the hang-gliding society?'

The Virgin

I stand outside the wheelchair guy's rooms, cursing Philip for talking me into wearing this top.

'What are you crying for?' he says, wiping my face with the sleeve of his trenchcoat. 'I'm not asking you to sleep with him or anything!'

'That's not funny, Philip. Don't be disgusting.'

The more I think about it, the more it seems like a pants idea. And what if he does agree to play Hamlet? How am I going to be able to act with someone who can't even tie his own shoelaces?

'Let's just get on with it, shall we?'

'I can't, not yet. I need to . . . fix my make-up.'

Philip smiles and hammers on the door again. 'No time for that, I'm afraid. It's Showtime!'

I gulp down a final mouthful of breakfast Twix. 'But I don't know what to say to him.'

'I'm sure you'll think of something,' says Philip, backing away from me. 'Remember to text me the moment he says he'll do it.'

'Where are you going?'

'I told you; I've got a breakfast meeting with my designer. She has some very exciting ideas for Elsinore.'

'You can't just leave me here.'

'You don't expect me to hold your hand, do you?'

'But I thought . . .'

Halfway across the quad he turns and bellows, 'Don't forget to ask him his hat size.'

The door opens. It's the 'lardy-arsed geriatric' that Philip warned me about. Last time I visited, he was scouring Oxford for mature Stilton. 'Well, hello. And to what do we owe this unexpected pleasure?'

'Oh, hi, I . . . sorry to bother you, is Michael available?'

'You'd better come in.' Philip's right; he does sound like a character out of one of Mummy's favourite black-and-white movies. But I thought he was joking about the baseball cap. 'And may I say how charming you look?'

41

'Thanks.'

'Sorry about the smell,' he says, gesturing at the figure in the wheelchair gliding slowly towards me. 'I could open a window if you like.'

'It's fine. I just want to speak to Michael.'

'But I'm forgetting my manners, you must excuse me. I'm Timothy, Timothy Salt.' He pauses, as if to suggest I should have heard of him. 'Michael's carer.'

The sweaty handshake is just about preferable to some of the slobbery kisses I've had to endure from Daddy's friends. 'I'm Anna Jenkins. I live on the next staircase.'

And now he wants to tell me his life story. 'Only temporary, you understand. In my other life, I tread the boards. But I like to get out into the real world now and again. And it doesn't get much more real than this, eh, Mike?'

I wish I had the nerve to use that expression of Philip's about not confusing me with someone who gives a fuck. 'Is that right?'

'You're the clarinettist, if I'm not very much mistaken.'

'Yes, sorry about that. I hope my practice hasn't been disturbing you guys.'

'Not at all, dear girl; the Mozart is one of my favourite concertos, and very tricky in parts, I believe.'

'Don't worry about him,' says the boy in the wheelchair, coming to a halt about two feet in front of me. 'He doesn't get out much.'

And this time I'm ready for him. This time, I behave like he's at least the hundredth horribly deformed little person I've seen this morning. This time, I refuse to be thrown by an unfortunate optical illusion that makes it look like the poor guy can't keep his eyes off my tits. 'Sorry to barge in on you like this, Michael, but have you got a minute?'

'I'll leave you two young things to it, shall I?' says his carer, with a stomach-turning wink. 'I need to speak to my agent, anyway.'

Now that I'm alone with him, I don't feel quite so up for it. This Aids ribbon usually serves as a sort of front-line contraceptive ('Isn't it a drag we can't be promiscuous any more?') but when I get really nervous, I find myself treating the tassels like late-twentieth-century worry beads. That smile of his is freaking me out. It's a terrible thing to say, but it just doesn't look right on someone in a wheelchair. 'So . . . Michael, how are things?'

'Fine, but I didn't think I'd be seeing *you* again.'

A vile blush spreads across my face like galloping syphilis. 'Oh, God, was it that obvious?'

'Don't worry about it. Most people get a bit fazed when they meet me for the first time.'

'I'm sorry, Michael; I think we might have got off on the wrong foot. I mean . . . oh, shit, what did I say that for?'

His squeaky laughter kind of reminds me of *The Chipmunks*. 'That's brilliant,' he says. 'You can come again.'

'What do you mean?'

'Most people treat crips like pre-watershed children. It's just nice to hear someone swearing for a change.'

'Is it?'

'I can cope with walking metaphors, you know.'

This is weird; we're almost having a normal conversation. 'When I came down to introduce myself last week, it was all a bit of a . . . shock. I shouldn't have just turned up like that. You see, I didn't realize you were a . . .' Oh, my God! What do they call them now? I know it's not disabled any more, but what on earth is it?

'Gommo, you mean?'

'No, no, of course not.'

'Two legs short of a cancan dancer?'

'I didn't mean it like . . . sorry, Michael, I think I'd better go.'

'No, don't,' he says, moving his wheelchair to block my exit. 'I hate it when people tiptoe around me, that's all.'

I reach instinctively for my Aids ribbon. 'OK, I'll . . . I'll try not to then.'

'Just treat me like a movie star, and we'll get along fine.'

He *is* taking the piss, isn't he? 'Yes, right, I . . .'

'What did you want anyway? And before you ask, I'm rubbish at netball.'

I smile politely, not quite sure if I'm supposed to laugh out loud. 'I've got a message from Philip Sidney.'

'Have you now?'

That is *so* tragic. It really does look like he's ogling me. His mouth falls open and a rivulet of dribble slides slowly down his chin. He doesn't expect me to wipe it, does he? 'Are you OK, Michael? You look . . . weird. Do you want me to get what's-his-name?'

Right on cue, the carer guy bursts out of his bedroom with a can of aerosol. 'Don't mind me,' he says, spraying maniacally, 'I thought this room could do with a bit of freshening up.'

'I'm sorry, Anna. What were you saying about Philip Sidney?'

'He thinks you'll make a wonderful Hamlet.'

Aerosol guy lets out an enormous stage guffaw. 'Heaven forbid.'

'Philip's asked me to play Ophelia. And I'm really hoping that you're going to do it too.'

'I don't think I'm quite . . .'

It's obviously part of the carer's job to finish his patient's sentences for him. 'Mike's decided that discretion is the better part of valour, haven't you, matey? I mean, let's be honest, Hamlet's a tough enough challenge for any . . . able-bodied actor.'

'But that's rubbish,' I say, half meaning it. 'You'd be good, Michael, I know you would.'

'My dear girl, I'm sure your heart is in the right place. But I would hate to see Michael humiliated. As I say, I have been in the business for some years. I do know what I'm talking about.' He saunters over to Michael and ruffles his hair. 'Tell her, old chum. You know it makes sense.'

Well, that's that, isn't it? He's never going to do it now. And quite frankly, I don't blame him. Philip will just have to find another Hamlet. And I suppose I'll have to come up with another victim for Mummy. 'Fair enough, then; if that's the way you feel, Michael, I'll go and tell Philip the bad news.'

The boy in the wheelchair stares hard at his carer before turning his attention back to my breasts and smiling sweetly. 'Do you know what? I think I've changed my mind. There can't be much to this acting lark, can there, Timothy? And with Anna as Ophelia, it could be very interesting.'

4

Country Matters

The Actor

When Simon Butterworth (who I can just about describe as my one remaining friend) finally got married, it was I who inherited his Purrfect Pussy. As the only born-again bachelor in the stag party, it was fitting that he should fling it towards me with all the care and precision of a bride, intent on ensuring that her bouquet should reach some deserving spinster.

He bought it, in a *semi*-ironic way, out of the back pages of *Club International* ('No real pussy purrs as purrfectly as this one') when he was going through one of his fallow periods. It's shaped like an American football, with a hole in one end (obviously) and at the other, a place for the batteries. One could imagine it cropping up in a 70s BBC 2 panel game, where a group of slightly posher than average celebrities would pass it around in an attempt to discover its purpose. '*Is it one of those things you use to make yoghurt?*' Of course it's nowhere near as good as the real thing, but it can preserve you from some of the more depersonalizing effects of marriage. Far more discreet than a blow-up doll, it sits demurely on my bedside table, ready and willing at the flick of a switch.

I've known Simon since the sixth form, so, when I first came by his Pussy, I saturated it in detergent and used a condom. As with my corporeal relationships, the safe-sex thing went out of the window after the first couple of dates. I don't wish to suggest that we're inseparable, but, right now, if I was the subject of *This is Your Life*, the Purrfect Pussy would probably be the surprise guest that they flew halfway across the world to be with me on my special day.

No doubt it would amuse SOWINS to learn that I haven't completely given up on *This is Your Life*. When my ex-wife uttered the words 'till death us do part', what she really meant was that she'd only stick around if I landed a part in a sitcom. Her final ultimatum, '*Get yourself a proper job or I'm out of here,*' was all the more heart-breaking for the fact that my agent (Bunny Michelmore at Bunny Michelmore Management) had just called to tell me I hadn't got the Tango commercial. Doubtless SOWINS would have something equally pithy to say about the Purr-fect Pussy. She always did make me feel a bit of a wanker.

As I roll these deathly thoughts around my mouth and spit them out in fear and disgust, I let the shipping forecast descend over me like a safety blanket. For how many other insomniacs and late-night masturbators is it a poem more soothing than the Lord's Prayer?

Michael is still out there, tapping away like a demented Dalek. He says he's got a work crisis, but I know full well he's playing one of those tedious computer games that every male under thirty seems to find so fascinating. I ought to be so angry with him, and yet all I feel is pity. It's not his fault that some lunatic thinks he can play Hamlet. Philip Sidney makes the director who cast Frank Bruno as the genie of the lamp look like a man of artistic integrity.

So I've decided to sit back and enjoy the spectacle. I've even agreed to accompany him to the Morley Fletcher Rooms for his first rehearsal. It's not in my job description, of course, but like the knee-jerk reaction that inevitably accompanies the words 'includes scenes which some viewers may find disturbing', I feel drawn to the nascent disaster, like men in anoraks to Clapham Junction.

And let's not forget, Michael is one of the few people who make me feel good about my sex life. Although the Purrfect Pussy is by no means Purrfect, the experience is a whole lot better than anything poor old Ironside will ever come across.

So, having paused to examine my testicles for any 'lumps, irregularities or changes in shape or firmness', I remove my favourite moggie from the bedside table. As the National Anthem swells to its glorious climax, I fumble for the switch.

The Quadriplegic

- WHERE ARE U?
- BARBADOS. WHERE ARE U?
- SITTING ON MY BED
- HOW ARE U FEELING?
- RELAXED

– WHAT ARE U DOING?

– LOOKING AT YOUR PHOTOGRAPH. ARE U REALLY THIS HANDSOME?

– NOT FOR ME TO SAY

– AND MODEST WITH IT

– WHAT ARE U WEARING?

– MY LITTLE BLACK DRESS.

– AND UNDERNEATH?

– JUST MY KNICKERS. SHALL I TAKE THEM OFF FOR U?

– DO U WANT TO?

– YES

– TAKE THEM OFF THEN

– THAT'S BETTER

– HOW DO U FEEL NOW?

– MEGA RELAXED. WHEN AM I GOING TO SEE U? EVEN AIRLINE PILOTS GET TIME OFF FOR GOOD BEHAVIOUR DON'T THEY?

– TELL ME ABOUT YOUR BREASTS

– THEY FEEL HARD

– WHY DON'T U TOUCH THEM FOR ME?

– OH MICHAEL. I WISH U WERE HERE.

– WHAT WOULD U DO IF I WAS WITH U?

– I'D GO AND LOOK IN THE FRIDGE

– WHAT'S IN THE FRIDGE?

– YOGHURT!

– THAT'LL DO NICELY

Other people's multiple orgasms give me the mother of all headaches. Voice recognition software is OK when you've got time to go back and correct yourself, but the wand is much better when you're trying to keep up with a girl in real time.

The Internet is the ultimate arena for the projection of alternative personas. It can also be a mega let-down. How many horny optimists have had their wet dreams shat upon from a great height when they've finally come face to face with their repugnant Internet lovers? How many eagerly awaited rendezvous in provincial hotels have come to a premature conclusion the moment the old swamp-donkey (who said she was a model) pops back to her room to fetch her glasses? I wonder what they'd do if Wheelchairboy showed up? Probably stick around for a drink, out of pity.

I still reckon the Net's just about the best thing that's ever happened to me. Of course, I trawl the porn sites from time to time – don't we all? In fact, if you're some kind of pervert, you can even find sites with guys and gals like me on them. But what I love about the Internet is that I get to try on a whole new set of heads – and more importantly a whole set of new bodies – without anyone ever suspecting that their favourite cyber-mate is a horribly deformed mutant from the planet Unequal Opportunities. Sitting at my keyboard, even I start believing I'm a 'real boy'. And not just any boy, either; I can be anyone I want to be: from Goths to gay vicars, my range is spectacular. There are a lot of saddos out there, all gagging to believe that you're exactly who you say you are. With so many of us about, I'm confident that the webcam will never really catch on.

Out in cyber-space, I can float like a butterfly and sting like a bee. In the real world, I'm about as manoeuvrable as a dog turd and as conspicuous as a wart on a supermodel. Teenagers are supposed to have this fixation that everyone's staring at them; with me it's actually true. When I wheel into that rehearsal tomorrow, I know for a fact that all eyes will be on me.

The Virgin

We called it market day. Every second Saturday of the summer term, they bussed the entire upper fifth to the boys' school on the other side of Tewkesbury. After a couple of juicy scandals (one of which made it to page six of the *Daily Telegraph*) the headmaster of St Dominic's decided that the boys' energies might be better channelled if they were allowed strictly limited access to suitable members of the opposite sex – a bit like a mass conjugal visit for the prisoners on death row.

At least that's what it felt like. For the rest of the year we were supposed be perfect young ladies, but for a couple of Saturdays in June we were required to dress up like high-class hookers and snog the boys of St Dominic's into the paths of true righteousness. Not that everyone felt the same as I did. I remember the excited babble as we swarmed onto the coach ('Cassie isn't wearing any knickers,' 'Isabel Barrett thinks you can get pregnant from a blow job!'), the overpowering smell of Chanel No. 5 and the screams of delight at the first sight of the rugby posts when we turned into the long drive that led up to Dracula's castle.

Although these so-called Fraternization Nights lasted

an agonizing three and a half hours, the non-alcoholic punch (rumour had it that a group of Dominican boffins were manufacturing their own ecstasy), the obligatory dose of whingeing Britpop from the school band and the dismal attempts at urbane witticism ('Can I park my Porsche in your garage?') were only a prelude to the all-important last five minutes.

The slow dance, or 'gentlemen's abuse me' as we called it, was a frenetic free-for-all in which the light show was momentarily shackled and our soft-hearted jailers turned a blind eye to the scenes of desperate debauchery on the dance floor. There beneath an impressive memorial to the old boys who gave their lives in two world wars, I prepared myself for an assault of a different kind: a tongue in my mouth, a hand on my bum, perhaps a clumsy attempt to unfasten my bra strap or, worse still, inky fingers trying to force their way into my pragmatically skintight jeans. I still wince whenever I hear Céline Dion.

But the slow dance wasn't the worst part. I soon worked out that a casual allusion to *The Mill on the Floss* was enough to confuse even the most amorous schoolboy, and an adolescent queasiness about the menstrual cycle ensured that the phrase 'Sorry, I've just come on' was a failsafe deterrent for inky fingers. And besides, Mummy loved to hear about the boys I'd snogged. She was always saying how much my letters cheered her up during the bad times. No, the worst part for me was right at the start of the evening when, one by one, we had to parade through a corridor full of expectant Dominicans whilst they checked out our cleavages, clapped and whistled like the crowd at

Twickenham and shouted lewd comments. I hated it; their eyes like lasers, burning into all my most private places.

So how does he cope? Michael, I mean. I saw the way everyone looked at him when we walked back to college tonight. The poor guy must get it the whole time. It would kill me, but he seems to take it all in his stride (oops!).

That's why I'm dreading the rehearsal tomorrow. I'm not cut out to be an actress. No wonder I can't sleep. What's that bit in *Hamlet*, '*perchance to dream*'? Tell me about it! Philip has promised to be gentle with me, but I've been having nightmares ever since he said we'd be spending the first part of the evening playing theatre games.

The things I do for Mummy!

5

The Actors are Come Hither

The Actor

Philip Sidney looks a prize prat in his black polo-neck sweater. I'm amazed he hasn't got a fold-up chair with 'Director' on the back.

'I don't want to do a read-through. I think we'll leave that sort of thing to Crewe Rep, don't you?' (Much amusement.)

It's a speech I've heard a million times before. It usually continues along the lines of: he's not going to do any blocking (because he's not directing traffic), followed by a solemn promise to 'let things grow organically'. Which is code for 'I haven't got a fucking clue.'

'What I want to do first, and what I think will actually be a lot more useful, is to consider the word "prison".' A murmur of approval goes round the rehearsal room. 'Denmark is a prison, yeah? OK, let's all get into a circle on the floor – apart from you, of course, Michael.'

'Thanks, Philip.'

'I want you to sit in the middle of the circle and be my sounding board. Every time anyone says anything, echo it back to them.'

This is not by any means the foul parody it seems. In five years' time it's quite conceivable that Philip Sidney will be dispersing similar pearls of wisdom to middle-aged thespians at one of our major subsidized theatres; each one of them eager not to appear set in their ways in the face of such youthful brilliance.

'Buggery.' ('Buggery.')

'Burglary.' ('Burglary.')

'Shadows.' ('Shadows.)

(Cliff and the . . .?)

'Monotony.' ('Monotony.')

The Virgin

God, this is horrid. When I first told him that Michael had agreed to play Hamlet, Philip said he'd 'love me for ever', but tonight he's treating me like something he'd wipe off his riding boots. How come he didn't make that obese slapper from St Hilda's improvise a porn movie? And what's it got to do with *Hamlet* anyway? No wonder I want to lose myself in a family pack of fun-sized Mars bars.

'Come on, Anna,' he barks. 'You're supposed to be a Serbian whore, not a refugee from *The Sound of Music*.'

'I just don't see the point, that's all.'

'Oh, so you don't see the relevance of the Balkans conflict to sixteenth-century politics, then?' He rolls his eyes at the girl playing Guildenstern, who obviously can't believe my ignorance.

At least Piers sticks up for me. 'Why am I taking my quadriplegic cousin to a prostitute anyway? It doesn't make sense.'

Philip mimes banging his head against the wall. 'Jesus, Piers, haven't you been listening to a word I've said?'

Michael's actually quite a funny guy. He told me just now that his mum thinks he'd make a brilliant prime minister. And he didn't even crack a smile. I expect he's enjoying getting out for a change. When you look like he does, you probably get used to the odd funny look. For all I know, he could be having the time of his life.

The Quadriplegic

The last sixty-eight minutes have been at least a trillion times more demeaning than the time I 'made a mess' in Santa's grotto. At most non-spacko social events they park me in a quiet corner and have the decency to whisper about me behind my back; here in the rehearsal room, Philip celebrates my spackocity at every turn.

'It's staring you right in the face, Piers. His whole body is a prison. I mean, how do you think that makes him feel?'

'Pretty rank, I should imagine.'

'So, now do you see what I'm getting at?'

'Oh, yah . . . abso-bloody-lutely,' says Piers, grudgingly. After his triumph in *The Elephant Man* he's still a bit peeved not to be playing the quadriplegic Hamlet himself.

Most of the time, people regard me as the opposite of a chimney sweep at a wedding. What I represent to ABs (crip jargon for able-bodied) is a nasty reminder of their fragile mortality. Isn't that why you reach for 50p every time you see an old lady with a collection tin outside Sainsbury's; as your insurance policy against getting cancer, or ending up lumbered with a kid like me? I might start hiring myself out to undertakers.

Philip has made it his mission in life to humiliate Anna. He orders her around like she's a Victorian scullery maid (for all I know, they still have one in the Sidney residence) and every one of his improvisations seems to revolve around her posing as a horny schoolgirl or a Romanian prostitute on the run from her (wheelchair-bound) pimp.

Anna does her best to laugh it off, but I can see from the way she looks at him that she's hating every minute of it. Take it from me, she is not cut out for a life in the sex industry.

'OK, people,' says Philip, 'for the last couple of hours I want to do some work with masks. We've done some really useful exercises around the concept of prison . . .' (Yeah, right.) '. . . and now I want to explore the idea that things are not always what they seem. "*Seems, madam? . . . I know not seems.*"'

Talk about hoist with my own fucking petard. I only agreed to do *Hamlet* so I could spend a bit of time with a 'real girl' and torture my corpulent carer, but Anna probably thinks I'm an evil sex pest, and the bald bastard at the back seems to be loving every minute of it. In fact, it's the first time I've seen De Niro smile since we got here.

'Now don't forget,' says Philip, 'show some respect for the mask.'

The Actor

Strangely enough, I've been through all this with an illustrious knight of the theatre. I was giving my Athenian soldier in his 'well paced but ultimately parochial' production of *The Suppliant Women*.

'OK, people, in a little while some sort of sounds might begin to emerge – grunts, perhaps.'

He said that when we first pulled on our masks we would be quite unable to speak, but that gradually, as we grew into them, we might achieve maturity, and eventually, perhaps, the gift of speech. He sat in front of us like a Renaissance prince or the non-schizophrenic Kray brother, the merest hint of a self-satisfied smile playing about his lips as before his very eyes we (remarkably) progressed from childlike mutes, through grunting Neanderthals, into fully fledged masked orators – just as he said we should. Never mind medical students, theatre directors could keep the sperm banks overflowing well into the twenty-first century.

I really shouldn't have worried about this. As the last actor is unmasked and Michael manoeuvres his wheelchair to the periphery of the circle, I know with thrilling certainty that Sidney's *Hamlet* is destined to be the crassest, most ill-conceived and all-round embarrassing production since *It's a Royal Knockout*. Coupled with a leading man who is both out of his depth and ludicrously miscast (think John

Inman and *King Lear*), and you will understand why I shall shortly be celebrating with my favourite tipple.

Philip Sidney is perplexingly upbeat. 'Thank you, people, that was fucking excellent. I just want to say that if we carry on like this, we're going to have a truly mind-blowing show on our hands. OK, before we all adjourn to the White Horse, I think we should end with a game of tag. Perhaps you'd like to join us, Timothy. I don't normally let anyone sit in on my rehearsals, so we'd all appreciate it if you'd deign to let your hair down – what there is of it – and join us.'

(Smart-arsed little bugger.) 'Thank you, Philip, but getting the big picture is really most illuminating.'

'Whatever happened to your inner child, Tim?'

'My outer parents bludgeoned him to death with the gas bill.'

The Quadriplegic

Philip and Piers hump me down the stairs outside the rehearsal hall.

'Where's Florence Nightingale?' says Piers. 'I thought this was *his* job.'

'Gone for a piss,' I tell him.

'He's probably got his head stuck down the bog looking for his career,' says Philip.

Piers puffs out his cheeks and does a hopelessly camp imitation of my carer. '"*I must* speak to my agent."'

'Yeah, travel agent,' says Philip, 'book himself a nice

Saga holiday.' He glances at his Rolex. 'Sure you're not going to join us, Michael?'

'Pubs aren't really my thing.'

He doesn't exactly bust a gut trying to talk me out of it. 'Take care of yourself, then. That was a bloody excellent rehearsal, by the way. Told you he was inspired casting, didn't I, Piers?'

Piers nods half-heartedly.

I'm always getting blockages of one kind or another (many of them life-threatening), so don't go thinking it means anything, but as soon as I see Anna walking towards us, head bowed like Mum at a prayer meeting, I get this lump in my throat.

'Look who it is,' says Philip, putting on a truly awful working-class accent. 'How much for a Lewinsky, doll?'

'Shut up, you idiot,' says Piers. 'Can't you see the poor girl's upset?'

'Well, you'd know all about drama queens, wouldn't you, Piers?'

'Piss off, Phil,' says Piers good-humouredly. 'Don't worry about him, Anna. He always treats his actors abominably. You should have seen what he put me through in *Elephant*.'

'I can't stand divas,' says Philip, prodding his nose stud with his index finger. 'They do my head in. Now can we just get to the pub, please? Some of us have actually been working tonight.'

'Yes, come on, Anna,' says Piers. 'I haven't finished telling you about the Scottish guy I met in Bangkok.'

Anna takes a pink paper tissue from her sleeve. 'I'd

really like that, Piers, but . . . some other time perhaps, if that's OK with you.'

'Oh yah, absolutely. We've got four more weeks of rehearsal, don't forget.'

'Please yourself,' shrugs Philip. 'You might use the time to think about those hang-ups of yours. No one likes a woman who bursts into tears every time you mention oral sex. Come on, let's get out of here.'

He disappears into the night, Piers skipping along behind. From the look on Anna's face, I'd hazard a guess that she's not using the time to consider her hang-ups – whatever they might be. But I wouldn't mind betting that, like me, she's just realized that four more weeks of *Hamlet* rehearsals are more than flesh and blood can bear. 'What's the matter, Anna, are you OK?'

Think back over your life and count up the number of times you've seen a grown man cry. I'm not talking about on telly – soap actors have it written into their contracts and doesn't the BBC just love a good old-fashioned natural disaster? No, think real life, as we like to call it, and add them up. So what did you make it – four, five? But I'll tell you what; I bet you can remember them all. I'll never forget Dad's pathetic display when the gutless bastard told me he was leaving: '*I'll still be here for you, I promise,*' he said, his face creasing up like Mother Teresa's. '*Chelmsford's only an hour and twenty-five in the Renault.*'

Now try the same thing with women. Can't do it, can you? It's like asking Mick Jagger how many models he's fucked. Some people say it's because women are more advanced than men, more in touch with their feelings.

Personally, I think that's taking things a bit far. I reckon I've got as much right to cry my eyes out as the next fashion victim, but, even if my tear ducts were fully functional, you wouldn't catch me turning on the waterworks. 'Please . . . please, Anna, don't cry.'

So how come I find the sight of Anna dabbing at her panda eyes so upsetting? How come I'd give my right arm (and throw in a couple of hardly used legs for good measure) just to change places with her soggy Kleenex? I'm completely paralysed from the neck down, and yet those tiny beads of moisture racing across her cheeks give me the feeling that someone's slowly twisting a knife in my guts. 'Come on, Anna. You mustn't let him get to you.'

'Its nothing. I'm . . . fine.'

'You don't look fine.'

'Why does he treat me like that?' Her voice is so brimming with vitriol that for some reason I feel like turning somersaults. 'Am I really so awful?'

'Of course you're not. If you ask me, you're the only one who knows what they're doing.'

She smiles and rubs my shoulder. 'Oh, Michael, you're so sweet.'

Trust me, it's not the sort of thing that any bloke in a wheelchair wants to hear. As terms of endearment go it's only marginally preferable to *You're really repulsive and I can't stand to be in the same room as you.* 'Yeah, cheers, thanks for that.'

'I'm sorry, I didn't mean to . . .'

De Niro bounces down the steps, fiddling with his flies and grinning inanely. 'Hello, you two. Enjoy the rehearsal?'

'Not really,' says Anna.

'I don't blame you, my dear. If I was playing Ophelia – and with young Sidney at the helm, that's not as outlandish as it might sound – I'd be less than enchanted to spend my first rehearsal masquerading as a child prostitute. And as for you, Mike,' he adds with a sly wink, 'I didn't know you had it in you.'

'I just wish I knew what Philip wanted,' says Anna. 'I can't think why he cast me in the first place.' (*I've* got a pretty good idea.) 'That's not true, actually, I do know why. He told me the other day.'

'Oh, yes,' says De Niro, smacking his lips like a tabloid journalist. 'What did he say?'

'It doesn't matter.'

The old ham rolls his eyes. 'I tell you what, Anna, I'd be more than happy to take you through your lines. After twenty years in the theatre, I do know a couple of tricks of the trade.'

'Thanks,' she says, shooting me a glance and mouthing the word 'help'. 'I might take you up on that.'

'Yeah, cheers, Tim,' I say, 'but Anna and me are going to walk back to college and run a couple of scenes together.'

'And I suppose you want me to sit in?'

'No!' says Anna. 'Erm, I mean, it would be a criminal waste of your experience at the moment – maybe in a couple of weeks' time?'

This seems to pacify him. 'As you wish. I was planning on taking a little liquid refreshment anyway.'

'Take as long as you like, Timothy. I'm sure Anna won't mind hitching me up to my computer.'

'Thank you kindly, young master,' says De Niro, touching his baseball cap like a comedy servant, 'but have no fear, I'll be back for bedtime. Toodle-pip.'

The Actor

A rather wicked thought flickers across my mind as I watch the odd couple disappear up Walton Street. I don't want to put anyone off their cornflakes, but just now I need a good chuckle, so what the hell? *Is this love's young dream that I see before me?* In a Channel 4 film perhaps; that gritty, fantasy world, where plucky northern housewives transform their lives, where unemployed miners regain their self-respect in feel-good strip cabals, and the quadriplegic always gets the girl. Sorry, that was in frightfully bad taste.

Someone told me that this part of town, to which I am strangely drawn, is where Jude (the Obscure) was supposed to have lived. With which literary character do you most identify? Juliet? Starsky and Hutch? It's full of Victorian terraces, rather grim, in as much as anything can look grim in Oxford. There's the occasional student coffee bar (checked tablecloths and pastel shades) but, on the whole, it has an empty quality, far removed from all that bloody architecture and the endless swarms of cocksure, middle-class kids with better A level results than me. By the way, there's only one place in Oxford where you can get a decent cappuccino. But if you think I'm going to tell you where it is, so you can muscle in on my favourite window seat, you can go and take a flying fuck.

'Oh, bollocks, what does she want now?' If it wasn't essential that my agent (Bunny Michelmore at Bunny Michelmore Management) be able to contact me 24/7, I'd have thrown this bloody mobile in the Cherwell weeks ago.

'Hello, Mrs Owen. I assume you're enquiring after Michael.'

I always get the feeling she's expecting me to tell her I've accidentally left him stranded on the hard shoulder of the M4 or something.

'How is he?'

'He's fine.'

'What about his bowel management, how's he doing?'

Given that all Michael has to do is shit and piss himself, I should have thought that question was more properly addressed to the chief cook and bottle washer. 'As I said this morning, everything's under control.'

'Good, good. I do worry about him, you know.'

Oh, really, I would never have guessed. 'I am doing my best, Mrs Owen.'

'Oh, yes, yes, please don't think that . . . You're doing a wonderful job, Timothy. Michael's very lucky to have you, it's just that he's my little boy and I wish I was still looking after him.'

Now there's something we both agree on. 'You ought to get out more.'

She laughs hysterically. 'I haven't been out for the last seven years – apart from church, of course. What on earth would I do?'

I was faced with the same dilemma when I left SOWINS, but I'm not about to suggest that she commandeers the female equivalent of the Purrfect Pussy. 'How about ballroom dancing? Or tiddlywinks, perhaps?'

'Michael said you were a funny person. Can I speak to him, by the way?'

'I'm sorry, Mrs Owen, he's with a lady friend.'

'He's what?' she says, sounding like it's a sure-fire sign that Armageddon is imminent.

'I told you about that ridiculous business with the play? Well, he's having a private rehearsal with Ophelia.'

'I'm sure he's got time for a quick word with his mother.'

'No can do, I'm afraid. I thought I should leave them to it, so I've popped out to the . . . that is, I felt I needed some space, so I'm taking a brief constitutional.'

I can almost hear her nodding sagely. 'Starting to get you down, is it?'

'Well, I . . .'

'I'm so sorry. I should have warned you about that. Caring for Michael can be a great joy, of course, but sometimes you just want to . . .' She sounds like a lapdog yelping. 'How are you, Timothy? Are you coping all right?'

It's been so long since anyone enquired after my mental state that I'm lost for words. If I allow myself to give the question some serious consideration, I could be struggling here. 'Well, I . . .'

'I'll pray for you.'

And when I turn the corner, there in front of me is the answer to a youngish man's prayers. The Fatted Calf is my refuge in a drab and unforgiving world. It's like *Stars in Their Eyes*; I'll walk into that pub a nobody, and after three or four pints, I'll emerge from the cigarette smoke feeling like Marlon Brando in *Streetcar* . . .

'Sorry, Mrs Owen, you're breaking up. Let's talk again tomorrow.'

The Quadriplegic

'*I loved you not.*'

'*I was the more deceived.* He points to the *what*? Fald-stool? Any ideas, Michael?'

'You'd better have a look in the glossary.'

I thought the whole private rehearsal thing was just a ruse to get rid of De Niro. I couldn't believe she actually wanted to go through with it. So here I am, with a real girl not two feet away from me; close enough to feel her breath on my face, close enough to see the pinky whites of her eyes.

'*Faculty, false fire* . . . no, doesn't say anything about faldstools.'

The strap of a white cotton undergarment has appeared in the V of Anna's black fluffy jumper. Perhaps if I was a real boy she'd self-consciously try to push it back in again, but with me she feels safe enough to let everything hang out. This is probably the nearest I'm ever going to get to first base. Why couldn't God – in his divine mercy – have seen to it that my fantasy life was as erotically challenged as the rest of me?

'Perhaps our director could enlighten us.'

'Oh, him,' says Anna, sinking slowly onto the sofa and

hugging herself like she's wearing a straitjacket. 'I doubt very much *he'd* be able to help.'

I've been trying to get round to this since we started. Every time Philip is mentioned, she goes all weird on me. What's the story, I wonder? 'Is there something you want to talk about, Anna?'

'Not really, I mean . . . you don't want to hear about my . . . do you?'

God knows why, but – along with dogs and homosexuals – women tend to regard quadriplegics as excellent confidantes. It could be because we're the ultimate captive audience, although I have a feeling that, despite the 'remarkable courage' wank-fest that people come out with from time to time, it's because all elements of competition go out of the window when you're wheel to wheel with a spaz. You might not want to admit to your next-door neighbour that your husband can't quite cut it any more, but I've had complete strangers giving me blow-by-blow accounts of their divorce proceedings.

'Come on, Anna. I won't bite, you know. Actually, biting's one of the things I'm quite good at.'

She picks up the Chelsea FC cushion that Dad sent me for my thirteenth birthday and clutches it tight to her stomach. 'I dunno, you'll probably think I'm a headcase.'

I puff into my controller and move a few inches closer. 'Try me.'

'I think what first attracted me to Philip was his incredible self-confidence.'

'It wasn't his natural modesty, then?'

She smiles, places the cushion on her knees and drums

on it like a tom-tom. 'He can talk about anything. George Eliot, Wittgenstein . . . *Home and Away.*'

'What about *Neighbours*?'

'You must have known we've been seeing each other.'

'Yeah, course,' I say, nonchalantly; grateful, for the first time in my life, that my body language can't betray me. 'Everyone knows you and Philip are an item.'

'Hardly,' she says, 'at least not after tonight.'

My broad smile on the other hand is a dead giveaway. 'I'm sorry to hear that.'

'I just want to know where I stand with the guy. I mean, I know we're not Romeo and Juliet or anything, but I thought we were a little bit more than just good friends.'

On my first day in college, there was a glossy brochure waiting for me called *Advice for Students*. De Niro took great pleasure in quoting from it at length and holding up the 'delightful' full-colour illustrations. It was packed with useful tips like how to procure an abortion, the correct way to insert a Dutch cap, helpline numbers for every variety of deviant, and a failsafe method for identifying syphilitic penises. If that wasn't enough to bring home to me how well and truly 'special needs' I am, then watching Anna sniffing into her sleeve and not being able to extend a consoling arm really rubs my nose in it. 'Oh, come on, Anna. It's not that bad.'

'All he wants is a bloody shag.'

Judging by *Advice for Students* that's pretty well par for the course. 'And you don't?'

'Yes . . . no . . . look, you wouldn't understand.'

'Because I'm a crip, you mean?'

'Because you're a bloke.'

It's probably the nicest thing that anyone's ever said to me. 'Cheers, Anna.'

She twists a lock of hair around her index finger. 'What I'm trying to say is that I'm a . . . I mean, I haven't . . . not because I'm religious or anything, I just . . .'

And finally the penny drops. 'Oh, right . . . I see.'

Her bottom lip is trembling again. 'I told you you'd think I was a headcase.'

'Course I don't.'

'Well, Philip does. When I said that . . . God, it makes me sound like a silly schoolgirl . . .'

'What does?'

'That I wasn't ready. That I wanted the . . .'

'First time?'

'Yep, wanted it to be, you know . . . special. He thought I was joking. Now he calls me "the last virgin in Oxford". Says it's why he cast me as Ophelia.'

Speaking as someone who will never have a first time, even an abusatory one, it's quite hard for me to be completely sympathetic, but I manage to put on my best caring-profession face – fuck knows I've seen enough of them. 'That's terrible.'

'Now he keeps trying to rub it in. Why do you think he made us do that improvisation about the prostitute? It makes me feel like going out and sleeping with someone just to get him off my back.'

'I'll tell you one thing, Anna.'

'What's that?'

'You're not the last virgin in Oxford. In ten years' time

you'll probably have six kids or something, but *I'm* never going to get my end away.'

She thinks for a moment. 'Yes, but that's because you're a . . . sorry, shall we press on?'

'*Get thee to a nunnery: why wouldst thou be a breeder of sinners? I am myself indifferent* . . . Anna, are you OK?' Her hysterical laughter stops me mid-iambic and I seriously wonder if she might not be a headcase after all. 'What's the matter?'

'That wallpaper, I've only just noticed it. How can you live with that?'

'They say you can get used to anything if you live with it long enough.'

'Sorry, Michael, I didn't mean to . . .' She leans towards me, her elbows on her knees. 'Do you mind if I ask you something?'

'Go ahead.'

'Have you always been – they don't call it disabled any more, do they – but have you always been, you know?'

'No, it just seems that way.'

'Then how . . . ?'

Whenever anyone asks me that question, I feel like a celebrity on an endless round of chat shows. Only I haven't got a new movie to promote, so rather than polish up the anecdote for Parky (the bastard lifeguard who just had to play the hero; the genius psychiatrist who pronounced that I 'might' get a bit depressed), I try to get it over with as quickly as possible. 'I was nine years old. It was an accident – chance in a million and all that. They said at the hospital I was lucky to be alive.'

This is the point at which most people get tongue-tied or start reminiscing about 'quadriplegics I have known'. Not Anna, unfortunately.

'Can you feel *anything*?'

'Anger, bitterness – a soupçon of despair now and then.'

'You know what I mean.'

I read on a website somewhere that it's best to be upfront at the beginning of any relationship. I can see that it probably makes sense to come clean about your love child, or 99 per cent of your sexually transmitted diseases, but there are certain skeletons that should always stay in the cupboard. 'I can't feel anything from my neck down.'

'Yes,' she says, stroking her cheek with the back of her hand, 'that's what I thought.'

There's a photograph, at home, of the three of us on Littlehampton beach. Whenever I pass it, I feel like I've seen a ghost. Dad lies buried up to his neck in the sand and I'm standing over him with a green plastic bucketful of sea-water in my hand and an enormous grin on my face. Mum (who looks pretty damned good in her flowery bikini) is kneeling in the background, offering up a Tupperware container of ham sandwiches, like one of the three kings.

'So, what do you think, Michael,' says Anna, a bit more chirpily. '*Did* Hamlet sleep with Ophelia?'

6

Spirit of Health or
Goblin Damned?

The Actor

The Fatted Calf is my kind of pub. I discovered it, quite by chance, the first week I was here. No log fires, no carefully selected secondhand books, and no bloody board games. No friendly joker of a landlord, no real ale, and above all no cast of eccentric regulars to brighten up my evenings with their autobiographical meanderings and homespun wit. Neither is it full of grunting louts in overpriced replica football shirts, but a disparate band of loners, cradling their drinks and peanuts, engrossed in the action like perverts at a peep show.

I've given up trying to ingratiate myself with the barmaid. 'Pint of Guinness and a packet of salt and vinegar, please.'

A jaded forty-something, she has the permanent look of a woman who's just tasted her first mouthful of sperm but can't find anywhere to spit it out. 'Hang on a minute. You're not Timothy Salt, are you?'

This is somewhat unnerving. She doesn't strike me as a person with a passion for regional theatre, and if she'd caught my Reverend Timms, surely she would have mentioned it weeks ago. 'I might be.'

She gestured towards the Gents. 'Someone over there wants a word with you.'

Who in God's name can it be: a hitman, hired by one of the many women I have wronged, an undercover agent from the Inland Revenue? As you will have gathered, I am not one of nature's optimists. I know it's not SOWINS in search of a rapprochement, or Tom Champagne come to tell me I've won the *Readers Digest* draw.

'Hi, I'm Nikki, Nikki Hardbody.'

My mouth opens, but I am reminded of Jacobi's magnificent tour de force in *I, Claudius*. 'H-H-H-H-H-H . . .'

She proffers a slim and perfectly manicured hand. 'It's great to meet you.'

'Hello there. C-C-C-Can I help you at all?'

'I do hope so,' she purrs, shooting a glance, if I am not very much mistaken, at the crotch of my chinos. 'I'm from Wellard Films.'

'Aaah.'

This is not how I imagined it. In my version it's Bunny Michelmore who calls:

'I think you'd better sit down, darling. You remember your Mr Scully [man in shop, episode 1,907] who witnessed the racist attack?' ['*There were two of them, white, must have been in their late . . . twenties. I didn't get a proper look cos there was a milk float in the way.*'] 'The producers liked him so much that they want to make him a regular.'

Even in what SOWINS referred to as my 'pathetic adolescent fantasies', the architect of my good fortune was never a drop-dead gorgeous thirty-something in a beautifully cut business suit with a black lacy T-shirt that allowed you a tantalizing glimpse of her jugs. 'You are Tim, aren't you?'

It's one of those moments of validation that I want to savour. If only Mum and Dad could be here. I hope at least that the barmaid is listening. 'Yes, I'm Timothy. But how on earth did you find me?'

'Everyone I asked said you'd be in the pub. Now, let me get you another one of those, and then we'll find a nice quiet corner and have a proper chat.'

When I was a very young actor, I made it a rule of thumb never to sleep with the director. This was largely to avoid unnecessary confusion with gentlemen of a certain age. In Nikki Hardbody's case, however, I might be prepared to make an exception.

'You're the guy that looks after Michael, right?'

'Well, yes, in a manner of speaking. But you needn't worry, it wouldn't be a problem. There are plenty of carers out there.'

I don't generally approve of women smoking, but with Nikki it's like watching a master class in fellatio. 'Michael's a pretty amazing young man, isn't he?'

'What . . . well, I suppose . . .'

'Did you know he has an IQ of 176?'

This doesn't feel quite right. It's like making love to a woman who keeps getting your name wrong. 'His mother might have mentioned it. I can't say I've given it much thought.'

She sips at her sparkling mineral water, leaving a crimson stain on the rim of her tumbler. 'I dug up the story in the *Croydon Advertiser*.'

'I'm sorry, I don't understand.'

'I'd shoot the whole thing on PD150 to give it a vérité feel.'

You get to a certain age and life starts eluding you. It begins with the subtle nuances, bits of the conversation that pass you by; then, almost overnight, you can't keep up with the contemporary allusions, it's years since you knew what the number one was, and you realize, to your horror, that you've taken to wearing Marks & Spencer jeans (with added Lycra). Nothing can stop you ending up with all the social awareness, tact and perspicacity of a High Court judge. 'You've lost me, I'm afraid.'

She smiles indulgently. 'You've probably seen some of my other work. *Kids with Cancer*? People said a lot of flattering things about it.'

'I don't think . . .'

'*Gerald to Beryl*? I was on the long list for a BAFTA.'

Now that *does* ring a bell. 'Wasn't it about the sex-change chappie? Didn't he end up doing panto?'

'Beryl was a very brave lady,' she says, pointedly. 'We became really close.'

And suddenly I'm thinking John Hurt; suddenly I'm

thinking amusing skits on *Children in Need*; suddenly I'm thinking *Best Newcomer*. 'Come on, Nikki, don't keep me in suspenders. What exactly did you have in mind?'

It appears Ms Hardbody is as excited as I am. She vacates her stool and joins me on the other side of the table, sliding across the fake leather towards me. I sense the warm promise of thighs. 'I want to make a documentary about Michael. I want people to understand exactly what it means to be a quadriplegic at Oxford.'

I wouldn't have lasted two minutes in the business if I hadn't perfected this simple technique. I believe young children have been known to survive immersion in the arctic waters by doing something similar. Whenever my agent (Bunny Michelmore at Bunny Michelmore Management) calls with bad news ('*Sorry, dear, the interest has cooled,*' '*Sorry, darling, they've decided to go with a name.*') I have learnt to put my whole body into a state of shutdown. It's an invaluable way of preserving one's dignity, and worked a treat when SOWINS said she didn't love me any more. Which is why, even as we speak, my face looks like I've just heard a mildly amusing anecdote, when inside I'm as angry and confused as McEnroe after a bad line call. '*You cannot be serious.*'

'It's got everything an award-winning documentary needs: a young guy who succeeds against all the odds, gorgeous setting – the Americans can't get enough of Oxbridge – plus the whole human angle. It's a really heart-warming story.'

If she dares to use the expression 'life affirming', I swear I shall spontaneously combust. I can just see her pitching the idea to the commissioning editor of Channel 4. 'I don't think that—'

'And what great characters, Jesus! You've got his batty religious mum who's still praying for a cure, the absent father we could go and doorstep, people love all that.'

Frankly, it all sounds about as entertaining as the annual digital rectal examinations for which I must submit myself when I reach the dreaded four o. 'Oh, I don't know.'

'And how, for the love of fuck, did he end up sharing his rooms with a failed . . . er, "resting" actor? It's zeitgeist on toast. We'd climax the whole thing with his performance in *Hamlet*. It'd be just great, great television.'

The temporary paralysis is wearing off; low-level peevishness will soon give way to full-blown fury. 'Look, Nikki, if it's *him* you want, what are you doing talking to me?'

'You and Michael must have become pretty close.'

'Are you trying to be funny?'

'I would never try and be funny with a guy as on the ball as you.'

'Yes, well, it . . .'

She squelches her cigarette butt into the ashtray. 'I don't want to go ahead with anything unless Michael's cool about it. The last thing I want is something in bad taste. I just thought that, with you two being so close, your input could be crucial.'

'In what way, exactly?'

Did I mention that, for a smoker, she has dazzling white teeth? 'I'd love it if you could sound him out. Show him what a fantastic opportunity it would be.'

'I should have thought you'd make a pretty good job of that yourself.'

Somehow she manages to move even closer. 'It needs to come from someone Michael trusts. I've had a few . . . set-backs lately.' She stares into her mineral water; I get this barely controllable urge to put my hand on her knee. 'Of course, it didn't help when Beryl . . .'

And now it's all coming back to me. 'That's right; the poor bloke couldn't handle his five minutes of fame. That's why he—'

'Beryl had a history of bipolar disorder. She was clinically depressed when we started filming. Her ex-wife told me as much at the funeral.'

'I'm sure that's a great comfort to you.'

She straightens her back and runs her hands slowly down her torso, like a dancer in a pop video. 'What would be very nice is if you could convince Michael to sign the consent forms. That way, if he does get cold feet (she smiles at the inappropriate metaphor), there won't be very much he can do about it.'

My ex-wife maintained that I would exhume my grandmother and flog off her collection of antique thimbles for a cough and a spit in *EastEnders*. I think, for once, SOWINS would be proud of me. 'Absolutely no way; Michael is a human being, not a piece of meat.' I inch sideways so that we're no longer joined at the hip, and bring my hand down hard on the table like what's-his-face in *Ice Station Zebra*. 'I will *not* be a party to it. Thank God that some of us still have our artistic integrity intact. And anyway,' I say, remembering a hard-hitting article in the

Daily Mail, 'this so-called reality television is on the way out. I can't see it lasting into the twenty-first century.'

She runs her tongue slowly across her top lip. 'Well, that's a pity. I had an idea that might have given your career a much needed boost.'

A shadow of doubt passes over the hostelry. 'How do you mean . . . boost?'

'Forget it. You're probably right. There's a lot more to life than a BAFTA.'

'No, wait,' I say, seizing her by the wrist. 'You might as well tell me what you had in mind.' (Pride is one of the seven deadly sins, after all.)

'I'll be straight with you, Tim. I was thinking John Nettles, but listening to you – your passion, your quiet dignity – I wonder if maybe we should get you in to do the voice-over.'

And suddenly I'm back to Jacobi's Claudius again. 'R-R-Really?'

'Yes,' she shrugs. 'Shame, that.'

'Now hang on a minute!' As you are probably aware, acting is about the toughest profession in the world. However, compared with making any headway in the voice-over game, it's a stroll in the park with a Harrods picnic hamper. Only a highly select coterie (Jarvis, Jason, McShane, Briers, Coogan, Laurie and the *Men Behaving Badly* gang) are permitted to gorge themselves on the rich pickings to be had in voice-over land. 'Perhaps I've been over-hasty.'

'Really?' she says, astonished yet delighted at the same time.

'Maybe disabled people deserve a prime-time platform.'

'You're so right.'

I'm anxious to establish a few ground rules. 'I take it that, as well as the voice-over, you'd want me to appear in this thing?'

'Absolutely,' she says, sucking on her slice of lemon and spitting the pips into her empty glass. 'Of course, Michael would be the central focus of the piece, but you'd be a major player, no doubt about it.'

'Well. I'd have to speak to my agent, of course – Bunny Michelmore at Bunny Michelmore Management – but I think I can probably help you out.'

'That's brilliant,' she says, patting me on my inner thigh, about halfway between my John Thomas and my knee. 'I think we're going to make a very good team.'

A pornographic image floats across the forefront of my mind. 'Yes, indeed.'

'You'll have a word with Michael then?'

'Absolutely,' I say, crossing my legs. 'Mike says he thinks of me as an older brother. If I can't talk him round, nobody can.'

I'm not self-deluded enough to actually believe this. However, I have an inkling that it may be in my best interests to let Ms Hardbody consider it so. Even if Michael didn't hate my guts, I have little doubt he would view the prospect of television immortality with as much enthusiasm as a course of abseiling lessons. No, the way I see it, there's only one person who's got a hope in hell of making him see sense. And doubtless she'll be phoning again before the evening's out. Into her hands I shall condemn my fragile spirit.

7

What a Piece of Work is a Man

The Quadriplegic

Mum has turned into a pushy showbiz parent. She holds the contract in front of me, smiling like a goblin damned. 'That's right, Michael,' she says. 'Just sign here . . . . and here . . . . aaand here.'

'Isn't it great, the way he does that?' says Nikki Hard-body, bending over me like one of those people who think they're good with children. 'Now, you are sure about this, aren't you, Michael? I don't want you getting into some-thing you're not happy with.'

'He's sure,' says Mum, 'aren't you, love?'

'Yes, Mum, quite sure.' I'd rather drown in a reservoir of my own vomit than be part of this Bambi's *My Left Foot* bollocks. Unlike practically everyone else in the world, my main ambition is not to make a turd of myself on TV. But since the poor cow's never going to get to cry at my wed-ding, it's the least I can do.

'Isn't this exciting? Soon the whole world's going to know about my wonderful son.'

'That's right,' says Nikki, taking the contract and slipping it into her Gucci handbag. 'And I have a hunch that the whole world is going to love Michael just as much as you do. You should have seen the great share we had for *Pepé, the Boy with No Nose.*'

'Yes,' says Mum. 'My heart went out to the poor little mite.'

Mum's been raiding the Littlewoods catalogue again. She's gone and got herself a new flowery dress and baggy pink cardigan, because she doesn't want to let me down. And she looks terrible. Back in the days when I was a real boy, we went on proper family holidays; a week in a guest house complete with half-board and tea- and coffee-making facilities in every room. Mum and Dad always dressed up for the evening meal; Dad stiff as hell in a jacket and tie, Mum in an almost fashionable dress and a gallon of the perfume she's still wearing now. They looked so out of place that, even though I was only eight years old, I couldn't help feeling sorry for them.

'I do look all right in this, don't I?' says Mum. 'It's not too much, is it?'

It's obvious that Nikki Hardbody isn't even on nodding terms with the Littlewoods catalogue. 'You look lovely, Valerie. You're everything I could have wished for, and more.'

'You'll make me blush,' says Mum, blushing.

'I don't want you to think of me as a director,' says

Nikki, 'but as a friend. That's what I love about this job. You get to meet such amazing people.'

Mum takes a paper tissue from her cardigan sleeve, and fusses about the mantelpiece, dusting the photograph of me and her with the Mayor of Croydon, and taking a quick peek in the mirror. 'I'm all of a tizzy,' she says. 'I've never been on the television before. Well, I was on *Songs of Praise* once, but all you could see was my hat.' She laughs, hopefully. 'I say, all you could see was my hat.'

Nikki grabs her camera, like a psychopath reaching for a chainsaw. 'Everyone feels nervous to start with. That's why I always work with the PD150. There's no crew getting under your feet all the time – just little me,' she smiles. 'Don't worry, after a while you won't even know I'm there – just like Sister Bernadette.' She points the camera in my face. A red light comes on. 'Now, we've got some lovely footage of Tim doing Michael's colostomy bag. Why don't I film the three of you having breakfast? Timothy,' she calls, 'is that coffee ready yet?'

'Just coming,' booms De Niro. 'Do you want to capture my entrance?' He's turned into this really scary Stepford carer; he can't do enough for me, and his conversation is peppered with 1970s superlatives and sycophantic banter – when the camera's running, that is. 'Here we are then. Do you know, Nikki, I've found this super little place in the covered market where they make a perfectly acceptable – light and crispy, but not too buttery – croissant. Why don't I feed Mike, and you two can get on with your coffee?'

'Aren't we forgetting something?' says Mum.

De Niro glances anxiously at the breakfast table. 'I might have some cherry preserve somewhere.'

Mum always likes to give thanks where it's due. 'Michael, would you like to say grace?'

It's a pity she's not so quick to apportion blame. 'Not really.'

Mum winks at Nikki. 'Someone got out of bed the wrong side this morning, didn't they, dear?' She bows her head and puts on her bank-manager-talking-to-an-important-customer voice. 'Dear Lord, we thank you for this food. And we just pray that you will bless Nikki and the wonderful work that she's going to be doing over the next couple of weeks. Amen.'

I've never had the courage to tell Mum I don't believe in God. What's the point? It would be as meaningless as if I decided to come out. I can't do any of the things Christians are supposed to feel guilty about anyway. Telling a quadriplegic not to kill is like instructing a blind man never to look at pornography. Mind you, it doesn't stop me having murderous thoughts from time to time.

Mum's inspecting a tea towel with the words 'A Gift From Poole' on the front. 'That's done well, hasn't it? Do you remember our holiday in Poole, Michael?'

'The one where Dad told you about Chelmsford, you mean?'

'Oh, was it?' says Mum, her face falling almost as quickly as Nikki can turn the camera in her direction and De Niro can launch himself into the frame. 'I don't remember.'

'Of course you do, Mum. It was our first – and last – family holiday after I became a crip.'

'I've told you not to use that word, Michael. You know I don't like it.'

Sometimes her Pollyanna routine does my head in. 'I think most women would remember the day their pathetic apology for a husband walked out on them, don't you?' I say, addressing the camera directly now and really enjoying it. 'You said you hoped he'd rot in hell, and after you'd blubbed for twenty minutes, that woman from the guest house gave you some brandy.'

I told you Mum was a cry-baby. 'Stop it. Stop it right now.' The constant tears have gouged deep trenches in the side of her face. 'You're not filming this, are you?'

'Of course not,' says Nikki, although the red light still appears to be on. 'Not if you aren't happy with it.'

'I'm not,' sniffs Mum. 'He gets like this sometimes. I'm sure he doesn't mean to, it's the medication, you see.'

'That's right,' chips in De Niro. 'I had an idea it might be the caffeine. Here, Mike, try some of this.' He tears off a piece of croissant and stuffs it down my throat. 'I expect he's still hungry, poor love.'

The Actor

Nikki wants to film the three of us enjoying a 'relaxed picnic by the river'. Apparently, if you put people at their ease, they're far more likely to spill their guts for the camera. Having practically ruptured myself humping

Michael and his chair across acres of Flanders mud, I'm certainly in no mood to spill mine.

'OK, finish your strawberries,' says Nikki, 'and then I'd like to do a little question-and-answer session. We'll start with you, Valerie, and then move on to Michael.'

'Sorry, Nikki,' I say, not wanting to make her look incompetent, but at the same time knowing that it needs to be said, 'you didn't mention my good self. When would you like me to do my piece to camera?'

Nikki looks almost as delightful as a model from the Next catalogue. Her black cowl-neck sweater and classic Levi's are in stark contrast to poor old Mrs Owen's Blue Cross Day ensemble. 'Sorry, Tim,' smiles Nikki, 'we'll do it later if you don't mind. Valerie's only with us today.'

'Can't let the Women's Prayer Group down, can I?' says Mrs Owen. 'Not after all the wonderful things they've done for Michael.'

'Fine,' I say, almost meaning it, but still mindful of the *Crimewatch* Incident, 'that way we'll have more time.'

'Yes, well, if you could just move Michael over there a bit, Valerie can squeeze in next to the picnic basket.'

'Not a problem. If I plonk him by the tree you can get a tight little three shot.'

Although I prefer not to speak of the *Crimewatch* Incident, it has impacted hugely on my approach to screen acting. Beppo the clown had done a runner. Doubtless you are unfamiliar with his work, yet it is a name that will in all probability haunt me longer than his young victims. It was my first telly. Imagine my joy at landing the role of the disgraced clown's agent. Unfortunately, the actual gentleman in question got it into his head that any association with his erstwhile client would be bad for Party People Enterprises, and the threat of legal action was enough to ensure that my beautifully understated performance ended up on the cutting-room floor. Since that time I have tried to ensure that no editor should be able to expunge me from the proceedings quite so effortlessly. Several years later, when my next big break came along, I contrived to stick as closely to Sooty as possible; consequently there was, at least, a small part of my anatomy in every shot. Which is why, at this very moment, I have assumed a position equidistant from Michael and his mother, leaning casually against a tree, pretending to be engrossed in *Be Your Own Psychotherapist in One Weekend*, à la Hamlet.

Nikki plays the off-screen interviewer; that annoyingly flat voice, which lulls its victims into a false sense of security and prompts them to unburden themselves in squirmingly graphic detail. 'How did you feel about that, Valerie, when you realized Michael was going to spend the rest of his . . . the foreseeable future in a wheelchair?'

'I think I felt angry . . . with God. It wasn't easy. I couldn't help asking, Why me? I didn't think I deserved it. I suppose I thought that because I'd always been a – it sounds silly, I know, but – well, a . . . a good Christian, whatever that is, that it shouldn't be happening.'

'So how did you manage to reconcile yourself to your son's . . . condition?'

'With God's love, and through a lot of prayer and fellowship, I gradually realized that he wasn't the millstone I'd first thought but a . . . well, a wonderful gift from our heavenly Father.' It's a concept I've always struggled with, but I do believe the glistening droplets welling up in the corners of her eyes are bona fide tears of joy. 'God was showing me just how much he loved me. Sorry, sorry . . . could you give me a minute?'

'Take as long as you like,' says Nikki, moving in for the close-up.

There's an exercise in *Be Your Own Psychotherapist in One Weekend*, which I defy anyone screwed up enough to buy the book to try. It involves getting both of your parents (or anyone you consider to have had an adverse effect on your life), sitting them in armchairs (I'm not sure how important the armchairs are, but the book is fairly specific), and then one by one outlining their crimes against you, before magnanimously forgiving them. There seems to be a basic flaw here: even if I just completed the exercise with SOWINS, it would take at least two years; if you add to that the casting department of *The Bill* and SOWINS's entire family, you can begin to see my problem. Observing Michael and his mother together, I have a hunch that my young charge might find the exercise equally time-consuming.

'That was spot on,' says Nikki, 'really moving stuff. Now, let me just sort out Michael's mike, and then we can get on with it.'

'She's so lovely, isn't she, Tim?' whispers Mrs Owen. 'She really knows how to put you at your ease.'

'Doesn't she just,' I say, taking a step to the left so that I'm directly behind Michael.

'How was I, Timothy? You must have done lots of filming. I suppose it's all a bit boring for you.'

'Well, you know,' I shrug, 'it is something of a busman's holiday, but I try not to get too blasé about it.' Her mouth forms an ooh shape. 'You were fine, by the way.'

'Was I really?'

'Absolutely. I think you're coming over very well.' Actors don't do sincerity; it's something we try to leave behind at the stage door. I'm sure the novelty of seeing real people speaking from the heart will soon wear off, but there's still a certain fascination in watching a nobody like Mrs Owen emoting so shamelessly. 'Did you actually mean all that stuff?'

'What stuff, Timothy?'

'About Michael being a "wonderful gift from God"?'

'Yes, of course I did,' she says, slamming the lid of the picnic basket. 'Michael's accident was the best thing that ever happened to us. God is love, Timothy. He doesn't let his children suffer unnecessarily unless he has a very good reason.' She starts maniacally gathering paper plates and plastic cutlery. 'If we don't see that reason straight away, it's our lack of faith that's to blame, not God.'

'Sorry . . . only asking.'

When I first clapped eyes on her, that fateful afternoon in East Croydon, Valerie Owen looked washed out and at least fifty years old. This bracing weather might be partially responsible for her healthy glow, but, in the cold light of an autumn morning, it's painfully apparent that there can be no more than a couple of years between us. Perhaps, after a few drinks, she could almost be attractive, in a Blanche Dubois sort of way. 'Look, Tim,' she says, 'I'm the one who should be apologizing, especially after the wonderful way you've been looking after my Michael.'

'Think nothing of it.'

'Oh, I almost forgot. I took your advice.'

What's she talking about? Ever since Simon Butterworth's frosty reception of my well-meant (but possibly ill-judged) meditations on the institution of marriage, I have done my best to keep my own counsel. 'What advice?'

'The other night on the phone, you said I ought to get out more.'

'Did I?'

'You know you did,' she says, patting me on the arm. 'Well, I've only gone and signed up for ballroom-dancing lessons. I've always wanted to, but of course, I've never had the time before.'

'OK, everyone,' shouts Nikki, 'can we have a bit of hush, please? Michael's all set.'

'Go on, love,' says Mrs Owen. 'Don't be nervous. If I can do it, you can.'

I pick up *Be Your Own Psychotherapist in One Weekend* and inch slowly towards the boy in the wheelchair.

The Quadriplegic

If this is God's plan for my life, it's a really crap plan. It's bad enough having to live it privately, but who in their right mind wants to see someone like me popping up at the end of the cornflakes adverts? Mum thinks it's wonderful.

That's her favourite word, have you noticed? I don't know what's worse: that horrible dress she's wearing or the frightening smile she pulls when she tells the world how being the little cripple boy's mother is like having all her Christmases and birthdays rolled into one.

'OK,' says Nikki, 'let's go for it. So, Michael, how are you finding Oxford?'

'It's all right.'

'Were you surprised when they offered you a place?'

'Not really.' (She could shake spunk from a stick in those jeans.) 'I have got an IQ of 176.'

'And where do you get your brains from, do you think?'

'Not my dad, that's for sure.'

'Why do you say that?'

'Because he's a thick tosser.'

'That's enough, Michael,' says Mum. I'm not sure if she's telling me off for bad-mouthing the man she once loved or for my use of the mild expletive. 'Go on, Nikki, ask him about his A level results.'

Nikki shows Mum the palm of her hand; the gesture of a concerned social worker anxious to let a difficult 'client' have his say. 'Hang on a minute, Val. I think we might have touched on something important here. Tell me about your dad, Michael. How do feel about him?'

'I don't feel anything about him. The bastard walked out on us. How do you expect me to feel?'

I don't need eyes in the back of my head to realize that Mum is chucking a mental. 'I won't have you talking about your father like that. I'm so sorry, Nikki. I don't know what's got into him today.'

'It's cool,' says Nikki, not even looking up. 'We can bleep it if you like. So what you're saying, Michael, is that you felt abandoned.'

'Too right I did. One minute he's playing happy spacky families and the next he's pissed off to Chelmsford and never wants to see us again.'

Mum throws herself in front of the camera, like that suffragette with the horse. 'It wasn't like that. Terry's a good man. It was . . . difficult for him.'

Nikki leaps backwards and carries on filming. (It could be my imagination, but, even through her black jumper, I could swear that those are erect nipples.) 'What do you say to that, Michael?'

'I say he should have tried harder. I say he's a pusillanimous cretin for treating us like that.'

I don't think it's going quite the way that Mum intended. 'How can you say that, Michael, after all that man's done for you?'

'You are joking, I hope.'

'Who do you think paid for the house so that I could look after you?' says Mum, looking straight into the camera. 'Who came up with the money for your first computer?'

'Big deal,' I say. 'What's a couple of grand hush money if it means not having to walk down the street with the Veg?' And suddenly I realize I've gone too far again. 'Sorry, sorry, Mum. I didn't mean to . . .'

Nikki looks like the cat that got the cream. 'Why don't we have a quick time out? It's getting a bit heated, isn't it?'

'You won't use any of that, will you, Nikki?' says Mum.

'Of course not, it's entirely up to you. I'm a serious journalist, Valerie, not some filthy tabloid hack. Now, I've just got one more question for Michael – don't worry, it's nothing heavy – and then I won't need you again until this evening.'

De Niro slithers even closer. 'Look forward to it,' he says. 'Great working with you, by the way.'

'OK,' says Nikki, 'this last one's just a quickie. Tell us about your dreams, Michael. What's your greatest ambition in life?'

What do you reckon? Win the Nobel Peace Prize? Kill my carer? Improve Mum's dress sense? Nah, don't think so. 'Oh, that's easy, Nikki.'

'Tell me about it.'

'I want to have an orgasm.'

8

Let the Candied Tongue Lick

The Virgin

'What the hell are you playing at?' says Philip. 'You're keeping everybody waiting.'

'Don't you ever knock?'

'I haven't got time for this, Anna. Now for the love of fuck, get your act together.' He stomps over to my CD player and karate chops the pause button.

'I was listening to that.'

'You were supposed to be there twenty minutes ago.' I register his sneer of disapproval as he spots the Snickers wrappers in the wastepaper basket. 'I can't believe how selfish you're being.'

As usual, Piers isn't far behind him. 'Anna, are you all right? Phil and I were really worried about you.'

'She's fine,' says Philip, tugging at his burgundy cravat. 'She just needs to get her arse into gear.'

Piers has spotted the photograph on my bedside table. 'Gosh, how adorable. What are their names, Anna?'

'Maggie and Tom. Gorgeous, aren't they?'

'We haven't got time for your fucking family history,' says Philip, throwing my boots at me. 'Nikki's going mental down there.'

'I'm not doing it.'

Philip looks like he's been slapped in the face with a wet kipper. '*What* did you say?'

'You heard me.'

His hand flies up to his mouth; he bites hard on his knuckles. 'I thought I'd explained all this. It's an art-mirroring-life kind of thing. Nikki wants to show how close you and Michael are getting.'

'Yes, but we're not . . . not really. I mean, he's a sweet guy and everything, but I'd hardly call us close.'

'God help us,' says Philip, kicking my Wallace and Gromit slippers across the floor. 'Look, the whole idea is that, even though he's in that bloody wheelchair, he can still have a half-decent social life. What's wrong with that?'

'It's not true, is it? You know as well as I do he spends virtually 24/7 sitting in front of his computer. That tart with the video camera's just using him.' (I've seen the way Phil looks at her. She's the sort of woman who ices her nipples before every business meeting.)

'Do I have to spell it out for you?' says Philip wearily. 'The more this film focuses on my production of *Hamlet*, the less likely it is to turn into a tedious diatribe about living with quadriplegia and the state of the National Health. I don't need to tell you how good that could be for my career.'

'Him and his brilliant career!' sniggers Piers.

'Shut up, you old queen, this is important.' Philip takes

97

my hand and strokes it with his index finger. 'Come on, Anna. All you've got to do is sit with him for a bit. As soon as the filming's over you can come and join us.'

'There's free cocktails all round,' says Piers gleefully, 'which means the boat club boys will almost certainly be getting their kit off.'

'Do it for me, babe,' says Philip. 'There's a good girl.'

This morning, I watched from the window as they led him away; his mother all over him like a tiresome waiter, the carer guy never more than two inches from his side, and that mini-skirted uber slapper filming their every move. Poor Michael; he looked just like I did when they carted me off to Toby Chamberlain-Webber's twenty-first. Just because he's in a wheelchair, doesn't mean he isn't entitled to a bit of privacy. 'No, sorry, I'm not coming. I don't feel comfortable with it.'

'Look,' says Philip, staring into my eyes like a stage hypnotist. 'If you do this for me, I'll come down to the Old Rectory.' He's already made it quite clear what a disgustingly bourgeois prospect that is. 'I'll even be nice to your old lady.'

Given Mummy's fragile mental state, it's too good an offer to refuse. 'Well, all right then, but I'm only staying half an hour.'

The Quadriplegic

Welcome to the Underground. I've not been down here before (too many fucking steps and the smoke's a real killer) but Nikki wants some footage of me enjoying a 'typical Oxbridge experience', so here I am in the student bar surrounded by my closest 'chums'.

And guess what: suddenly I'm the most popular guy in Oxford. Everyone who's anyone is here: the admiral of the college punt (aka Piers) is sitting by the jukebox with Philip Sidney, and half the boat club are shuffling about with their trousers around their ankles singing 'The Cucumber Song'. *'It's green, it's long, it looks just like my dong, CUCUMBER, CUCUMBER!'*

If I wasn't paralysed, all this backslapping would be getting on my nerves. Last week they melted into the woodwork when they saw me coming, now they're calling me Mike and telling Mum what an amazing guy I am. Is it because they've come to realize that, underneath it all, I'm just the same as they are, or could it be the lure of a fleeting appearance on Channel 4 and Nikki's kind offer of free Flying Fucks (two shots of vodka, cranberry juice, Bols Blue and a 5mm spoonful of Night Nurse) for the evening?

Mum doesn't care much for Flying Fucks. She cradles her orange juice, looking as out of place as a quadriplegic donkey in a nativity play. 'Isn't it wonderful,' she says. 'I didn't realize Michael had so many new friends.'

'Yes,' says Anna, glancing over at the jukebox, 'he certainly seems to have made his mark.'

'I'm so pleased for you, love,' says Mum. 'He's always found the social side of things a bit tricky.'

'Oh, right,' says Anna. 'I would never have guessed.'

Nikki thought it would be rather nice to see Hamlet and Ophelia socializing. Anna looks like she'd rather be anywhere in the world than sharing a table with Mum and me. I don't know why she bothered.

De Niro hasn't left my side all evening. He stands guard over my chair, like a puritanical chaperone. 'How are you feeling, old chap? Would you like me to wipe your mouth for you?'

'You did that two minutes ago.'

'He's wonderful, isn't he?' says Mum. 'Do you know, Anna, I was really worried about leaving my little boy with a stranger, but I've got to admit, Tim here's a real treasure.'

'One does one's best.'

Nikki is wearing a T-shirt with 'Dirty Slag' on the front. 'OK, everyone, I just want to try one last set piece, and then we can all get down to some serious drinking.' (Cheers from the boat club crowd.) 'Tim; push Michael over to the pool table, would you? We haven't got time for all that faffing about. And Anna, could you park yourself on the arm of his wheelchair?' De Niro drags me backwards across the bar. Anna follows reluctantly, but opts not to sit on my spaz-chariot. 'Right, the two guys playing pool sink a couple of balls and then the chappie in the cravat . . . sorry, I forgot your name.'

'It's Sidney, Philip Sidney, as in . . .'

'Yeah, whatever. You bring Michael a cocktail, pat him on the back, then he smiles and cracks a joke and, Anna, I want you to piss yourself laughing. All rightee, any questions?'

'What joke do you want me to tell?'

'Don't worry about it, Mike. No one will hear you anyway. This will all be part of the video montage section.

I'm going to use that Ian Dury song – in an ironic way, of course. "Spasticus Autisticus", *you* must know it.'

'Sorry, Nikki,' says De Niro, 'just a small thing. Wouldn't it be better if Philip handed *me* the cocktail and then, after Mike's told his joke, I can stick the straw straight in his mouth. I am his carer, after all.'

'Yes, all right, if you must,' says Nikki, biting her bottom lip. 'Now, can we get on, please? OK, places everyone, camera rolling . . . aaand action.'

Anna stares at her Doc Martens. Philip Sidney walks stiffly across the Underworld and hands De Niro my drink. Nikki thought that if everybody sucked their cocktails through stripy straws it would make me look more normal, but after the initial kiddies' tea party hilarity, everyone except Mum dumped the straws anyway, and the boat club boys are pouring their Flying Fucks into pint glasses.

De Niro coughs loudly, and twitches like a lunatic. 'Your joke, Michael, your joke,' he hisses, in a loud stage whisper.

'Oh, yeah. OK, there's this quadriplegic, right? And it's his birthday.'

'And cut. Sorry, Mike,' says Nikki, 'we'll have to lose the quadriplegic joke. Don't want to offend anyone, do we?'

'You said no one would hear me.'

'It's the lip-readers, I'm afraid. There's always someone who writes in to complain. The deaf buggers haven't got anything better to do. OK, people, let's go again, shall we?'

The Virgin

Thank God that's over. The moment Nikki Hardbody shouts, 'OK, everybody, it's a wrap,' I slip under the pool table and make my getaway. I thought Michael was joking when he said his mother was like an older, non-singing version of Julie Andrews, but after half an hour of her honey-coated saccharin, I feel like topping myself.

I pick my way through a drunken scrum of rugger buggers, expecting a few words of sympathy from my director/boyfriend. Philip greets me with a leery smile and a hand on the arse. 'Don't they make a lovely couple, Piers? The virgin and the quadriplegic, it's a marriage made in heaven.'

Piers giggles and slides down his chair. 'You could say that.'

'Inspired casting I'd call it,' says Philip, patting his lap and gesturing me to sit down on it. 'Have you named the day yet, Anna?'

I take the seat next to Piers and try not to look as pissed off as I feel. 'Valentine's Day, most probably.'

'But how remiss of me,' says Philip, waving his glass like a rat-arsed best man. 'I forgot to congratulate you on your charming, putative mother-in-law.'

'Stop it, Philip. It's not funny.'

'On the contrary, I find the whole scenario most amusing.'

'You owe me for this.'

'I said I'd come down to Toad Hall with you, didn't I? What more do you bloody want?'

Piers looks none too happy about the idea. 'You mean you two are really going to spend a weekend together?'

'I said one night,' snaps Philip. 'I can't afford a whole weekend in the middle of a rehearsal period.'

'Well, that's great,' says Piers, sounding even less convincing than his Horatio. 'I'm . . . so pleased for you.'

Philip's voice somehow manages to rise above the drunken cacophony. 'She still won't screw me, you know. Think I must be losing my touch.'

Ever had the feeling that the whole world is laughing at you? Just as I'm about to die of embarrassment, good old Piers flies to the rescue. 'Where are your people from, Anna?'

'Hampshire.'

'Do you know the Chamberlain-Webbers?'

'Absolutely. Mummy and Auntie Pru used to be great chums.'

'James and I were at school together.'

'Gosh . . . really?'

'Oh, God,' says Philip with a huge yawn. 'Is there anything more tedious than the incestuous ramblings of the middle classes?' (Daddy says that the true aristocrats don't need to be snobs; Philip must be the exception that proves the rule.) 'If it's small talk you're after, maybe you'd be better off with Gommo over there.'

'Maybe I would,' I say, glancing across at Michael and his sainted mother. 'At least he's not a stuck-up wanker.'

'Well, he couldn't be, could he?' says Philip, roaring with laughter. 'I'd say that was something of a physical impossibility. In fact, there's not really a lot he can do.' He waves drunkenly at Michael and gives him the thumbs-up. 'All right, mate?'

'At least he's got a decent sense of humour,' I say, trying to sound like a feisty heroine. 'At least he doesn't treat people like pieces of meat.'

'So go out with him then,' shrugs Philip. 'I can see you've got the hots for the bloke.'

'Maybe I will.'

'Now that I would like to see,' says Philip, lurching to his feet. 'Still, I suppose it would end up exactly the same as one of *our* dates.'

'What do you mean?'

The corners of his mouth twist upwards into a sly smile: 'Totally shagless, of course!'

'Why do you always do this to people?' says Piers. 'You were exactly the same with that girl from St Hilda's.'

'I guess that's just the kind of guy I am,' mutters Philip. 'Now, if you've quite finished, I'm going to put a song on the jukebox.'

Piers smiles sympathetically and clicks *The Archers* theme with his tongue. 'By the way, I got you something, Anna.' He reaches into his waistcoat and pulls out a Ripple. 'I know you're a bit of a chocolate fiend.'

'Oh, Piers, I could kiss you.'

A flicker of concern dances across his face. 'No need for that, old thing. And you mustn't worry about Philip either. I know how much he's looking forward to meeting your parents – he told me so himself.'

The Actor

The party rages around us. Thanks to yours truly, filming is finally over for the night. It's quite possible I could warrant a writing credit. If I hadn't stepped into the breach with my joke about the two prostitutes on Brighton Pier, no doubt we'd still be at it.

Michael looks deeply peeved. Five minutes ago they were his bezzy mates, but now they seem quite content to let him sit in the corner and watch with Mother. SOWINS maintained that the expression 'tight-arsed' might have been invented for me; however, looking across at the woman who can make one Britvic orange last an entire evening, I'm beginning to feel like something of a libertine.

'To make you come, just stick it up your bum, CUCUMBER, CUCUMBER!'

Luckily for Mrs Owen, the young gentlemen of the boat club are not au fait with the articulation exercises in *Voice and the Actor*. 'What on earth is all that about, Timothy?' she says, pulling at the cuffs of her cardigan. 'They're not really singing about vegetables, are they?'

'It's what passes for undergraduate humour these days.'

'That's right,' says Nikki Hardbody, downing her third Flying Fuck, 'unlike the sophisticated wit of Timothy here. "One swallow doesn't make a summer" – very droll, Tim, very droll.'

I'm not so out of touch that I don't realize the legend on Nikki's T-shirt is supposed to be ironic, but I can't help hoping it has some basis in truth. Just because she has 'Dirty Slag' tastefully emblazoned across her chest, doesn't necessarily mean she's taken a vow of chastity. 'One does one's best.'

'And I think you're doing very well, Timothy,' says Valerie Owen. 'And so does Michael, don't you, dear?'

The young gentleman in the wheelchair is not quite so keen to endorse my credentials. 'Haven't you got a train to catch, Mum? I don't want you to miss it.'

'That's very thoughtful of you, love. But don't worry; it's not until five-and-twenty to. I've got heaps of time.'

Michael looks as fed up as I feel. There's no way I can start having a crack at Nikki with the 'moral majority' sitting opposite. 'Michael's right,' I say. 'You really shouldn't risk it.'

'You hear that, Nikki?' says Mrs Owen, proudly. 'Now I've got two young men looking out for me – how about that, eh?'

Nikki inhales deeply, like a world-class athlete, and puffs out a thin plume of smoke. 'Good on you, Val.' Although I'm cautiously optimistic that Nikki may be partial to the mature type, I'm still hoping she registered the two 'young' men comment.

'I tell you what,' says Mrs Owen. 'I'll just finish my drink, and then, perhaps, I'd better be making tracks.'

Despite the fact that he's been known to hand out crap presents like chummo there, I'm thinking that maybe there is a loving God after all. Things get even better when someone puts an old favourite of mine on the jukebox.

'God, I love this song,' says Nikki, shaking her boobs like a slightly worse-for-wear go-go dancer. 'It reminds me of the old college bop.'

'Were you at Oxford too, then?' says Mrs Owen.

Just for a moment Nikki's knockers are becalmed. 'No, no, I was at the other place.' She stares up at the ceiling and sings along to the chorus of 'Like A Virgin' in a husky tenor. 'Jesus, that was a long time ago.'

Michael appears to have gone into hibernation, Mrs Owen is still smarting from the profanity, and Nikki looks to have succumbed to a nasty dose of nostalgia. The whole evening is taking on a regrettably maudlin feel.

Anna's arrival at the table of doom is a welcome relief; that is, until I clock the puffy eyes and the ubiquitous Kleenex. 'Hi,' she says, distracted for a moment by the whoop of laughter that goes up by the jukebox, 'how's it going?'

'Very nicely, thank you, dear,' says Mrs Owen. 'We're having a good old chinwag, aren't we? Why don't you join us?'

'No,' says Anna, rather too emphatically. 'Actually, I just wanted a quick word with Michael.'

The three able-bodies at the table turn towards her in unison: 'What about?'

'I was thinking of going for a pizza,' says Anna, looking over her shoulder at the jukebox. 'I wondered if Michael might like to tag along.'

'I don't think so, dear,' says Mrs Owen. 'He finds that sort of thing a bit of a strain.'

'I'm not sure young Anna here realizes what it entails,' I add, with feeling.

'I know he's not a dab hand with a knife and fork, if

that's what you mean,' says Anna, somewhat tastelessly. 'Come on, Michael. What do you say?'

'Tell her, love,' says his mother, 'you don't want to be out on a night like this.'

'Yeah, yeah, that'd be really nice,' says Michael. 'I love pizza.'

'I think it's a stonking idea,' says Nikki. 'I mean, just because he's in that chair, doesn't mean the poor kid shouldn't have a social life. You don't mind if I film it, do you?'

'Yes, we do, actually,' says Anna. 'I think we've all had enough of that for one night.'

'Please yourself,' shrugs Nikki. 'Little Pepé, the boy with no nose, didn't like me filming him eating to start with, but he soon got over it.'

'What about your medication, Michael?' says Mrs Owen. 'You know what happens when you eat at this time.'

'You'd better take these, Anna,' I say, reaching into the baby changing bag that I carry with me on all Michael's little expeditions. 'These ones are for before the meal. And he'll tell you what to do with this when he's finished.'

'OK, cool,' says Anna, stuffing the packets of pills into her orange rucksack, obviously keen to get out of here. 'See you back in college, Timothy – and nice to meet you, Mrs Owen.'

Valerie Owen smiles unconvincingly and stabs the back of her hand with a cocktail stick. 'Don't forget your Colosac, Michael!'

Nikki slugs down another Flying Fuck as Ironside and

his dinner-date make their way to the door, unmourned by their contemporaries.

The Flying Fuck (or Flying F**K as it is coyly titled on the blackboard behind the bar) has nothing to do with acrobatic sex. Judging from Nikki's conversation, it derives its name from the fact that once you've imbibed a few you cease to give a fig for the sensibilities of those around you. Under certain circumstances, I will allow that the story of Beryl the transvestite's taste in lingerie could be (mildly) amusing, but I share Valerie Owen's distaste for Nikki's anecdote about Pepé, the boy with no nose.

'It just slipped out,' giggles Nikki. 'Thank Christ, his parents didn't speak a word of English. Otherwise I'd have been in dead shtuck. Anyway, it was that Channel 4 guy's fault for asking me how he smelled.'

'I'd better pop to the little girls' room,' says Valerie Owen. 'Don't want to miss that train.'

'Terrible!' repeats Nikki, proving once again that there is no such thing as a new joke. She watches Valerie Owen disappear into the Ladies before sliding towards me and whispering conspiratorially, 'Can you believe that woman?'

'I know what you mean,' I reply, sympathetically, 'but I'm sure you can salvage some of her best bits. She's not that bad, is she?'

'Not that bad?' says Nikki incredulously. 'Not that bad? She's a fucking wonderful gift from our heavenly father.'

'I'm not with you, Nikki,' I say, suspecting it's something to do with the 'good is bad' thing that passes as accepted wisdom amongst the under thirties. 'What do you mean?'

'The silly cow's a total nightmare. She's got everything, the terrible clothes – I mean, what does she think she looks like? – the 1950s shop-girl accent: "Isn't it *wonderful* that my darling son shits into a plastic bag?" (Nikki's impression is cruelly accurate.) 'I knew it was going to be special, Tim, but I didn't think it was going to be this good.'

'So all that's good, is it?'

'She makes Sister Wendy look well-adjusted. The woman's a complete joke, the public will love her. They adore anyone who makes them feel intelligent. And what about all that stuff about Michael's dad – talk about getting her knickers in a twist. It's gold dust, that is.'

'I thought you said you weren't going to use any of it.'

'You're joking. Why do you think I got them to sign those consent forms? I'm not making that mistake again,' she adds, bitterly. 'If Beryl's wife had let me film his funeral the sodding BAFTA was in the bag.'

It's another one of life's cruel paradoxes: my slim chances with Ms Hardbody increase with every drink she downs, and yet the more inebriated she becomes, the less alluring she appears. Still, as Simon Butterworth once said (and I think rightly), '*A fuck is a fuck is a fuck*.' 'Did I ever tell you my Hamlet joke, Nikki?'

'No,' she says, reminding me of SOWINS whenever I suggested a euphemistic early night, 'I don't think so.'

Humour is the last resort of the ugly and impecunious, but needs must and all that. 'There's this young method actor playing Hamlet. After a rehearsal, he asks the chap giving his Polonius if he thinks that Hamlet slept with Ophelia, and the old pro replies, "In my day, dear boy, invariably." Not that that's going to happen in *this* production,' I add waggishly.

'No,' whispers Nikki, 'but wouldn't it be great if it did.' My attempt at humour seems to have jolted her into sobriety. She jumps to her feet and slings her handbag over her shoulder. 'Sorry, Timbo, got to get back to my hotel. Do you know the Bath Place? You'll have to come over for a drink sometime.'

'Let's grasp the nettle while it's hot, shall we?' I say, struggling for a metaphor that doesn't sound like code for 'Fancy a shag?'

'That'd be nice,' she says, 'but not tonight, eh? I need my beauty sleep. The kids from *Fame* are letting me film their first run-through tomorrow.'

'How did you get Sidney to agree to that?'

'Oh, I have my methods,' says Nikki, smiling enigmatically. 'Thanks for today, Timothy. You've been bloody fantastic. I don't know your work, but I feel sure I'd like to use you again sometime. Ciao.'

'Don't go yet,' I say, marvelling at her perspicacity, and then clutching at a passing straw. 'What about Mrs Owen? Don't you want to say goodbye?'

Nikki is already on her way to the door. 'Do it for me, will you, Timmy? I can't face another second with that dozy bitch. Tell her I've got Spielberg on the line if you like. I'm sure you'll think of something.' Even the lads on the floor freeze mid-drinking game to watch the rise and fall of Nikki's derrière as it makes its way towards the exit.

Valerie Owen emerges from the Ladies, raincoat belted like an evacuee. 'Where's Nikki?'

'She had to leave, I'm afraid – something to do with work.' I'm not used to lying for other people (except Simon Butterworth when he was having that affair with the marriage counsellor) so I'm amazed she doesn't smell a rat. 'But she sends her apologies.'

'Isn't that nice,' says Valerie Owen, reaching for her shopping basket. 'She's wonderful, isn't she? Nothing's ever too much trouble. Did you know she was paying all my train fares?'

'Good old Nikki.'

'Talking of which, I'd better be on my way. It's not far to the station, is it?'

'No, no, I'll point you in the right direction if you like. That is, normally I'd walk you there myself, Valerie, but I've got rather an important appointment.'

'That's quite all right, Timothy,' she says, offering me her hand. 'I know how precious your time must be.' Somehow it would seem churlish not to take hold of her delicate fingers. 'Cheery bye then. I'm so glad Michael's got someone like you looking out for him. I can't tell you how grateful I am.'

I shrug modestly. 'You're very welcome. And please, feel free to call me any time.'

A quarter of an hour later, I'm sitting in the Fatted Calf with my second pint of Guinness, feeling ever so slightly guilty that I didn't escort her to the station.

9

The Primrose Path of Dalliance

The Quadriplegic

Oxford's nothing like East Croydon; there are a lot more *Observer* readers for a start. Venture into the Arndale Centre and chances are that the happy shoppers will react to me in one of two ways. First up there's good old-fashioned repulsion; shock horror followed by a sudden interest in the window displays. (I include in this the sniggering taunts of frightened schoolchildren.) The other one is pity: the sympathetic smile, the forced conversation, the traffic cop who pretends to book you for speeding. The repulsion I can deal with. It's the pity that really pisses me off.

Here in Oxford, on the other hand, I'm often met with what people imagine to be the perfect, liberal response. No patronizing friendliness, not even the slightest hint that they wouldn't be anything but thrilled if you asked for their daughter's hand in marriage. The only thing that gives them away is that, in their anxiety to prove they're treating you exactly the same as a normal person, they hold the look just a tiny bit too long.

But tonight is rather different. With a fit girl like Anna by my side, even I can see we make a pretty unusual picture. Luckily, she's far too preoccupied to notice the funny looks we've been getting. 'Who does he think he is anyway?' she says, holding the door for me. 'That guy's so up himself it's not true.'

'You mean Philip, I suppose?'

She stands in front of the 'Please Wait to be Seated' sign, nodding angrily to the 1980s soundtrack. 'Who else would have put on that bloody Madonna song?'

Pizza Express (my number one choice) is up a load of stairs so we've ended up at a place near the theatre, which has one of those crap punning names (Pizza the Action, Piece of Pizza, or some such) and black-and-white photographs of 1950s Hollywood stars on the wall.

Mandy, our waitress, looks about twelve. 'Table for two, is it, madam?' she says, doing her best not to stare.

'Yes, thanks,' says Anna.

'Would you like smoking or non-smoking?'

'Non-smoking, please,' I say, just to show her that I've developed the power of speech.

'If you'd just like to follow me.'

On the other side of the restaurant they've pulled three tables together, and what looks like an office outing is in full swing. Young guys in colourful shirts smoking cigars, and girls with loud voices and bare legs crack 'in' jokes and indulge in flirtatious banter. Two waiters arrive with a flaming birthday cake, and the whole group lurches into a drunken chorus of 'Happy Birthday, Dear Julie' for a girl in a red dress, who's turning a shade of green.

Mandy leads us to a secluded alcove next to the Gents. 'Can I get you something to drink while you're looking at the menu?'

'I don't know about you, Anna,' I say, trying to sound sophisticated, 'but I fancy a glass of wine.'

'Are you allowed wine?'

'Afraid I might get legless?'

Anna smiles. 'Go for it.'

'OK, then, we'll have half a bottle of house red, two glasses and a straw, please . . . oh, and a glass of tap water.'

Mandy looks bemused. 'What do you want a straw for? . . . Oh, yeah, right.' She lingers uncomfortably, transferring her weight from foot to foot, trying to find the right words. 'Er . . . does he need a knife and fork?'

'No, it's OK,' says Anna, 'Michael can share mine.'

Anna turns out to be a great feeder. A lot of people just keep shovelling it down until it's all gone. This is slightly less frustrating than the 'chew everything a hundred times' school, or the 'constantly wiping your mouth with a napkin' mother-and-baby method. Anna seems to have a natural feeling for the nuances of eating. She knows exactly when I need to pause for breath, and even does that thing of saving a nice bit of pepperoni for the last mouthful. It's a luxury I'm seldom afforded.

'What do you want to do when you get out of this place, Michael?'

'I thought we were going back to college.'

'No, silly,' she says, folding her napkin into a water lily. 'I mean, what do you want to do when you leave Oxford?'

'No one's ever asked me that before.'

'Why not?'

'Because most people assume I'll end up in a home somewhere. Mum used to say that if I prayed faithfully enough I'd be able to walk again, but I was never that stupid.'

Anna mimes playing the violin. 'Oh, come on, there must be something you want to do.'

'I always fancied being the brainy one in an American high-school series. You know, the nerd in spacksavers who all the cool kids take the piss out of? Then one day I had a reality check.'

'I'm sorry,' says Anna, twiddling the stem of her wine-glass, 'that must have been hard for you.'

'Yeah, as soon as I realized how shit my American accent was, I knew it was never to be.'

'I wanted to be an air hostess.'

And suddenly, I'm transfixed by her breasts again. She's done her best to camouflage them underneath that baggy jumper, but all I want to do is bury my head in them and feel the warmth. 'Actually, if you really want to know, Anna, I'm going to write.'

'That's brilliant,' she says, sounding like she means it.

'Not a lot else I can do, is there?'

'What sort of stuff? I mean novels, poetry . . . ?'

I don't know where it comes from, but I find myself replying like it's something I've known all my life. 'Theatre, I want to write for the theatre.'

'Yes, of course,' she says, 'I should have guessed.'

Writing is, after all, the ultimate revenge; better than violence, better than sex. And I am the ultimate fly on the wall. Wheel me into any room, and after about twenty minutes people forget I'm there. That's why I've got this flair for dialogue. I had a ringside seat for some of Mum and Dad's biggest bust-ups. One time, they were halfway through 'making up' before Mum remembered where she'd parked me. 'Maybe I'll dedicate my first play to you, Anna.'

'Thanks, that's really sweet of you.'

'What about you? How do you see your life panning out?'

'Well, if I take after Mummy, I can look forward to a lifetime of manic depression and chemical dependency, but if I turn out like Dad, I'll probably end up as a promiscuous megalomaniac with a gardening fetish.'

'I must meet your family sometime.'

'Mummy's always on at me to bring a "chap" down for the weekend. She says if I don't meet someone at Oxford, I never will.' A malicious grin flickers across her face. 'Serve her right if I turned up with someone like you.' She buries her face in her hands the moment she releases what she's said. 'Oh, bums . . . sorry, I didn't mean . . . oh, God . . . look, Michael, I really am . . .'

She continues burbling apologetically until one of the office party stumbles past us, on his way for a piss. 'That your boyfriend, darling? Good in bed, is he?'

For a moment, Anna looks like she's going to burst into tears. 'Yes, he is, actually. So why don't you take your pathetic little tool to the lavatory and go fuck yourself.'

I didn't realize she had such a way with words. The office boy seems just as stunned as I am. As he slopes bogwards, Anna turns to me and explains: 'I've got this really annoying little brother.'

And now it's my turn to be embarrassed. 'Sorry, Anna, have you got my Colosac?'

'That sachet thing?'

'Yeah.'

She fumbles around in her orange rucksack. 'It's somewhere here. Yuk, I'd forgotten I had that. Yes, here you go. What do you want me to do with it?'

'Just empty it into my glass of water, if you don't mind.'

'What is it anyway?'

You have to become immune to this sort of thing. Like diabetics who casually shoot up at dinner parties. Only with Anna, for some reason, I don't really feel like discussing the details of my bowel-management programme. 'It's a laxative. I tend to get a bit . . . you know.'

'What, constipated?'

Mandy has plonked the bill and some little round mints on a saucer in front of Anna.

'Yeah.'

'Tell me about it,' says Anna, reaching for a mint. 'Ever since I told Daddy I wasn't going to read law, I've had terrible trouble with my shitting. The doctor said it was IBS – irritable bowel syndrome?'

'I read about it on the Net.'

Mandy waits patiently, but I sense she's getting increasingly uncomfortable.

'Don't worry, Anna, I'll get this.'

*

On the way back to college, I do something that would normally make me puke. I take an inventory of the moment: every sight, every sound, every feeling. That way I can recreate it for myself when I'm all dressed up with nowhere to go. I note the way Anna treads on the inside of her foot, the shape of her nose, the colour of her hair and the way her breath explodes into the privileged Oxford air. In Beaumont Street, a loud, posh bloke declaims, 'Piss off, Rupert, she's taken,' a pub band pumps out Bowie and, miraculously, I feel my perennially pissed-off countenance relaxing into the beginnings of a smile. What's totally incredible is the way these cold grey buildings, which yesterday seemed only claustrophobic and depressing, have suddenly taken on the golden hue of vintage Disney.

'Why are you doing it, Michael?'

Shit, I hope she can't read my mind. 'Doing what?'

'This documentary thing. I don't understand why you're doing it.'

'Didn't you hear what Nikki said? I'm striking a blow for the differently abled.'

'That bitch. Come off it, Michael.'

'If you must know, I'm doing it to please my mum.' Anna nods gravely, as if she understands exactly what I'm talking about. 'She thinks God'll get a kick out of seeing the little cripple boy on the box.'

'Oh, my God.'

We make the last part of the journey in silence. And all the way I'm trying to figure out what Anna's 'Oh, my God' means. Is it because she's sickened by the thought of a television quadriplegic, or could it be an expression of sympathy? Search me. I never bothered learning about female psychology. I always thought that knowing the Top Twenty from 1954 to the present day would be more useful. Everything I know about the opposite sex, I've learnt either from my mother or from Internet porn. Faced with a real woman, I'm beginning to wish I'd done my homework.

'Goodnight then, Michael,' she says, holding open the door to my rooms. 'Thanks for a nice evening. It really took my mind off things. We must do it again sometime.'

'Yeah, that'd be good.'

'See you at the run-through tomorrow.' She holds her hand in the air and makes it tremble melodramatically. 'I'm so nervous, aren't you?'

'Not really.'

It's only when she bends down and kisses me on the cheek that I start getting panicky. It doesn't do for quads to get attached to anything. When he, she or it starts legging it, you've got fuck all chance of catching them.

The Actor

'Aren't you going to suck me off before you put me to bed, Timothy?'

It was a short-lived affair; Simon Butterworth normally goes in for thrusting city girls with a penchant for entry-level sadomasochism, not altruistic fair-traders like Jennifer Jane. Jennifer Jane (or JJ as I steadfastly refused to call her) smelt of orange peel, and worked with mentally handicapped children. I remember her saying that although they struggled with basic syntax, most of the kids could swear like troupers before they were into grown-up nappies. I'm not at all surprised that Michael constantly assaults me with a crude barrage of double entendres, but I refuse to be flummoxed by them. 'Oh, very well then, if you really think it's necessary.'

'I'm getting a bit blocked up.'

'And how was your meal with the delightful Anna?' I say, reaching reluctantly for the suction machine and feeling a bit like the comic at the end of a panto who gets a kiddie up on stage and asks him if he's married.

'Good, thanks.'

'Hope you didn't do anything I wouldn't do,' I say, loosening his straps and preparing to winch him onto the bed. 'It's always a bad move to go too far on a first date.' You see, I'm trying to keep the mood as light as possible, because it doesn't get much more disgusting than this. And please remember, ladies and gentlemen, that I'm only getting a couple of quid above the equity minimum. 'The eagle has landed,' I intone through my cupped hands. 'I repeat, the eagle has landed.'

I roll him onto his front and start drumming on his back to loosen the mucus, just as Mrs Owen instructed. This part of the operation is vaguely therapeutic; it's the next bit – where I stick the nozzle in his mouth and hoover around until the container is full of his greeny-coloured snot – that is particularly sordid. 'Are you sitting comfortably? Then I'll . . .'

'. . . . .'

'Sorry, old chap. You'll have to speak up. I can't hear a word you're saying.'

Without his microphone, he has to bust a gut to make himself heard. 'Tell me everything you know about women.'

OK, so I've had a few drinks, but I could have sworn he just said . . .

'Please, Timothy. Tell me what you know about women.'

There's an amusing Christmas novelty publication which consists entirely of blank pages, and goes under the title *Everything Men Know About Women*. Personally, I would have little difficulty in filling several pithy volumes on the subject of the opposite sex. However, as I hoover around at the back of his mouth, Michael's seemingly reasonable request throws up a couple of pertinent questions: First of all, why in the name of Jehovah does he want to know about women? And second, perhaps less obviously, why ask someone whose first love dumped him for the second-eleven goalkeeper, whose marriage proved shorter running than an Andrew Lloyd Webber flop, and whose most durable relationship to date has been with a battery-powered piece of plastic?

'Michael, old chap, you've come to the right man.'

The snot jar brimmeth over. Michael is tucked up in his undulating bed, eyes half-closed, doubtless suffering from information overload but grateful, I'm sure, for what can only be described as a master-class in the art of love.

'Remember, Michael, one of the reasons you should

never try and make contact with your first love – apart from obvious things like she's probably married, with children who have violin lessons, and a husband called Clive – is that the older you get, the easier it is to categorize them. I can't tell you how painful it is to discover that the gloriously eccentric, incandescently attractive individual who you thought you'd worship for ever was just a middle-class horsey with overtones of RAF.

'And don't forget, your first arty fuck-up may seem a rare and exotic species – and the sex is invariably fantastic – but believe me, as soon as you see that copy of *The Bell Jar* on her bedside table you should run like buggery.

'What I think I'm saying is that it's a jungle out there – dog eat dog, every man for himself. And this is the frightening part, Mike: there are no rules. Oh, sure, I can give you a couple of pointers – they hate it if you call their bluff and start talking about your feelings, and on no account should you attempt to share the contents of your Dream Diary – but like I said, what can you do if one minute she's telling you she's not ready for commitment and two weeks later she's married to a man from the motor trade?

'And don't get me started on oral sex. Now there's a bone of contention. You see, Michael . . . Michael? Yes, well, maybe that is enough for one day. I suppose some of that should be on a strictly need-to-know basis. I mean, it's not as if you're actually going to be able to use any of it.'

I turn out the light. And I'm actually feeling quite pleased with myself, until I suddenly remember SOWINS's frank appraisal of my people skills. Who am I trying to kid?

If twenty-two months of marriage taught me anything, it's that I don't know the first thing about women.

The Quadriplegic

When people think they've got to know me (and a crippo 'chum' can be a nice little calling card for the concerned liberal) one of the first things they ask is, 'Can you walk in your dreams?' I get it nearly as often as, 'Could you have children?' When I'm in the mood, I spin them some half-arsed crap about slow-motion prancing through poppy fields. But the truth is, I don't dream much – you have to sleep for that.

If anything was going to set me yawning it was the lamentable tragedy of De Niro's love life. The trouble is, when the lights go out and it's just me and my amazing dancing bed, I lie awake and brood.

The night I was born (4.50 a.m., 6lb 7oz), Dad staggered punch drunk into the hospital car park and celebrated with a miniature cigar. He was always boring me shitless with that story: '*I turned on the car radio, Mikey, and do you know what the first song I heard was? "I Can See Clearly Now"*.' (He couldn't sing, my dad, but he liked to have a go.) '*I knew then that everything was going to be OK*.'

So how come he can't bear to look at me? How come the only contact I ever have with him is a crap birthday present and a tin of Quality Street at Christmas? Stupid dickhead; stories ought to mean something, but they never do.

Mum genuinely believes that God's up there helping her find the best-value bananas in Tesco's. She's got this keyring with WWJD on it: 'What would Jesus do?' Once you've sussed that, everything else falls into place. Finding meaning in life comes so much easier when you're terminally stupid. It's all very well for the able-bodied brigade to wank off about karma, and how we spackers must have been Adolf Hitler in a previous life, but the problem of suffering is a lot more difficult to come to terms with when you're the one in pain.

And I thought I knew all about pain. So imagine how delighted I was to discover a brand new agony I hadn't even thought of. Unrequitable love has to be the shittiest torture in the book. Even if (miracle of miracles) she did like me, there'd be nothing I could do about it. Talk about a head fuck.

And you know what the worst thing is? Even a complete spastic could see that the only sensible course of action is to steer well clear of Anna, and try not to give her a second thought. But I can't wait to see her again. So I lie in the dark, reliving every moment of our conversation in the restaurant, counting the minutes until the run-through tomorrow.

IO

What a Rogue and Peasant Slave am I

The Actor

I can't tell you how much I've been looking forward to this. All through the day I've caught myself humming snatches of that song from *West Side Story*. Although I've sat in on a couple of rehearsals, it's only tonight, when they run it for the first time, that I'll be able to get a true picture of just how appalling this production is really going to be. There's nothing more elevating than someone else's theatrical disaster; when it comes with an 'I told you so' attached, it's little short of thespian paradise.

Philip Sidney has gathered his troops about him for one of his rousing pep talks. Unlike his pathetic band of sycophants, the only reason I'm basking in his shadow is because I'm pretty sure it's being filmed. 'All right, people, now listen carefully. This evening we're going to try and stagger through the first half. Nikki will be sticking her oar in from time to time . . .'

(Nervous laughter.)

'But essentially this is for you. I don't want you to think about an audience at all. We've got another three weeks for that – thank fuck! So just feel your way carefully, and above all be brave! Now, before we start, Piers is going to take us through the salute to the sun and some chi kung.'

Piers, our reluctant Horatio, is clad only in black Lycra. I pose satirically behind him as he takes the entire company (apart from our Twinkle, of course) through the first few pages of *Teach Yourself Some Eastern Bollocks*, which he pretends to have picked up in India during his gap year. There's far too much of this sort of thing if you ask me. It starts in the big companies (how else do you fill eight weeks of rehearsal?) where you'll often see a movement guru instructing some queeny old ham in the ancient art of standing on one leg, and breathing (from the diaphragm) with a finger up your arse. Like the professional foul, it's only a matter of time before it works its way down to the lower leagues.

As for the idea that stepping onto the stage to play King Lear is as hazardous as negotiating a minefield, that's a story put about by literary thesps about to play King Lear. Acting is basically showing off, a way of getting women to sleep with you (or men in the case of our literary thesps). Bravery is nine years in the chorus of *Evita* – as well as being professional suicide, of course.

'OK, people,' shouts Philip Sidney, straddling a chair at the front of the hall and opening a tattered notebook, 'clear the stage, please. Let's get this show on the road.'

'*Who's there?*'

'*Nay, answer me. Stand and unfold yourself.*'

I can't help shivering when I hear the familiar opening words. Every night (over the dressing-room tannoy) they would provoke in me a sort of depression that didn't lift until the arrival of Fortinbras, five and a half hours later. They were starter's orders for thirteen minutes of frantic green-room bitching time with the other courtiers, before our next entrance in Act I scene ii. I shift uncomfortably on the hard plastic chair and try to remind myself that tonight is strictly for pleasure.

At least Philip Sidney has had the good sense to cut half of it. But apart from that, what can I say? The concept is both crass and ludicrous, the acting too dreadful for words, and the direction virtually non-existent. It is, in fact, all that I had hoped for.

Nikki flits in and out of the action; bending athletically to capture a close-up of Bernardo, her low-cut top enough to distract the most hardened professional. I amuse myself by rehearsing my sardonic voice-over ('*Unfortunately, good intentions are not the only prerequisite for a theatrical triumph*') but in the end, the whole thing is so delightfully abysmal that I slip into a sort of reverie. I can hardly wait for the first entrance of the wheelchair Prince.

Next, something terrible happens.

I'm not sure when it hits me because, as I say, I'm in a state of coarse-acting-induced nirvana. Hamlet's entrance, the low hum of his wheelchair cutting across the chasm of Claudius' first dry, is indeed a joy. When he finally opens his mouth ('*A little more than kin and less than kind*') his peculiar, high-pitched, badly amplified voice is so incongruous that I have to laugh out loud. When the court exit (not to appear again until II.ii) and he's alone onstage for his first soliloquy, it's almost as if I've died and gone to heaven.

But, ludicrous though he looks, I have to admit that (unlike Gertrude and Polonius) he does appear to know his lines. What's more, he makes pretty good sense of them. Even Piers isn't nearly as bad a Horatio as he could have been. I'm not sure how they do it, but, between them, they manage to establish a genuine sense of camaraderie, which as a thirty-nine-year-old who's lost contact with all but one of his old friends, I find somehow rather touching.

It's also quite a good play. Although, as I've said, I appeared in it for nearly a year, thank God the director wasn't one of those cruel bastards who makes the whole company turn up for every rehearsal. Consequently, my knowledge of the chamber scenes is somewhat sketchy. But the poignant father/son relationship, the whole idea that you might somehow atone for the indignities suffered by a parent, is particularly prescient. I wish I could have done that for *my* dad – too late for that, of course.

And there's something different about Michael. I can't quite put my finger on it. He can only move his head, for God's sake, and yet, though it pains me to say it, I suddenly realize I'm no longer watching the patient from hell, but a different person altogether. I suppose it must be what people call acting. Put *me* in a Charles Fox, eighteenth-century vicar's costume, give me a funny Yorkshire accent and a limp, and it's still me. I won't bump into the furniture, they'll hear me in the balcony, and if the line's funny

I'll probably get a laugh. The trouble is, underneath it all, it's still Timothy Salt in a silly frock.

I have tried it, a couple of times, feeling things, but it's awkward and messy and, to be perfectly honest, not my cup of tea. So pretty soon I'm back to thinking, 'What's the next line?' 'Where am I going to eat between shows?' 'If he gets a move on and dies I won't have to change at Acton Town.' What's more, I've always found it pretty hard to believe that any actor could start feeling like someone else. But by the time Michael arrives at *what a rogue and peasant slave am I*, it's clear he's going to be a sensational Hamlet.

It gets worse. Anna turns out to be a really affecting Ophelia. Her voice isn't quite up to it, but she has a gaucheness and vulnerability that's spot on. Together, however, they have what is known in television circles as 'chemistry'. So much so that by the time he's packing her off to a nunnery, I feel moisture on my hot cheeks.

In my mind's eye I see hordes of critics beating their way down to Oxford, all desperate for a piece of the action. I see him and his wheelchair shining out from the Saturday supplements, interviews with Melvyn Bragg and guest appearances as the token cripple on *Inspector Morse*. I cannot let this happen. I simply cannot let it happen.

Suddenly I can't stand it any longer. I stumble, silently sobbing, from the Morley Fletcher Rooms, and I don't stop running until I get to the Fatted Calf.

11

For this Relief

The Quadriplegic

'Where's Laughing Boy?' says Nikki, barging in without knocking and flopping down on the sofa.

'He's getting ready for his audition.'

'You are joking, I hope. Who in God's name would want to waste thirty seconds of their valuable time with that old dugout?'

I'm actually in the middle of bringing a single parent in Reading to an earth-shattering climax. I stab rapidly at the keyboard with my wand, and bring up the screensaver. Looks like poor old Kelly-Marie is going to have to wait. 'He's been in his room for the last two hours. Do you want him?'

'God, no,' says Nikki, sounding as if I've just suggested a threesome. 'If there's one thing I can't stand, it's creepy middle-aged men.' I turn to face her, trying not to look guilty. Short skirts suit Nikki. When she uncrosses her legs, I get a sneak preview of black stocking tops. 'It's you I wanted to see, Mike.' She takes something from her hand-bag and conceals it behind her back. 'I'm going to be away for a couple of days, so I got you a little pressie.'

(It'd better not be a fucking hat.) 'What did you want to go and do that for?'

De Niro launches into a chorus of 'Hey Jude'. It sounds like Mum's horrible CD of that opera singer murdering ABBA songs.

'Shit,' says Nikki, 'I hope he's not doing that at the casting.'

I almost feel sorry for the bloke. He was pacing around the lounge at six o'clock this morning rehearsing his line. '*More Stilton? Don't mind if I do! With new fast-acting Flatuleeze, I can have my cheese* without *cutting it.*' And it sounded terrible. No wonder he's shitting himself.

Nikki gestures towards De Niro's bedroom and raises an eyebrow. 'That's part of the reason I got you a present really. You've been bloody magnificent, Michael. I don't know how you've managed to put up with him.'

'He's not that bad.'

Right on cue, De Niro begins his vocal warm-up: 'In Tooting two tutors astute, used to toot to a tune on the flute.'

'You're going to love this, Mike. He actually thinks I'm going to let him do the commentary for *Wheelchair of Fire*.'

So that's what he meant about getting into the voice-over game. 'Aren't you, then?'

She tosses back her head and lets out a deep-throated guffaw. 'I wouldn't let him near a trail for hospital radio, let alone a major new documentary. Don't worry, John Nettles has been pencilled in for weeks.'

'I don't think Timothy will be very happy about that.'

'This is grown-up land, Mike, not some male menopausee's wank fantasy.' Nikki has these totally amazing legs that stretch right up to her armpits. 'All the same, I'd be grateful if you didn't mention it just yet.'

'Whatever you say.'

She steps towards me, careful not to blind herself on my wand, and crouches at my feet like she's going to propose. 'Those things you said, down by the lake, about how you dream you can walk . . .' (If she comes any closer, I'll get a good look down her blouse.) 'They were truly humbling. And sitting in on your tutorial today was a great privilege. Pity that joker had to stick his oar in.'

He's only here to empty my colostomy bags, but for some reason, De Niro felt the need to share his views on Restoration comedy with my tutor. 'Glad you enjoyed it, Nikki.'

'Did you know that Professor Bradshaw was a consultant on *Nuns Who Stray*? He did a lovely piece to camera about sixteenth-century menstruation rituals.' She takes a green plastic object from behind her back. It looks like the gizmo for a radio-controlled car. 'I almost forgot, here's that present I told you about.'

'What is it?'

'You said something, the first day we were filming, that really moved me, Mike.'

'I did?'

Nikki nods gravely. 'My heart went out to you that

morning, Michael. And I just really wanted to do something to help.'

I hope she realizes I was joking about Disneyland. 'What did I say?'

'You said your greatest ambition in life was to have an orgasm.'

'Yes, but . . .'

'So I did a bit of research on the Net, and I think I might have come up with the answer.' At the flick of a switch, the green plastic thing whirrs into life. Nikki waves it triumphantly in my face. 'It's the Fecundimatic Vibrator. I've heard some terrific things about it.'

'Would you mind switching it off, please? What is it, anyway?'

'It's a revolutionary semen-retrieval system,' says Nikki, sounding like someone off the shopping channel, 'specially designed for guys with SCIs. No unsightly cords,' she runs her finger along the shaft and across the tip, 'it's battery operated. That's the applicator, and there's the indicator light that tells you if you're applying too much pressure.'

'I don't believe this.'

'Fantastic, isn't it? And there's something like a 45 per cent success rate. You see, your partner holds it against the root of your penis or perineum – or possibly,' she winces, 'in the anal passage, and hey presto!'

Just for once, I can't wait for De Niro to get his arse out here. 'You're not serious.'

Nikki is waving the thing around like a lightsaber. 'Sounds too good to be true, doesn't it, Mike? I'm not denying there can be the occasional unpleasant side-effect:

dysreflexia, restlessness, phantom pain . . . fatality even. But it's got to be worth it, hasn't it?'

I ought to be more disgusted than that bad-tempered bloke in Tunbridge Wells, so why do I find myself obsessing over a pointless side issue? 'I haven't got a partner anyway.'

'That's easy,' smiles Nikki.

'What, you mean *you* . . . ?

'Christ, no! I was thinking of the delicious Anna.'

'You what?'

'Oh, come on,' she says, ruffling my hair, 'it's perfect. I saw how great you looked together at the run-through. And anyway, *I* couldn't do anything because I'd be filming, wouldn't I?'

'That's disgusting.'

'No, Mike,' she says solemnly, 'it's beautiful. It's a marvellously positive image of a disabled man coming to terms with his sexuality. You know, a lot of people said I shouldn't have shown Sister Bernadette masturbating, but it was so tastefully edited that we got some incredible feedback.'

'What makes you think Anna would be interested anyway?'

'Because you've got so much to offer, Mike.'

'What, like free parking, you mean?'

Nikki pretends to be shocked. 'You mustn't sell yourself short.'

'Just get that fucking thing away from me. I don't want anything to do with it, OK?'

'I'm so sorry, Michael,' says Nikki, the hint of a tear in

her voice. 'I thought you were serious about this. Why don't you think it over? I'll pop the Fecundimatic down on the mantelpiece here. Let me know if you change your mind.'

De Niro sweeps into the room looking like the Incredible Hulk just before he burst out of his clothes. 'Well, how do I look?'

'Nice suit,' says Nikki, turning towards me and slipping a finger down her throat. 'What a fab decade the eighties was.'

'I bought it for my wedding,' says De Niro, fussing at the knot of his enormous tie. 'Thankfully, it proved somewhat more durable than the marriage itself.'

'A little bird tells me you've got an audition,' says Nikki. 'What are you up for?'

'Er, well, it's a commercial actually,' says De Niro, tugging on his earlobe, 'for some new dyspepsia lozenges, which is great because my agent – Bunny Michelmore at Bunny Michelmore Management – once told me that I looked like a man with permanent indigestion.' His hollow laughter doesn't quite ring true.

'Anyway,' says Nikki, 'I've got a plane to catch. I'm flying out to Paphos for a couple of days. The lesbian holiday reps are getting married, and Sheena has asked me to give her away.'

'How very elevating,' sneers De Niro.

'I'll see you guys later then,' says Nikki, resting her hand on my shoulder. 'And don't forget what I said earlier, Mike. You could be an icon for disabled men everywhere – wouldn't that be fab?' She walks slowly to the door. 'Oh and Timothy, have you ever thought about working out? It might do you good.'

De Niro is so preoccupied with his audition that he doesn't seem to register Nikki's parting shot. Flushed and slightly breathless, he paces the room like a bad actor, pausing in front of anything shiny enough to bear his reflection, and breathing on his hand and sniffing it. 'All right, Michael, this is it. Now listen carefully. Philip and Anna are coming here at eleven for a rehearsal, and then Anna's going to stay on to give you lunch and see to your . . . ablutions. But don't worry, she's raring to go, and I promise I'll be back before six.'

Every morning for the last week, Anna has been observing my bowel and bladder management. If I'd been at all squeamish about having an audience, I would have died of embarrassment years ago. But I still hated having her there. It didn't help that she seemed so fascinated by the whole thing. 'Good luck for the audition.'

'Fingers crossed, eh?' He checks his flies for the umpteenth time. 'Right, I'd better be off. Are you still using the computer, or do you want me to take your Dalek thing off?'

I suddenly remember Kelly-Marie. 'No, thanks, there's something I need to finish first.'

12

The Secrets of My Prison House

The Quadriplegic

Herr Director crouches against the wall, roll-up glued to his bottom lip, occasionally sharing some of the wisdom he picked up at the Nazi Academy of Dramatic Art – or was it Winchester? 'For fuck's sake, Anna, just act *better*.'

'I'm doing my best,' she says, flopping over at the waist and slowly coming up again (vertebra by vertebra) just like Piers does in his warm-ups. 'I told you I wasn't really an actress.'

Philip says the Hamlet/Ophelia thing isn't really working, so we're having some private, remedial rehearsals in my rooms. I just want to smash the arrogant bastard's face in. Why does she let him talk to her like that?

'It's no use; you'll have to find another Ophelia.'

Philip morphs into 'good cop' directing mode whenever it suits him. He takes Anna in a sickening embrace, wipes away her tears and plants a tender kiss on her forehead. 'Trust me, babe, you can do it. Look, I'm sorry I shouted. It's only because I care so much. You don't know how much this thing means to me.'

'It means a lot to all of us,' sniffs Anna.

'Well,' *I* think you're doing really well,' I say, hating the way she rests her head on his shoulder. 'Even Timothy said he thought you were going to be a brilliant Ophelia.'

'And we all know what an expert old Fuck-face is,' snorts Philip. 'Look, it was a bit better that time, but I still don't believe in you as a couple.'

'Funny that,' I say, 'I thought we were perfect casting for one of those coffee ads.'

'Yeah, nice one, Mike. Now, why don't we try it again? And this time, make it more real, OK.'

Anna begins in a feeble whisper, '*My lord, I have remembrances of yours that I have longed long to rede-liver.*' But it looks like Ophelia's going psycho about twenty pages too early. She tugs at the roots of her (recently hennaed) hair. 'It's all very well to say make it more real, but couldn't you give us a tiny clue? You are the fucking director.'

Philip Sidney head butts the wall, satirically. 'How many times do I have to say it? It's all in the punctuation. Shakespeare tells his actors everything they need to know.'

'That's rubbish,' says Anna, 'and you know it. I mean, who is this girl? What's happening in this scene? I just don't get it.'

'Well, that's pretty obvious,' says Philip.

'And what does she see in a nutter like *him*?' she says, pointing in my direction.

'*Frailty, thy name is woman*,' intones Philip, like it's the answer to everything.

'Don't give me that,' screams Anna, 'just tell us how to make it work.'

Philip has a malicious grin on his face. 'You're not going to like this.'

'Try me,' says Anna.

'Well, if it was anyone else, I'd be advising them to get bladdered and fuck each other's brains out. But seeing as it's *you*, well, you see my problem? I'm not talking about Mike, of course,' he adds, hastily.

'Not this again,' says Anna. 'This is so boring.'

Philip looks across at me and nods vigorously. 'Tell me about it. Did you know that Miss Cartland here is saving herself for Mr Right?'

'Can't we just get on with the rehearsal?' I say. 'This isn't getting us anywhere.'

'No,' says Anna, 'I've had enough. Sorry, Michael, do you mind if we do this another time?'

'Yeah, sure, cool.'

'Come on, babe,' says Philip, patting her on the bum, 'one more time, eh?'

'No. And keep your hands to yourself. I'm not in the mood, OK?'

'Ha,' snorts Philip, 'that's what you always say.'

'Just go!' says Anna. 'I can't stand to be with you when you're like this.'

'Have it your way then,' says Philip, backing towards the door. 'We'll talk about this at the Old Rectory.'

Anna watches in silence as he swaggers across the quad. She blows onto the window and scribbles 'bastard' in the condensation. 'Sorry about that, Michael. He gets on my nerves sometimes.'

This is the moment when a real boy would make his move; a consoling arm, a friendly squeeze, perhaps even a kiss (no tongues) if the arm goes down OK. Words are totally crap for this sort of thing, and so is the cuddly-cripple-boy smile that women over sixty find so appealing. 'Don't worry about it.'

'Tell you what,' says Anna. 'I know we can't . . . well . . . do what Philip said, but we could get pissed together, couldn't we? Don't go away, Michael, I'll be right back.'

She reappears, five minutes later, with a Marks & Spencer's bag, a bottle of champagne and a portable CD player. 'Hope you like Monteverdi.'

Anna's lying on the sofa, mug of champagne in one hand, smoked-salmon-and-cream-cheese bagel in the other. 'Did you know that Piers was gay?'

'Is he?' I say, trying to focus. 'Never really thought about it.'

'Oh, come on,' says Anna, 'you must have seen the way he looks at Philip.'

'Not really.'

'He does that thing with his lips.' She pouts like a fish. 'He did it the other day when he forgot his lines.'

'Oh, yeah, that was so funny. When he started trying to

ad-lib in blank verse, I thought he was going to have a heart attack.'

'Don't!' says Anna, sucking cream cheese off her index finger. 'He's a really sweet guy actually. He was ever so nice when I told him about Mummy.'

'Why, what's up?'

She squints at me through the hole in her bagel. 'Doesn't matter, it's really embarrassing.'

'Come on, Anna, you can tell me. Embarrassment's my middle name.'

'Daddy's been weeing on the compost heap again.'

I feel as rough as a badger's arse. My eyes won't open properly, this classical-music bollocks is doing my head in, and I'm sure she just said something really weird. '*What* are you talking about?'

'He only does it to annoy her.'

'I think you'd better explain, Anna.'

It's one of those waving-or-drowning moments; at first she looks like she's going to cry her eyes out, but a nano-second later she's laughing her head off. 'In the beginning, he took his wee down the garden in an old whisky bottle. He'd read about it in the *Telegraph* or something. "No use wasting money on one of those fancy activators when a drop of Jenkins '97 will do the job just as well."'

Pastor Reg was always warning us about the evils of alcohol. 'What are you on about?'

'Mummy thought that if the neighbours saw him pour-ing bottles of whisky away, they'd assume that *she* had a drink problem.'

'And has she?'

'No,' giggles Anna, 'but she's been back on the Prozac ever since Daddy discovered Viagra. Anyway, he promised he wouldn't use the bottle again, and next thing we knew, he was up on the back wall with his cock out.' She rolls off the sofa and stumbles towards me. 'Here, have some more champagne.' She manages to get some of it in my mouth; the rest trickles down my chin. 'Whoops . . . sorry.'

'So your mum's not happy, right?'

'Mummy's never happy, that's the problem. I'm just terrified that if Daddy pushes her too far, she might do something silly.'

'I bet my mum's sillier than yours,' I say, wishing that Anna would have a go at my chin with a damp cloth. 'One summer, we were halfway to Winchelsea when she made Dad turn the car round and drive all the way home because she thought he might have left the bog seat up.'

'I liked your mum. I bet she's really proud of you.'

'Mum's not that big on pride.'

She scrabbles around in her Marks & Spencer's bag. 'Hey, I almost forgot; I brought down some strawberries – hope you like them.'

'Love them,' I say.

'Scuse fingers.' I get a sort of shivery feeling as she rips off the cling film, places a ripe berry between her lips and bites off the stalk. 'Open your mouth and close your eyes and you shall have a *big* surprise.' When Anna withdraws her hand from my mouth, I touch the end of her fingertips with my tongue, and she smiles at me. This is about as good as it gets.

The Virgin

This is the moment I've been dreading. Even after half a bottle of champagne and the first two acts of *The Return of Ulysses*, I'm still not sure I can do this. As soon as he finishes that last strawberry, I'm going to have to bite the bullet.

'I suppose we'd better get on with it then,' I say, trying to sound like it's the most natural thing in the world.

Maybe Michael's as nervous as I am. 'You don't have to if you don't want to.'

'I do want to,' I say, taking a quick peep at his flies. 'I don't want to mess it up, that's all.'

'Don't worry, you'll be fine.'

I take a deep breath and try and do it in time to the music. To start with I'm all fingers and thumbs, but I eventually manage to prise open his Velcro flies and slide his trousers down to his knees. So far so good, just don't look down, girl – at least, not yet. 'Now where's that bottle thingy?'

'Timothy left it on the coffee table.'

'Right, yes, here we are. Let me see now.' This time I need to keep both eyes open. But do you know what? I'm not frightened at all. His little pink . . . addendum is such a far cry from Philip's burgundy battering-ram that I don't even flinch when I take it by the throat and slip it into the specimen bottle. 'Are you ready for this, Mike?'

'Go for it.'

It feels wrong somehow, but I aim for the sweet spot,

an inch or so beneath his belly button. 'Nothing's happening. What's wrong?'

'You don't have to be quite so gentle, Anna. Go on; give it a bit of welly.'

'I'm frightened of hurting you.'

'That's the one thing you could never do.'

What a sweet thing to say. This time, I'm determined to get it right. I focus for a moment before sinking my hand into his lily-white belly. A second later there's a reassuring tinkling sound. 'Yes!' I shout, so pleased with myself that I almost break into a little victory dance. 'Look at that, I've done it.'

Michael doesn't seem quite so ecstatic. 'What do you want, a medal?'

'I thought you'd be pleased.'

'This is my life, Anna, not some stupid fairground attraction.'

'I'm sorry,' I say, holding the specimen bottle up to the light. 'I just got a bit carried away. Wow, is it always that colour?'

'Think your dad might want some Owen '99 for his compost heap?'

I love the way he manages to joke about it. 'You're so brave, Michael.'

'Where do people get the idea that you deserve the Victoria Cross just because you spend your life in a spaz-chariot? I just get on with it, that's all.'

I wish he'd learn to take a compliment. 'I think you're amazing. I mean, you're really funny, you hardly ever complain, and how you manage to cope with all *this* . . . quite frankly, if it was me, I think I'd . . .'

'Kill myself? And how would I do that exactly?'

'No, that's not what I meant at all. All I . . .'

'Would you mind pulling my trousers up, please?'

'Yeah . . . sure.' He looks just like Maggie after I've taken one of her toys away: sad eyed and reproachful. All I want to do is bring a smile to his face, but instead I struggle silently with the Velcro, and try to psyche myself up for the 64-million-dollar question. 'Michael, do you mind if I ask you a big favour?'

'Try me.'

In the end I just blurt it out. 'I want you to come down to the Old Rectory to meet my parents.'

'What?'

'I know it's a big ask, but Philip and I are supposed to be going down on Friday and staying overnight. It would be really nice if you could come too.'

'Why?'

'Well, because . . . because Mummy and Daddy would love to meet you and . . .' That sounded so much more plausible when I practised it earlier. 'OK, OK, it's because I want to teach that bastard a lesson. Philip thinks he's going to have me all to himself.'

He looks at me with those big brown eyes. 'Oh, right, I get it.'

'But it would be really lovely to have you there, Michael. We could even do a bit of rehearsing if you like. *Please*, say you'll come.'

'I don't think so. Playing the gooseberry in a wheelchair doesn't sound like much fun to me.'

The weird thing is, I actually want him there. 'It wouldn't be like that.'

'I'm sorry, Anna, it's much too complicated. I don't exactly travel light, you know.'

Somehow, it just wouldn't be the same without him. 'I could look after you, I know I could. I've done all right today, haven't I? Come on, Michael, it's only for one night. You might even enjoy it.'

'I'll have to think about it.'

The Quadriplegic

And I'm still thinking about it eight hours later, when the door crashes open and a gun-wielding New York cop bursts upon the scene. 'OK, you motherfucker, FREEZE!' Except that it isn't a New York cop. It's a worse-for-wear, middle-aged man with two pointed fingers in the pocket of his ill-fitting, double-breasted suit.

'You said you'd be back before six.'

'You what?' says De Niro, still amused by his humorous entrance.

'I've been sitting here for the last two hours.'

He totters towards the sofa. 'Yes, I'm terribly sorry about that, old dog. I popped into the Fatted Calf for a swift half, and I must have lost all track of the time.'

'You're supposed to be my carer.'

'Yes, and don't I bloody know it,' he says, crash landing

on the sofa and sending up a cloud of dust. 'Which reminds me: your dear mama phoned again. You'll be pleased to hear the dancing lessons are progressing most satisfactorily.'

'*Anything* could have happened.'

'Yes, well, it didn't, did it?' snaps De Niro. 'Look, would you mind awfully if we save the post-mortem for tomorrow? I've had a bitch of a day.'

He loosens his trouser button and belches. I'd say the answer to my next question is fairly obvious.

'How did your audition go?'

'Bunny will be furious,' he says, sinking his fist into my Chelsea cushion. 'The buggers didn't even get me to read.'

'Why not?'

'Apparently I don't look sophisticated enough for the father of the bride. Can you believe it?'

That one's so easy I don't even bother to answer.

'I hate bloody weddings anyway.'

'You were married once, weren't you, Timothy?'

The ghost of a smile flickers across his forlorn features. 'She was a dancer. We met in panto – *Babes in the Wood*. I was giving my Will Scarlet. It was the happiest six weeks of my life. Even Scunthorpe can be relatively tolerable when you're in love.'

'How did you know you were in love?'

'Oh, the usual: constant throbbing erection, intellectual paralysis, a sudden penchant for singer-songstresses, and the complete demolition of the emotional Berlin Wall that was supposed to protect me from such things.'

It sounds so familiar – apart from the throbbing erection, of course. 'So what happened?'

'We got hitched that July. Of course, it didn't last. My brother was right, as usual: "You'll never hang onto a bit of totty like that, Tim." Well, as soon as the *Cats* crowd got their claws into her, our marriage didn't stand a chance. Anyway, I never talk about it.' He stares into the distance like a shell-shocked war poet. 'Now, I expect you're hungry. Why don't I fix us both a snack?'

'No, thanks, I think I'm a bit hungover.'

'Don't say the delicious Anna has been leading you astray.'

'We had a bottle of champagne with lunch.'

'You want to be careful, old chap. She probably wants to have her wicked way with you.' His forced laughter swiftly dissolves into a flatulent silence. 'Sorry, that was below the belt, I do apologize.'

I've been dying to tell someone all day: 'Anna wants me to go down to Hampshire to meet her parents.'

His double chin hits the floor. 'Good grief, what on earth for?'

'I don't know. To make Philip jealous, I think. What do you think, Timothy, should I go?'

'Look,' he says, massaging his temples with his pudgy fingertips, 'despite what I might have implied the other day, I'm probably not the best person to ask. How do *you* feel about the idea?'

'It would mean staying overnight, which could be tricky, but Anna thinks she could cope with the . . . well, you know.'

For a man I would have described as dead behind the

eyes, the transformation is incredible. 'Oh, so you'd be making a night of it then?'

''Fraid so.'

'And when would all this come to pass?'

'Friday.'

'Perfect,' he says, plumping my Chelsea cushion and placing it carefully back on the sofa, 'it'll give me a chance to celebrate my birthday in style.'

'Your birthday?'

'Yes, the big four o. Don't look forty, do I?'

'So you think I should go then?'

'That's entirely up to you, of course. But let's face it, Michael, what have you got to lose? And I for one wouldn't want to miss out on an opportunity to get one over on Master Philip Sidney.'

Just before De Niro switches out my light, he says something really weird: 'I don't quite know how to put this, Michael, but the thing is, whatever may or may not happen in the future, I want to assure you that, well – it really is nothing personal.'

13

A Dream of Passion

The Actor

I wait until their train is a dot on the horizon before pulling out my phone. My text today is '*Far better ask and be refused, than not ask at all*'. (*Be Your Own Psychotherapist*, Chapter Nine: 'My Family and Other Anima'.) Besides, I'm quite sure the gods are smiling on me. With no Ironside around to cramp my style, it's the best opportunity I've had since the casting department of *The Bill* were looking for a slightly overweight, balding man (forties) who was prepared to have rats crawl over his naked torso.

'Yah, who is it?' She sounds half asleep. I get a tantalizing vision of Nikki Hardbody, all tricked out in black, lads' mag suspenders.

'It's Tim here.'

'Who?'

It's a bugger having to compete with the station announcer. Fortunately, it's glaringly obvious which one of us has read *An Actor Speaks*. 'Timothy Salt? Your voice-over artist for *Wheelchair of Fire*?'

That seems to rouse her. 'It's not Michael, is it? He is OK, isn't he? God, that's all I need.'

'Michael's fine. He's going down to Hampshire with Anna. How was Lesbos, by the way?'

'What did you say?'

'How was Lesbos?'

'Never mind that. Are you telling me that those two are spending the night together?'

'In a manner of speaking, I suppose . . .'

'Hamlet and Ophelia are getting it on, and I wasn't told about it? Jesus Christ, I don't believe this.'

'It was a spur-of-the-moment thing, Nikki. And anyway,' I add, trying to console her, 'I don't think you should go reading too much into it.'

'Are you kidding? A couple of shots of those two walking into the sunset would be like gold dust. Do you know what happened to the ratings when little Dylan's mum started screwing his oncologist?'

Things are not going quite the way I intended. 'Well, I'm afraid they won't be back until tomorrow. And seeing as I haven't a clue where they're staying,' I lie, fairly convincingly, 'I suppose you and I will be at a loose end tonight?'

Nikki sounds distracted. 'How can I get them into bed together without it looking tacky?'

Why's she getting her knickers in a twist about the most unlikely alliance since King Kong and Fay Wray? Perhaps she'll come to her senses when I make her an offer she can't refuse. 'Rather serendipitously, it's my birthday today.'

'Come on, Nikki, *think*.'

'And I was rather hoping you might care to join me for a celebratory meal.'

'Mustn't waste our last two weeks together.'

'We could meet in the Fatted Calf for pre-meal drinks if you like.'

'Yeah, yeah, if you like. Now first, we've got to get his stupid mother onside – can't do anything without that dopey cow's approval.'

OK, so it sounded a bit like SOWINS acceding to my lovemaking, but I'm sure there was an affirmative in there somewhere. 'Well, that's marvellous. Tell you what, why don't I meet you in the Fatted Calf at about eight?'

'What?'

'The Fatted Calf? About eight?'

'Yeah, yeah, whatever.'

I ring off before she has time to change her mind. Maybe life really does begin at forty.

The Virgin

Philip shivers and bites on his knuckles. The poor love doesn't see why he should have to put up with the guard's van just because Michael does. 'God, it's cold in here,' he whines. 'I don't think I can stand much more of this.'

But he knows he can't say anything, because he doesn't want to upset the golden goose. He sees Michael as his passport to theatrical immortality, especially since that tart Hardbody arrived on the scene. Isn't it amazing how a few false promises ('*You're so talented, Philip. I'd love to work with you on my first feature.*') and a pole dancer's wardrobe can turn a bloke into a slobbering idiot.

'Why don't you go down to the buffet and get Michael a coffee?'

'Yes, all right,' he says, pulling up the collar of his trenchcoat. 'Don't worry, I may be some time.'

You should have seen him when I broke the news that Michael would be joining us. OK, so I'd just started my period, which always sharpens my sense of *Schadenfreude*, but I couldn't believe how good it felt to watch his Daniel Day-Lewis cheekbones rearrange themselves into a petulant frown. It felt even better when I remembered what he'd said to me the previous night: '*If you use those things you're technically not a virgin anyway, so Christ knows why you're making a five-act tragedy of it.*'

'What's the matter with *him*?' says Michael.

'He's not a happy bunny. He's still sulking because I won't let him do what bunnies do best.'

Michael has this gorgeous, open smile, which practically lights up the guard's van. I'm not being funny. I mean, I know, physically, he hasn't got a lot going for him, but that smile of his is to die for. 'I don't suppose I'm his favourite quadriplegic right now.'

'Probably not.'

'That's good then. I hate the way he talks to you.'

'Oh, Mike, you're so sweet.' To tell you the truth, I'm a bit in awe of the guy. The more I get to know him, the more amazing I realize he is. There's a Zen-like stillness about him. Like that poem, he always manages to keep his head when everyone around him is losing theirs.

'I think it's time for my medication, Anna.'

'No probs,' I say, reaching for my rucksack.

'You're getting good at this.'

When the actor guy begged me to look after Michael while he went for his audition, my first reaction was to head for the hills. Quite frankly, I've never been that good with excreta, not even Maggie and Tom's, but as soon as I saw Mike lying there, tubes all over the place, it began to make sense. He looked so helpless, like a magical, talking baby. And the funny thing is, I knew exactly how he felt. All I wanted was to keep him safe.

Daddy's waiting for us at the station, in the horse-box. He doesn't look best pleased when he clocks our two enormous suitcases. 'Bloody hell, Pumpkin, I didn't realize you were staying for a fortnight.' He looks so archetypically upper middle in his ancient Barbour that I'm quite sure Philip is staring straight down his nose stud at him.

'They're Michael's,' says Philip, overdoing the put-upon-baggage-handler routine. 'He doesn't believe in travelling light. It's Philip, by the way, Philip Sidney. As in . . .'

'Chuck them in the back, there's a good man. Then come and give me a hand getting young Michael here lashed to the mast.' Daddy always resorts to nautical jargon in a crisis. 'You are Michael, I suppose?'

'No, I'm the other quadriplegic.'

'Jolly good,' says Daddy.'

They trundle him up the ramp into the horsebox and secure his wheelchair with some of the blue nylon rope that Maurice the handyman uses in the orchard. 'You'll be all right in there, won't you, old son? It's only twenty minutes to the village.'

Michael's voice echoes out of the darkness, 'Yes, thanks, Mr Jenkins,' and Daddy heaves closed the doors.

'Wait a minute, Daddy. I want to go in the back with Michael.'

'Don't be ridiculous, Pumpkin, there's nowhere to sit. And between you and me, it could do with a damned good hose-down in there.'

I'm uber-sensitive to whiffy odours just after I've come on, so I reluctantly join Daddy and Philip in the front seat.

'How's Mummy?' I say, trying to sound cool about it.

'After the Oxbow Incident, you mean?' says Daddy, crunching into third gear. 'Well, you know your mother, Pumpkin. It never rains but it pours.'

Philip flicks through a copy of *Horse and Hound*, obviously storing up every detail of Daddy's bourgeois ramblings to beat me with later. His aristocratic features gleam superciliously in the late morning sun. He's never more attractive than in the middle of a major strop.

'Pumpkin tells me your people are from Sussex,' says Daddy, trying to change the subject. 'I wouldn't be at all surprised if our paths had crossed at some point.'

'I doubt it,' says Philip loftily.

Although I didn't have what you might call an idyllic

childhood, I still get a warm, sticky feeling when we turn into the drive and I get my first glimpse of the Old Rectory. 'Nearly there, Michael,' shouts Daddy, banging on the back wall.

'God, I hate excessive wealth,' mutters Philip under his breath. He's capable of quite staggering hypocrisy when he feels like it.

Mummy is waiting by the stables in her 'vont to be alone' shades, smiling bravely and clutching my bratty brother, Barnaby, who's allegedly recovering from a dose of chickenpox. Even Maurice has wandered up from the meadow to stare at us.

'Where are they?' I say, trying to conceal my disappointment.

'Here they come,' says Daddy, pointing towards the old barn.

'Hello, my babies,' I squeal, as Tom and Maggie (our faithful black labs) bound up to welcome me with their lovely sloppy tongues. I've missed them so terribly. They're living proof that it's actually possible to love someone without trying to run their lives for them. 'Who's going to give their mummy a lovely kiss then?'

I can't help noticing that Philip recoils slightly when Maggie tries to make friends. I suppose I always assume that anyone I'm attracted to is bound to be potty about animals. But that's the least of Philip's worries. Mummy is on him in a flash.

'You must be the young man that Anna is so sweet on. And I can see why.' She grabs him by the shoulders and plants kisses on both his cheeks. 'I'm Camilla. Welcome to the Old Rectory.'

'It's Philip, Philip Sidney, as in . . .'

'And where's the other one?' says Mummy, almost certainly raising an eyebrow behind her shades. 'Your little charity case?'

'He's not my charity case, Mummy. And his name's Michael.'

Mummy flashes Philip the smile she uses to present the prizes at the village show. 'Anna Panna's always had a weakness for waifs and strays.'

'Give us a hand, Maurice,' says Daddy, struggling with the ramp.

Maurice lumbers forward, shirttails poking through his flies as per usual.

'You all right in there?' says Daddy, jumping into the horsebox.

Two minutes later, Michael appears at the top of the ramp.

The Quadriplegic

Tonight, Matthew, I'm going to be Quasimodo, the Elephant Man, Stephen Hawking and Frankenstein's monster all rolled into one. Even though it stinks of stale stallion's piss, and I wanted to puke the moment 'Daddy' banged me up, I'd have given my right ear to stay in that horsebox. What in the name of fucking fuck made me think that this was a good idea? But you'll have to excuse me, my public awaits.

'Jeepers creepers,' says the woman with the eye complaint. 'Oh, I am sorry.'

'Look,' says the little kid who hasn't twigged it's rude to point, 'it's ET.'

'Shut up, Barney, you little creep,' says Anna, blushing furiously.

'Now, now, Pumpkin,' says her father, 'I'm sure Michael knows that Barnaby doesn't mean it.'

Philip Sidney stands smirking like the cock-of-the-house, and the old man in the boiler suit shakes his head and slopes back to the big field. Just when things couldn't possibly get any shittier, two monstrous hell-hounds plant their muddy paws on my wheelchair and scour my face with their disgusting slobbery tongues. And I honestly believe I'm going to die. 'I can't breathe. I think I'm going to . . .'

'That is *so* sweet,' says Anna. 'They've really taken to him, haven't they, Mummy?'

'You've got a couple of friends for life there,' adds 'Daddy'.

'Just get them off me, PLEASE!'

'I think Mike's in trouble, Mrs Jenkins,' says Philip Sidney, probably not wanting to see his Hamlet torn apart before opening night. 'Shouldn't somebody . . . ?'

'Tom, Maggie, DOWN!' bellows Mr Jenkins, scaring the crap out of me, but also having the desired effect.

'Perhaps we should go inside,' says Anna's mother, taking Philip by the arm. 'My darling daughter tells me you're a budding Sir Peter Hall. How exciting. Why don't you tell me all about it over lunch? Oh and please, call me Camilla.'

Camilla Jenkins can't conceal her disgust. Perhaps she should have thought more carefully about the luncheon menu. Anna made a good stab at feeding me the lemon sole, but bread-and-butter pudding with crème anglaise (à la Delia) is the last thing you should serve up for a quadri-plegic.

'Can *I* feed him now?' says Barnaby Jenkins, his face almost as well custarded as my own. 'Go on, Mummy, please.'

'I don't think so, darling.'

'You don't mind, do you, Michael?' says the hyperac-tive ten-year-old. 'I could do aeroplanes if you like.'

'Why don't you go and play cricket on the railway track?' says Anna.

'Why don't *you*?' says Barnaby.

Anna wipes my face with a well-starched napkin. 'Sorry, Michael, I told you he was a pain in the arse.'

'She said "arse", Mummy, did you hear her, she said "arse"?'

'Barney's the "little miracle" that was going to bring Mummy and Daddy closer together again. But as you can see,' says Anna, gesturing to either end of the enormous kitchen table, 'he only succeeded in pushing them further apart.'

'Coffee, anyone?' says Mr Jenkins, commencing the long walk to the Aga.

Philip Sidney shows his contempt for bourgeois convention by attacking his bread-and-butter pudding with a fish knife. 'Thank you so much, Camilla. This is superb.'

Camilla Jenkins looks like a sadder, thinner version of her daughter. 'I'm just delighted to see you in the flesh, Philip,' she simpers. 'I didn't think Anna would ever meet a suitable young man. Now tell us some more about this documentary of yours. It sounds fascinating.'

'Strictly speaking it's about Michael,' says Philip grudgingly.

Camilla Jenkins casts a dubious eye in my direction. 'Oh, really, why on earth would anyone want to . . . ?'

'But Nikki, that's the director, has promised faithfully that my *Hamlet* is going to be the centrepiece. It's a massive boost for Histrio-Mastix, I don't mind telling you.'

'Bernard and I can hardly wait,' says Camilla, glaring at her husband who is crossing the kitchen balancing a cafetière on a National Trust tray. 'Careful, you clumsy oaf, that's Mummy's best china, as well you know.'

'Ah, yes,' says Mr Jenkins, 'the Beast of Bodmin, God rest her soul.'

'Granny Devonshire thought that Mummy married beneath herself,' adds Barnaby helpfully.

'And she never tired of reminding me of it,' says Mr Jenkins, angrily downing the plunger. 'The City was far too vulgar for the likes of Granny D. Didn't stop the old witch sponging off me though, did it?'

Camilla Jenkins dabs her eyes with a napkin. She looks more like her daughter than ever. 'Now do you see what I'm talking about, Anna Panna? Twenty years of marriage and he still treats me like the hired hand. No wonder Dr Prideaux is so worried about me.'

Mr Jenkins walks, wearily, to the door. 'You'll have to excuse me, gentlemen, while I abandon ship.' He turns to his wife with a gleam in his eyes. 'Nature calls. If you want me, you'll find me at my compost heap.'

'Tell Maurice I need him in the pantry,' Camilla shouts after him. 'The dishwasher's playing up, and we can't do anything about dinner until he's seen to it!'

As soon as her husband is out of earshot, her hostess-with-the-mostest smile is up and running again. 'Why don't you take Philip for a walk, Anna? It's a lovely afternoon and Maurice says he's seen that kestrel again. I'm sure you could do with a bit of private time, eh, Philip?'

'Yes, indeed,' says Philip Sidney, with a huge metaphorical wink.

'What about Michael?' says Anna.

'Does he like videos? Yes, of course he does. How about *Bedknobs and Broomsticks*? Anna Panna used to love that film, didn't you, darling? Barnaby can show him the games room. I'm sure they'll get along famously.'

'Give us a ride,' says Barnaby, jumping onto the back of my wheelchair.

'Leave him alone, you little beast,' says Anna. 'Let me give him his coffee.'

That bloody kid's worse than the fucking dogs. 'Come on, Michael,' he shouts, 'I'll show you my spots.'

And just for a moment I almost wish I was back in Oxford, listening to one of Timothy Salt's tedious stories about how he almost got the lead in *Gone with the Wind*.

The Virgin

Dinner was a nightmare. (You should try feeding lobster to the severely disabled.) Mummy entertained Philip with her yucky Mrs Robinson act, and afterwards, Daddy actually had the nerve to ask me to play the piano – like I was Jane Austen or something. 'Come along, Pumpkin. I didn't cough up for all those lessons with Madame what's-her-name so that you could hide your light under a bushel.' I bashed my way through a couple of Mozart sonatas, careful not to catch Philip's eye as he stared mockingly into his brandy.

Philip was the worst of the lot (worse even than my little brother, who's now decided that poor Michael looks like a character out of *Star Wars*). The moment he clapped eyes on the Old Rectory, I could sense his contempt. 'Manners Maketh Man' might have been his old school motto, but some of the things he said this afternoon were simply unforgivable: '*Oh dear, Daddy, I think I need a shit. Better get Maurice to pop up from the meadow to wipe my arse for me.*' Considering his family probably owned half of Sussex, he had a bloody nerve.

Poor Michael, it must be awful for him. At eleven o'clock, everyone except Mummy (who's retired early with a Temazepam) troops along to the Day Nursery to put him to bed. 'It's all hands to the pump then, is it?' says Daddy.

'Will his legs fall off if I pull too hard?' says Barnaby.

'Just keep out of it, you little gobshite,' I say, remembering an expression I picked up from an alternative comedienne at Toby Chamberlain-Webber's twenty-first.

'Now, Michael, we're just going to lift you onto the bed. Is that OK?'

'I can hardly wait.'

'Right,' I say, 'I'll take his head, and you two can do the body. On my count, we'll swing him onto the bed.' Daddy and Philip stand there like melons, waiting for me to take control. 'Come on, guys, let's get on with it. One, two, three!' I can't believe how light he is. He hovers above Barnaby's old Postman Pat duvet like a magician's lovely assistant.

'That wasn't so bad, was it?' I say, reaching for Michael's belt. 'Now let's get you sorted, shall we?'

Daddy twiddles his thumbs, just like he does when he spots a woman breastfeeding. 'We'll leave you to it then, shall we, Pumpkin? Too many cooks and all that. Come along, Philip, how about a nightcap?'

'Good idea.'

'Night-night, Michael,' says Barnaby, following them to the door. 'May the force be with you.'

Poor Mike; his spindly legs are so out of proportion with his body, and his pale skin looks even more emaciated alongside that pink-faced Postman. Hasn't the guy had enough to deal with without my family treating him like a circus act? I'm so angry I can hardly speak. 'Sorry, I mean . . . sorry . . . I'll just get you . . . sorry.'

But preparing him for bed is like one of those walking meditations that Piers is always talking about in his warm-ups. It's just nice to spend some time with a guy who doesn't lunge at you every five seconds. As soon as I feel the warmth of his colostomy bag, the tight knot inside my stomach begins to unravel. By the time I've brushed his hair and sorted out his PJs, I'm completely chilled. 'I'm so sorry, Michael. I should never have brought you here.'

He sounds so cute without his microphone. 'Don't worry about it. I've had a great time.'

'No, you haven't.'

'OK, it's been total crap, but at least your boyfriend looks pissed off.'

'I don't think Philip likes me very much right now.'

'Then he must be an idiot.'

'Oh, Michael, you're so sweet.'

'I wish you wouldn't keep calling me that.'

'But you are,' I say, tucking him in and kissing him on the forehead. 'You're the only one around here who really understands me – apart from Maggie and Tom, of course.'

'Goodnight, Anna.'

'Nighty-night. I'll be back in a couple of hours to turn you over.'

'*Flights of angels sing thee to thy rest!*'

Have you noticed how some people can make you feel good about yourself? I practically dance upstairs to my bedroom, forgetting for a moment the inevitable trials to come.

Five minutes later, I hear three sharp knocks on my door. Philip doesn't wait for an invitation; just saunters in, modelling a 'Never Mind the Bollocks' T-shirt and a massive mushroom in his Calvin Klein boxers. 'So, Miss Jenkins, we meet again.' He reeks of self-satisfaction and Daddy's second-best brandy.

'You can't come in. Mummy will go crazy if she finds you up here.'

He closes the door behind him and turns the key in the lock. 'I don't think so. And anyway, it seems to me that "Mummy's" halfway there already.'

'That's not funny,' I say, suddenly wishing I wasn't wearing these daggy old jim-jams. 'You shouldn't make jokes about mental illness.'

'Come on, babe, it's probably just what the old girl needs to cheer her up.'

'What do you want anyway?'

He slips his silver cigarette case onto my bedside table. 'Isn't it obvious?'

His body language says it all. 'Come on, Philip, do we have to go through this again?'

'I thought that was what tonight was all about.'

'You said you didn't mind waiting.'

'Yes, but not until bloody Godot turns up.' He lies back on my bed, still grinning at his Samuel Beckett joke. Lashings of antiperspirant can no longer disguise the disgusting odour of testosterone. 'All right then, babe, have it your way. I can wait, if that's what you really want. Come on, let's have a cuddle. I just want to be close to you.'

'Are you sure about that?'

He climbs under the duvet and kisses me tenderly on my earlobe. 'I'll wait for ever, if that's what it takes.'

Thirty seconds later I feel a cold hand in my pyjama bottoms.

'What are you doing?'

'Come on,' he groans, 'you know it's what we both want – just enjoy.'

'Look, for the last time, I'm not ready for this, OK? And anyway we can't.'

'Why not?'

'I've got my period.'

'No worries, babe,' he says, reaching for his cigarette case. 'I've slept with loads of women on the blob. Some of them really got off on it.' He bites into the condom wrapper like a ravenous tiger. 'These ones are specially ribbed "for your ultimate pleasure".'

'If you come anyway near me with that thing, I'll call Daddy.'

I'd never really noticed his thuggish laugh before. 'I'm sure "Daddy" would pay me handsomely for breaking you in.'

I'd always assumed it was just something that actresses did in plays, but I can't tell you how good it feels when the flat of my hand makes contact with his designer stubble. 'You bastard, Philip. I thought you were supposed to be a gentleman.'

For some reason, my last comment seems to have touched a nerve. He climbs out of bed and walks slowly towards my dressing table. 'So that's it,' he says, his mood deflating as rapidly as the mushroom in his boxers. 'I knew it.'

'What are you talking about?'

He sits in front of the dressing-table mirror, examining the red handprint on his cheek. 'Don't try and deny it. You posh tarts are all the same.'

'I don't understand.'

'Like fuck you don't. I never did buy that ridiculous little virgin act of yours. I know why you won't shag me. It's because I'm working class.'

'Is this some kind of a joke?'

'What gave me away this time? Passed the sodding salad bowl the wrong way, did I?'

For a second, I think it might be one of his horrid improvisations. 'You can't be working class. You were at Winchester.'

'Winchester comp,' he mutters. 'Huh, told you I went to a good school.'

'What about your estate?'

'Heard of the Stanmore, have you? It's the sort of place that Nikki Hardbody would wet her split-crotch panties over.'

(At least he's come to his senses over that uber-bitch's dress sense.) 'And why would she do that?'

'An award-winning documentary on every street corner: smack-heads and joyriders, tarts without hearts and right-wing politics, can't scratch your arse without a youth worker trying to sign you up for rapping lessons – she'd love it. I can just see her hanging out with some thirteen-year-old Kylie and her brown babies.'

'But why would you . . . ?'

It pours out of him, like a soliloquy. (That's another thing I thought they only did in plays.) 'Don't know Winchester, do you, Anna? It's a bit of a shithole, actually. You've got your townies and your squaddies beating the crap out of each other in the Broadway on a Saturday night . . . and then there's your college boys. I used to follow them around: rich wankers with credit cards and loud voices who ponce about the place like they own it, arrogant dickheads who look straight through you – unless they want you to serve them in McDonald's or die for them in one of their wars, of course.

'And you know what? I envied them. *I* wanted to sleep with birds called Emma, *I* wanted to make the rest of the world feel like shite, I wanted to direct neglected masterpieces at the National Theatre, *I* wanted a voice that everyone would listen to. So I ditched 'Loser Phil' – Psycho's kid brother off the Stanmore – and became Philip Sidney, as in anyone I fucking wanna be.'

Why are some people so obsessed with class? Why can't they just be happy with who they are? 'I still don't understand. There are plenty of guys like you in college, and none of them are ashamed of their background.'

'Oh, you think so. Well, let me tell you: Oxford's full of middle-class tossers dropping their aitches, and making out they're working-class heroes because they've been to a couple of football matches.'

His self-pity is so much less attractive than his blind arrogance. 'So what's your problem then?'

'It doesn't work the other way round, does it? Breeding tells, eh, "Pumpkin"? I mean, look at the way you treated me.'

'That had nothing to do with class.'

'Come off it. Why else would you keep turning me down? Cock-teasing went out with Jane fucking Austen.'

'I've had enough of this.'

'Going to break the bad news to Mummy, are we?'

All I want to do is get away from him. 'I've got to see Michael, he needs turning over.'

'I don't know what you're bothering with him for. He's just as much of a prole as I am.'

'You know what, Philip? I feel sorry for you. I didn't realize you were such a snob.'

He stands between me and the door, his shrivelled testicles peeking out from the bottom of his boxers. His voice is taut with desperation. 'Promise me you won't tell anyone about this. It would be disastrous for company morale, and I'm sure we both have the best interests of the production at heart.'

'Yes, all right,' I murmur, fumbling for the key and making a mental note never to take anyone at face value again.

The Quadriplegic

When the wind's in the right direction, I smell like an old people's home: air-freshener mingled with industrial disinfectant but, underneath, a suspicion of something rotten in the state of Denmark. Anna's unexpected arrival brings with it a fragrant combination of jasmine, camomile, ylang-ylang, patchouli, spearmint toothpaste, fresh apples and that powder they put on babies' bums.

'What are *you* doing here?'

She clicks on the Thomas the Tank Engine table lamp.

It flares in my face like a torturer's anglepoise. 'I've come to roll you over.'

'You've only been gone five minutes.'

'I'm sorry,' she says, 'couldn't sleep.'

'That makes two of us then; must be all the excitement of having a different ceiling to stare at.'

'Sorry, didn't quite catch,' says Anna, moving into my field of vision, clutching the top of her pyjama jacket like she's got an irrational fear of vampires. 'I'll come closer, shall I?'

'Take a pew.'

She perches on the side of the bed. A few more inches and I could feel the warmth of her breasts on my face. 'Oh, Mike, why are men such arseholes?'

'Thanks a lot.'

'Not you, Michael. I don't mean you . . . you're different.'

'Well spotted.'

'Most guys just want to stare at my tits all night.' Her whole body is quivering, like a little kid after his first swim in the sea. 'I hate being out of control, you know? All my life, it seems like whatever happens to me, it's because someone else is pulling the strings, not because I want it for myself. It does my head in.'

'How do you think I feel?'

'Scared, I guess,' she says, hugging herself.

'I ought to be used to it by now,' I say, wishing I could run my fingers through the purple streaks in her hair, 'but being trapped in this totally crap body doesn't get any

171

easier. Especially when there's something you really want to do.'

'Like what?'

'Oh . . . I don't know.'

'Come on, you can tell me.'

(Not without making her throw up, I can't.) 'Oh, you know . . . swim with the dolphins, punch our director smack on that toffee-nose of his.'

'Maybe it's not made of toffee after all.'

'Come again?'

'Oh, nothing,' she smiles, 'it's not important. Who wants to talk about Philip Sidney anyway?'

'Philip Sidney?'

'You don't mind if I stay with you for a bit, do you, Mike?'

'Be my guest. Hang on a minute, what are you . . . ?'

Anna peels back Postman Pat's head and squeezes in beside me. 'Mnn, toasty! Come on, we can run through some lines if you like: *You are keen, my lord, you are keen . . .*'

Imagine arriving at the most beautiful oasis in the world, and not being able to drink. 'I'm sorry, Anna. I don't think this is a good idea.'

'Can't you breathe or something?'

'No, it's not that. It's just . . .' (What is this, Beauty and the fucking Beast? Who am I trying to kid?)

'Is that light bothering you? I'll turn it off, shall I?'

'Yeah. Look, Anna, what I was going to say was . . .' She must be a mind reader. Why else would she be pissing herself? What's so funny?

'What do you think Philip would say if he could see us now?'

'"Be more real"?'

'Yeah, that'd be right.'

Her warm breath is burning a hole in the back of my head. If I don't say something soon, I'm going to have a heart attack. 'The thing is, Anna . . . God, this is hard . . . but . . . Look, you mustn't think that just because I'm paralysed, I don't have . . . feelings.' (Well, she's certainly not laughing any more.) 'I really . . . don't take this the wrong way . . . I really like you, Anna. I know it's the last thing you want to hear right now, but you've got to see that this is difficult for me . . . I . . .'

'Shhh . . . it doesn't matter.'

'You mean . . . you don't mind?'

I feel her lips on my neck. 'I think I might feel the same way about you.'

'That's impossible.'

'Why? This is nice, isn't it?'

'I suppose . . .'

'It feels pretty good to me. Let me stay with you, Michael. You'll let me stay, won't you?'

The Virgin

'I guess so, Anna. If that's what you really want.'

I close my eyes and snuggle up to his cold, lifeless body. The last time I felt warm and safe like this, I was seven years old. You probably won't believe it, but I was quite the little

Daddy's girl. Every Saturday morning, we'd wander into the village to pick up his *Telegraph* and a Curly Wurly or something for me. He'd sit on the bench in the corner of the swing park opposite the church and shout encouragement from behind the business section: '*Come on, Pumpkin, you can go higher than that.*' I loved the feeling of his weekend stubble on my fingertips, the stench of his illicit cigar, and the delicious sense of complicity when he whispered, '*Better not tell Mummy I've been smoking, eh, Pumpkin?*'

Mummy chose my clothes and taught me never to say thank you to waiters, but Daddy was special. He was the one I wanted to amuse with my silly stories about Whoops A Daisy Eddie, the Clumsy Teddy, he was the one I wanted to impress with my grade three clarinet pieces. Only a child could believe she'd feel that way for ever, only a child could fail to see that untainted happiness is like a really impressive sandcastle – it's only a matter of time before someone sticks their boot into it.

'A lady never reveals her age, Anna Panna,' Mummy smiled, as she buttoned me into my Snow White outfit. I knew it was her thirtieth because Daddy told me when he was showing Maurice where to put the ice sculptures: '*Better not mention it to your mother though, eh, Pumpkin?*'

'I like your hair, Mummy,' I said, amazed that she'd gone blonde overnight. 'You look ever so pretty.' It was true. She was the spitting image of Lady Diana. A few years later, all they'd have in common was their eating disorders.

Daddy came as Napoleon. He looked really handsome in his uniform. I couldn't wait to dance with him to the hideously expensive swing band he'd hired. After the meal (I was banished to the children's table; Toby Morton was telling jokes about his bum and willy) Daddy thanked the wonderful caterers and said some sweet things about Mummy: 'Every morning, when I wake up next to her, I have to remind myself what a lucky man I am – as does my mother-in-law. And I'm sure you'll all agree that my lovely wife Camilla makes an absolutely ravishing Lady Di. God bless her, and all who sail in her.'

I never did get to dance with him. After he and Mummy had foxtrotted round the marquee a couple of times to 'Lady in Red', he disappeared into the crowd to charm the ladies with his 'Not tonight, Josephine' routine and entertain the gentlemen with tales from the stock exchange. I sat beneath a trestle table with a bowl of pavlova, hiding from Toby Morton and his ugly sister, and hoping that Daddy hadn't forgotten the clarinet solo I'd prepared.

I don't know why I went back into the house. I didn't develop my IBS until the lower fourth, so I can only assume I needed a wee. The band was playing 'The Teddy Bears' Picnic'. A tired little teddy bear hauled herself up the banisters. And I would probably have fallen asleep on the landing if I hadn't heard noises from the guest room.

(You know, when I told Philip this story, he laughed like a drain and made one of his clever-clever comments about something in the woodshed. I must have been off my rocker to think I'd get any sympathy out of that hard-hearted sod.)

They really were the strangest sounds I'd ever heard: one deep and guttural, the other breathless and squeaky, but both marching to the same tune, a tune that was getting more *allegro vivace* by the second. I stood outside the door trying to decide whether to investigate. When a woman's voice screamed out, 'Yes, yes, *yes*,' I took it as my cue to enter.

'Bloody hell, Pumpkin, don't you ever knock?'

It was only years later that I was able to appreciate the glaring anachronism. Napoleon was standing at the rear; in front of him, on all fours, an arch-backed, pre-Jean-Paul-Gaultier Madonna – aka the lady from the pony club, aka the head caterer.

'Why are you hurting Mrs Chamberlain-Webber, Daddy?'

'I'm not hurting her, Pumpkin,' he said, still pumping. 'I'm just helping her find her contact lens, that's all.'

'Are you really?' I said, wondering why they hadn't tried the more obvious places first.

'That's right, now run along, Pumpkin, there's a good girl.'

Madonna laughed maniacally. I couldn't wait to get out of there.

'One thing before you go,' whispered Napoleon, pulling up his white breeches. 'Better not tell Mummy about this, eh, Pumpkin?'

I had no intention of mentioning it to anybody. I didn't even want to think about it, let alone relive one second of the whole sick-making episode. But a few days later, curiosity got the better of me, and I couldn't resist asking Mummy if it was possible for a lady to lose a contact lens up her front bottom. Mummy didn't think that it was.

Daddy and I were never as close after that. We didn't have our little secrets any more, and he was always too busy to play with me, or too exhausted after one of his running battles with Mummy. A year later, Barnaby was born, and the rift was complete. Daddy devoted all his energies to the burbling brat in the Babygro, and I gradually realized that he wasn't my hero any more.

And quite frankly, Mummy needed me. Post-natal depression gave way to something more permanent, and I made it my mission in life to alleviate her misery. I suppose, in a way, I felt responsible for it, so I spent every hour of the day trying to please her. Which was silly really, because the one thing I had learnt was that you should never rely on another person for your own happiness.

Well, I'm right, aren't I? No matter who it is, they'll always let you down in the end. That's what's so lovely about a dog. A dog loves you for who you are, not who they want you to be. People aren't like that; people only want to use you until something better comes along.

Or have I just been looking for the wrong kind of person? There must be at least one man in the world who isn't full of shit. There must be at least one man in the world who wouldn't walk out on me.

The Actor

Meanwhile, back at the Fatted Calf, desperation is setting in. So I call her mobile. Something tells me it's the closest to intercourse I'm going to get with her tonight. 'Hi, Nikki Hardbody at your service,' she purrs, her sexy rasp reminding me of the shapely masseuse in one of those Confessions books I found so stimulating as a boy. 'I'm afraid I can't take your call right now, but – *please* – leave me a message after the beep, and I'll get straight back to you. Go on, you know you want to. Ciao.'

I'd planned calling my autobiography something self-deprecating like *A Talent to Abuse*, but *Trying Not to Sound Too Desperate* would probably be a more apt summation of my life so far. 'Nikki, hi, it's er . . . Tim here . . . Timothy Salt. Sorry to call you again so soon . . . I'm sure you must be on your way. I'm in the Fatted Calf . . . still . . . wearing a red carnation . . . ha. Now, I'm afraid Bellini's will *probably* have had to let our table go. So, er, why don't we have a quick birthday drink before closing and then move on to college for coffee? Yah . . . good . . . that's it . . . er, over and out.'

I return to my pork scratchings, consoling myself with the thought that this particular episode of the naff sitcom which is my life can't possibly be anything like as tragic as the *Guess Who's Coming to Dinner* scenario playing out in the Jenkinses' household even as we speak.

My inner optimist is wondering whether to have another crack at the forty-something divorcee who works the bar, but something tells me she'd find the prospect about as alluring as an all-male production of *As You Like It*. And anyway, Nikki could still make it. I didn't get where I am today by giving up on lost causes.

I could lie to you and say that sitting alone in a pub is a new experience, but you wouldn't believe me. It was once, though. The first occasion is engraved on my mind, nearly as deeply as the remark (the more hurtful for its casualness) which precipitated it: '*Some of your friends are quite successful, Timbo, why aren't you?*'

Simon Butterworth came round in his old Renault. *Cats* was only in its 5 billionth year, so we had a couple of hours before my less than Purrfect Pussy got back from the theatre. You can count on Simon in a crisis. He's a bloody good solicitor too. I could give you his number if you like. In fact, I've asked him to be my executor. In the event of my sudden demise (and God willing a regular glove up the arse and a few extra helpings of broccoli should keep the Grim Reaper at bay for a while yet) I've instructed him to seek and destroy my collection of pornography. I'd hate Mum to find it. Ten years ago this would have been such a Herculean task that I would have felt obliged to appoint Pickford's as my executors, but the day after SOWINS and I got engaged – poor romantic fool that I was – I made a huge bonfire and burnt the lot. Considering it included several quite rare foreign issues, I suppose it was a wanton act of cultural vandalism.

Of course, SOWINS wouldn't have had the guts to tell me to leave. That would have meant sharing responsibility for the failure of our marriage. She just kept dropping gentle hints like, '*Maybe some time apart would do us* good,' or, '*There was a rather nice flat-share in yesterday's* Guardian – *did you see it?*' So it was I who was forced into the ridiculous subterfuge, and it wasn't long before SOWINS had created an official version of events, in which she starred as the plucky, abandoned wife, and I guested as the pathetic commitment-phobe.

Simon went through SOWINS's underwear drawer while I chucked a few clothes into my going-away bag and did the hoovering. I couldn't decide whether to rearrange the magnetic letters on the fridge (yet another hint, I suspected, that she wanted kids) to spell 'goodbye'. In the end there was only one o, and, knowing SOWINS, if I'd put 'Godbye' she would have thought I was trying to make some sort of pseudo-intellectual, theological comment.

Driving back across London, Simon tried to cheer me up by singing that song we wrote in the sixth form common room after the school production of *HMS Pinafore*:

> '*We sail the ocean blue,*
> *And our saucy ship's a tanker,*
> *And it's clearly plain to see,*
> *Mr Willcock is a wanker.*'

Butters had only just met Yvonne (the putative replacement for the Purrfect Pussy). No man alive would have expected him to stay in and console his oldest friend at the expense of a night with a new woman. Rather than sit silently sobbing in Simon's love-nest (every few minutes you could hear the distant rumble of the Northern Line) I decided to brave the pub opposite. Nowadays, drinking alone is no biggie, even all ponced up in this wedding suit. But that first time

– when I wasn't weeping wordlessly into my Worthington's, that is – I felt obliged to perform an elaborate waiting-for-someone pantomime; looking at my watch every few minutes and turning round each time the door opened. I never was much of an actor.

'Last orders, ladies and gentlemen, please.'

'Bollocks, bollocks, bollocks.' Nikki's definitely not going to show up now. My forty-first year to sodding heaven and all I've got to show for it is a twenty-five-yards swimming certificate and a rich crop of nasal hair. The barmaid's tired announcement sends me on my customary, narcoleptic schlep to the bar. It also gets me started on another favourite obsession: last times.

Up to a certain age, life is all about new experiences: first love, first car (one and the same in Simon B's case), first encounter with a stroppy tradesman. The terrifying thing about '*last* times' is that, quite often, you don't know that that's what it is when you're doing it. Last last orders, last visit to the Tower of London, last haircut, last episode of your favourite soap, last swim in the sea, last wank, last laugh (the longest?), last piss, last attempt to repair a faulty electrical appliance, last breath. I mean, how many last times have I had already?

'Cheer up, pet,' says the barmaid, with the special smile she reserves for certified losers, 'things can't be that bad. You're still here, aren't you?'

'I'm afraid you have the advantage, madam.'

'There's only one reason a man wears a suit like that.'

'I'm sorry, I don't catch your drift.'

'Well, you've had your day in court and they didn't send

you down – been a lucky boy, if you ask me. Same again, is it?'

That's the trouble with my autobiography at the moment; it's a treasure trove of self-deprecatory incident, but a little lacking on the Oscar nomination and 'starlets I have shagged' front. 'Yes, that's remarkably amusing, but if you must know, I've been waiting for a young lady.'

She obviously finds this a less plausible explanation than the criminal one: 'Yeah, right.'

'And she's obviously been unavoidably detained. She works in television, you see.'

'Yeah, right.'

'We were going on somewhere. Believe it or not, it's my fortieth birthday.'

For some reason she seems to find this my most unlikely assertion of all. 'Yeah . . . right.'

'I'm sure there's a perfectly rational explanation for her absence but . . .' And I'm on the point of admitting what a pathetic fraud I am – and probably fessing up to nicking that racehorse as well – when something rather miraculous happens. Never before have I been so happy to hear that vulgar ring-tone. 'In fact,' I say, producing my all-singing mobile with a theatrical flourish, 'that's probably her now. Hello, darling . . . lovely to hear your voice.' I beam triumphantly at the barmaid. 'You're breaking up, I'm afraid. Sorry, Sausage, I'm going to have to take you outside.'

No prizes for guessing that it's pissing down.

'Timothy? Is that you?' says Valerie Owen. 'I think I'd

better call you back. It's a terrible line. I could have sworn you just called me—'

'No! Don't do that, Valerie,' I say, turning up my jacket collar. 'It should be all right now – how's that?'

'Much better, dear. So, how's Michael?'

'He's gone down to Hampshire with Anna for the night. I probably should have mentioned it, but Mike didn't want to worry you.'

'That sounds nice,' she says, breezily. 'Anna's lovely, I'm sure she'll look after my Michael.' (I wasn't expecting her to take it so well.) 'But I expect you're missing him, aren't you, Tim?'

'Well . . .'

'It does get easier. I should know.'

'Does it?'

I push my way through a crowd of pissed-up college boys. This being Oxford, they're in the middle of a heated debate about Britten's *War Requiem*.

'Oi, watch it, baldy,' says a spotty wag in corduroy.

I scurry into the night, like a closet homosexual in 1950s London. 'Piss off, crater face – no, not you, Valerie!'

'Are you all right, dear?'

'Not as such,' I say, realizing that I'm being honest for a change. 'It's my birthday, actually.'

'You should have said something, Timothy. I would have baked you a cake.'

And now I really am breaking up. Insults I can take, but sympathy I find almost impossible to cope with. 'I'm forty years old, I look fifty, I can't even get myself a bloody

Flatuleeze commercial, and I've just been stood up by my dinner date – how's that for many happy returns?'

'Fancy standing up a lovely chap like you,' says Valerie indignantly. 'The silly girl must be out of her mind.'

'You think so?'

'I *know* so. Tell you what, Timothy. I'm coming to see *Hamlet* in a couple of weeks. I know it's not the same, but after the show, I'm going to take you for a special birthday drink.'

I haven't the heart to tell her that there's not going to be any *Hamlet*, at least not the five-act tragedy that she's expecting. 'Thanks, I'll hold you to that.'

'Of course, Shakespeare's not really my cup of tea. I prefer a nice musical – Andrew Lloyd Webber or something like that.'

'Did I tell you my ex-wife was in *Cats*?'

'I didn't realize you'd been married, dear.'

'It was a long time ago, Valerie, another country and all that. And besides, I never talk about her.'

By the time I've outlined my full marital history (including some previously unpublished material about my perceived inadequacies in the bedroom and DIY departments) and Valerie has explained, once again, how ballroom dancing has brought her out of herself, and what a wonderful teacher Mr Hornbrook is, I find myself standing outside Gloucester College.

'Gosh, is that the time?' she yawns. 'I think I'd better hit the hay, dear. It's the paso doble tomorrow. I wouldn't want to let Mr Hornbrook down.'

'Yes, good luck with that. And er . . . well, thanks.'

'Whatever for?'

'For listening. I know I go on a bit.'

'Don't be silly, Timothy, I've enjoyed it. Next time I see you we can have a proper old natter.'

'I'd like that.'

'And Tim, you mustn't get upset about those other things. It's just a question of finding the right person. If you want your boiler fixed, call a plumber.'

'I'll bear it in mind.'

'Don't worry, I'll pray for you.'

The Quadriplegic

Breakfast is going great. I don't know what Anna's mum is on, but the wicked witch of the west seems to have morphed into the good fairy overnight: 'How about another one, Michael?'

'Yes, lovely, thank you, Mrs Jenkins.'

'Please, call me Camilla,' she says, spearing an organic Cumberland sausage on a giant fork. 'Everyone else does.'

'You're pretty chirpy this morning, Mummy,' says Anna.

'Do you know, darling, I rather think I am. I haven't felt this good for donkeys'.'

'That makes two of us then,' says Anna, winking at me as she places a forkful of wild mushrooms in my mouth.

'Daddy and I couldn't be happier for you, could we, Bernard?'

Mr Jenkins is feeding the dishwasher: 'Absolutely, Pumpkin, good for you.'

'Where's Philip?' I enquire innocently.

'He was up with the lark,' says Mrs Jenkins. 'Maurice ran him up to the station in the van.'

'Why didn't you tell me he was in his college first boat, Pumpkin? If I'd known he had to be back for training, I wouldn't have kept the poor chap jawing half the night.'

'Such a polite young man,' says Mrs Jenkins. 'You've done really well for yourself, Anna Panna. A girl couldn't wish for a more suitable boyfriend.'

'Philip's not my boyfriend, Mummy,' says Anna. 'Michael is!'

'Well, shiver me timbers,' says Mr Jenkins, almost dislocating his thumbs.

Camilla Jenkins opens her mouth, but nothing emerges. The only sound is that of a half-cooked Cumberland sausage rebounding on the flagstones.

The Actor

I was so despondent this morning I barely stooped to examine the consistency of my post-Brazilian-blend stools. What was it D. H. Lawrence said about recklessness being man's revenge on a woman? I shan't be favouring Nikki Hardbody with a second bite at the cherry.

Perhaps I should have expected it. Then again, we are talking about the man who fondly imagined there to be a paucity of porky, middle-aged Equity members prepared to expose themselves for a colony of rodents. As my agent (Bunny Michelmore at Bunny Michelmore Management) said at the time, '*Sorry, darling, some of them had had ten years' vermin experience. In the end, it came down to that.*'

You will probably gauge my mental state by the fact that I haven't even dipped into *Be Your Own Psychotherapist in One Weekend*. I mean, we all *know* the things we could do to make us feel better: Go on a low-fat diet, take regular exercise, cut down on alcohol, meditate daily, stop watching so much telly, cultivate meaningful, mutually supportive friendships, stop being secretive, give up caffeine (do me a favour!), read a good book, develop a religious faith and always live in the present. The trouble is, eating pizza, watching *Match of the Day*, drinking Australian wine, regular masturbation, *Trisha*, losing touch with your school friends, bottling it all up, freshly ground coffee, reading the tabloids, agnosticism and brooding on the past, come so much more naturally. Which is why, as soon as I finish my fifth cup of Brazilian, I'm going to settle down in front of some daytime telly and fire up the Purrfect Pussy.

'Have you seen them yet?' she says, bursting through the door with her camera cocked. 'I haven't missed them, have I?'

'What are *you* doing here?'

'I can't believe it. It's absolutely amazing.' She might conceivably have popped into my fantasies at some point, but after last night, it's absolutely amazing that Nikki Hardbody has got the gall to show up in my rooms.

'What is?' I say, deliberately not clocking her skintight jeans and skimpy crop top.

'Michael and Anna, they're a couple. Can you believe that?'

I never thought I'd see a woman like Nikki skipping. 'No.'

'Well, it's true,' she says, polkaing over to the mantelpiece. 'Philip just told me – isn't it fab?'

'No.'

'What's the matter with you guys? Philip looked like shit until I explained what this means.'

'What *does* it mean?'

'Are you kidding? Hamlet and Ophelia in lurve? I knew the whole *Hamlet* thing was going to be great, but like I said to Philip, with those two playing happy families, every serious journo in Britain is going to want a piece of it. 'Who knows,' she smiles, taking a green plastic object from the mantelpiece and testing the tip with her tongue, 'Michael might be needing the Fecundimatic after all.'

'Yes,' I say, pointedly, 'dealing with women is enough to give any man a headache.'

Nikki's obviously too thick skinned to see what I'm driving at. She waltzes over to the window and rips open the curtains. 'How can you live like this? It's like a funeral parlour in here.'

I'm going to have to spell it out to her. 'If you must know, I'm still recovering from last night.'

'Out on the piss, were you?'

'I wasted my whole evening waiting for you.'

The penny finally drops. 'Oh, that,' she shrugs, 'sorry about that. I was running late. Something came up. Another time, perhaps – you don't mind, do you?'

Before I can produce a suitably vitriolic retort, the door swings open and in glides Romeo, followed by his breathless prom queen lugging a couple of suitcases.

'Well, look at you two,' says Nikki Hardbody, circling her prey like a hungry piranha. 'Don't they look fantastic, Timothy?'

'That's one word for it,' I say, stepping between the star-crossed lovers into a rather tasty three-shot.

'Come on then,' says Nikki, winking so hard that she must be coming down with Tourette's syndrome, 'how was last night?'

'Fine, thanks,' blushes Anna.

'Aren't you going to tell your Auntie Nikki all about it?'

'All about what?' says Michael.

'Well,' says Nikki, zooming in for the close-up, 'a little bird tells me that Hamlet and Ophelia are more than just good friends – is this true, Mike?'

When you think about it, it's in rather poor taste. Michael glares at Nikki, refusing to dignify her puerile innuendo with a response.

'Yes, it is, actually,' says Anna, stepping forward and putting her hand over the lens. 'Michael and I are a couple – so what? Now if you don't mind, we'd like a bit of privacy.'

'Oh, yah, absolutely,' says Nikki. 'But sooner or later we're going to have to be upfront about this. What would you say to a weekend in Paris?'

Michael advances towards her, like an angry Dalek. 'We don't want anything, OK. Just leave us alone, can't you, or I'm backing out of the whole thing.'

'Well, you did sign the consent forms,' smiles Nikki, 'but of course, if that's what you want. Forget Paris, nothing's going to top *Hamlet*, anyway.' She pauses and squints up at the ceiling. 'Christ, what's that awful noise?'

It starts slowly, like a vintage steam engine, gathers speed and shudders towards an uncontrollable climax. What is that hollow sound, which seems to shake the very fabric of this venerable establishment and turn all eyes in one direction? Ah yes, it's the sound of my own hysterical laughter; the laughter of a man for whom life has, long since, ceased to make sense; the laughter of a man who's done his homework and knows exactly how he's going to put a bloody great spanner in the works.

14

The Play's the Thing

The Quadriplegic

'That's better,' says Anna, applying yet more hair gel and flicking my fringe up into a quiff. 'You want to look your best for opening night, don't you, babe?'

'I just want to get it over with.'

'Not nervous, are you?'

'Not really, but it's going to be great not having that camera shoved up my dung trumpet every time I want to fart.'

A flicker of concern flashes across my girlfriend's face. 'You don't need your bag changed, do you, babe?'

'No! I'm fine. Timothy did it before you arrived.'

Anna scowls at De Niro's bedroom door. 'That's good. We're all set then.'

'Looks like it.'

She kisses her fingertips and places them on my mouth. Her fingers smell of chocolate. 'You happy?'

'Yep.'

'Me too,' she smiles.

Don't get me wrong; it's totally the best thing that's ever happened to me. What sort of an ungrateful bastard do you take me for? Anna's a brilliant girl: she's kind, she's funny, she's a dab hand with a surgical hoist. I just don't understand why she wants to spend so much time with me. And why does she have to tell me how she feels every five minutes? It's not like I can do anything about it.

'God, Mike, I'm shitting bricks. Mind you, I've been doing that for the last ten years. Did you know Philip had a guy from the RSC coming?'

'So you two are talking again then?'

'He said it was for the good of the show.'

'That was big of him.'

And I've got a confession to make: I don't find Mozart even slightly relaxing. In fact, all that plinky-plonking makes me so tense I want to scream. I'm not even that delirious about French films; what's wrong with *EastEnders*?

'Oh, yes,' says Anna, reaching into her rucksack and pulling out a plastic pig with a ribbon round its neck. 'I thought I'd give you this now. I've only got cards for the others. Isn't he gorgeous?'

'Yes, he's . . . great, thanks a lot. I never had my own pig before.'

Anna wipes a space on the mantelpiece with a pink tissue. 'I'll put him here, shall I, next to your what-do-you-call-it?' She examines the Fecundimatic, holding it up to the light like a rare jewel. 'What is this thing anyway?'

Anna made me promise we'd always be completely truthful with each other, but there is such a thing as being too honest. 'Nikki thought it might help with my headaches.'

'You haven't got a headache, have you, babe? Do you want me to rub your neck?'

'No . . . thanks, I'm fine.'

'You'd better wear that scarf I bought you.'

'OK then.' At first, it was quite cool when she bought me stuff; now I'm starting to feel like Wheelchair Barbie. I know she only does it because she wants me to look nice, but I wish she didn't want to change my outfit every five seconds.

'When are you seeing your mother?' she says, wrapping my new Gloucester College scarf tight around my neck.

'Not until after the show, thank God. She won't like it anyway.'

'Why not?'

'Because her son dies at the end, and Barry Manilow didn't write the music.'

'Why does she bother turning up then?' says Anna, doing that flouncy thing with her shoulders.

'Nikki says she's got a surprise for her at the after-show party.'

'Mummy's not coming, of course. Daddy says she's hardly been out of her room since our visit.'

'I wonder why?'

'Don't worry about her, it's not important.' She takes my head in her hands and stares into my eyes. There's something I've been meaning to say to you, Michael.'

It's never a good sign when someone looks me in the eye. It's usually the build-up to one of those '*I'm afraid you're never going to walk again'* or *'Me and your mother just don't love each other any more'* moments. 'You'd better say it then.'

She kisses me softly on the lips. 'Thank you.'

'What for?'

'For making me feel good about myself. You've been amazing.'

'Whatever.'

De Niro bursts out of his bedroom wearing a demented smile and a truly terrible tie with what looks like a plague of rats on it. 'Hello, you two, all set for your big night?'

He's been a total pain in the arse lately with his constant bloody cheerfulness. I think I preferred it when he was a miserable old sod. Don't tell me he's found someone desperate enough to grease his weasel.

'Actually, I'm really nervous,' says Anna. 'God knows how I'm going to get through the madness scene.'

A strange smile breaks out on De Niro's face. 'You needn't worry about that, dear heart. That is . . . I must have seen at least a dozen Ophelias in my time, and I don't think I've ever seen mental illness better conveyed.'

'It runs in the family,' says Anna bleakly.

I'm so eager to get out of here that my wheelchair is already halfway to the door. 'Come on, Anna, we need to be off. Philip wants to do an extended warm-up.'

On our way out, De Niro gives us a camp, one-handed finger wave. 'I'll see you two on the green then. And don't forget, have a lovely show.'

The Actor

'I know I'm going to,' I whisper.

Oh, by the way, do you like my lucky first-night tie? SOWINS gave it to me when I was understudying in *The Mousetrap* – hence the hamsters. Not that it proved in the least bit propitious. Despite a psychopathic murderer in our midst, the cast proved sickeningly durable. Even Dickie Burford managed to get some poor bugger to give him a lift during the traditional tube strike.

Which brings me rather neatly to the subject of my top two phoney acting clichés; next time you're watching the box, look out from them:

1) THE END OF THE PHONE CALL: Instead of hanging up immediately – as one does – the actor stares dramatically at the receiver, as if eyeballing the person he's just spoken to.

2) THE SLOW SLIDE DOWN THE WALL: Used to denote a state of extreme anguish, and often followed by the theme tune. The actor ends up level with the skirting board in a crouched foetal position, head in hands, sobbing. This requires terrific balance and upper-leg strength. If you ever come across it in real life, chances are that Halley's Comet will be illuminating the proceedings.

So what of the passing of time? As the camera pans around my dismal little room, perhaps it could zoom in on a growing pile of dirty coffee cups, come to rest on a newly acquired moustache, or maybe simply focus on Miss

November in my Page Three calendar and the box containing an enigmatic exclamation mark. Except, of course, I'm rather meticulous about domestic hygiene, I can't stand facial hair, and it dawned upon me many moons ago that Page Three girls are like a red rag to a bull as far as the type of women I generally shag are concerned.

Yet make no mistake, this is no ordinary 'day in the life'. This is the day I have been waiting for since I first clapped eyes on the Wheelchair Prince. My physical circumstances may not have changed much in the last few weeks, but my emotional journey – as one of those chain-smoking lady directors with a penchant for theatre games and onstage buggery would describe it – has been enormous. No acute observer could have failed to notice the carefree spring in my step, the cheerful alacrity with which I have performed my thankless duties, and my almost avuncular observation of Hamlet and Ophelia's burgeoning intimacy. Never, I believe, since Burbage himself was giving his legendary Dane, has a performance of *Hamlet* been so eagerly awaited. In fact, so bright has been my demeanour, that I do believe when *Wheelchair of Fire* is broadcast, I shall be receiving some pretty saucy letters from ladies of a 'certain age'.

Don't get the impression, however, that I have been completely idle. My improved self-image has marked a significant upsurge in my masturbatory activities, and as well as my regular evening visits to the Fatted Calf I've also managed to fit in some lunchtime drinking. Of course I've continued to ensure that I feature in every single shot of *Wheelchair of Fire*. You wouldn't believe how difficult it was to persuade Nikki that a romantic meal *à deux* should feature yours truly as the solicitous waiter. On top of all that there's been a certain amount of fine tuning involved. Although my master plan has a beautiful simplicity to it, the timing is crucial, and I've spent many a long evening perfecting the logistics.

But now, as darkness falls and the burnt-toast smells begin to pervade the atmosphere, all that remains is to park myself in front of *Countdown* and do just that. When zero hour arrives, I shall skip to the theatre like a frisky unicorn; and having first popped my head round to bid Michael 'break a leg', I shall take up my seat in the front row.

The Virgin

As soon as we step into the theatre (or Methodist Hall to be more accurate) that slag, Hardbody, descends on us like Cilla Black. 'Don't you two look fab? So come on guys, tell me all about it?'

'About what?' I say, managing to avoid her attempts to sucker me into a theatrical embrace.

So instead, she waves her tits at my boyfriend. 'Mike's always got a cheeky grin on his face these days, haven't you, mate?'

'No, I haven't.'

'There's no need to be bashful,' she says, patting him on the head. 'You two have got a really good thing going. The British public are going to love you, I know they are.'

That woman is so transparent she should have her own

double-glazing company. 'Would you mind not touching his hair, please? I spent a long time working on Michael's quiff.'

'I bet you did,' she says, turning it into a pathetic innuendo as usual. Michael's just as keen to get shot of her as I am. But she throws herself in front of his wheelchair, batting her eyelids like a French whore. 'Michael, before you go, I just wanted to say thanks.'

'What for?'

'For everything really: your patience, your . . . sense of humour, and above all for letting me into your life. It's been a real eye opener.'

All true, of course, but she's only using him, just like the rest of them. Wait a minute; it looks like there's more. Just how far is the Channel 4 bike prepared to go in her pursuit of fifth-rate television?

'It's an overused word, Michael, but in your case, I don't think it even comes close: you're a true hero, I really mean that. If we don't get a BAFTA nomination for this, I'll be bloody furious.'

'Oh, Mike,' I say, kissing his neck so that bloody floozy's in no doubt as to whose boyfriend he is, 'I'm so proud of you.'

'Don't let me down,' she says, suddenly sounding a lot more sincere. 'You won't believe who's going to be out there tonight. We've got *Channel 4 News*, the *Guardian*, Radio Oxford, that gorgeous guy from *Newsround* – not to mention your lovely mother, of course.'

'Don't remind me,' says Michael.

'And that's not all. The *Richard and Judy* psychologist

wants to do a phone-in on sex and the disabled, and *Blue Peter* are working on a special "make" of your wheelchair for *Children in Need*. Isn't that cool?'

What a sad person Nikki Hardbody is. Underneath that rock-hard exterior, I have a feeling there's something much more messed-up inside. I'm just going to have to do a bit of digging. 'What about you, Nikki? Have you got anyone special coming along – a boyfriend – husband, perhaps?'

'I'm a strong woman,' she says, biting her bottom lip. 'Some men find that quite threatening. But don't worry, Anna; *you'll* never have that problem.'

I smile sympathetically. 'So that's a no then, is it, Nikki?'

'I thought you two had a warm-up to get to,' she snarls.

The Quadriplegic

Philip Sidney has come as Count Dracula. He's wearing an Oxfam dinner jacket with a vampire's cloak and strategically placed Aids ribbon. He's dyed his hair black and looks so pale I could swear he's got make-up on.

'Acting is as simple as falling off a log. It's getting up on the log that's the difficult part.' (Confused grins.) 'You have all worked . . . fucking hard. Believe me, we've got a shit-hot show on our hands. OK, so we had a couple of problems in the dress, but they weren't seminal. I don't care if you forget your lines, miss cues even, but what I *do* need is for your hearts to be right. If you get things right in here,' he pats his chest, 'then everything else will fall into place.'

Piers's hand shoots into the air. 'Sorry, Phil, just a small thing.'

'Yes?'

'When are we going to rehearse the curtain call?'

Philip bites on his knuckles. 'We're not doing one.'

'Why not?' says Piers, tossing back his golden locks. 'I think we deserve it, especially Mike and Anna.'

'Because this is not the fucking West End,' says Philip. 'Some of you might go in for all that bourgeois crap – isn't that right, Anna? – but this isn't about egos, Piers, it's about respect.'

'But you just said we'd all worked so hard. Can't we even do a little walk-down?'

'*No*,' says Philip. 'Now this is what I want to happen: during the blackout, Rosencrantz and Guildenstern will put Hamlet back in his wheelchair. As the lights come up, you will form a circle and stare at the audience. I don't want any bowing or cheesy grins. That will destroy everything we've been working for. Stage management will bring the lights up and down a couple of times, and as soon as you hear the first bar of "Jailhouse Rock", move swiftly off.'

'Well, I hope you know what you're playing at,' says Piers, stripping down to his purple leotard. 'Now I suppose you want me to take this warm-up?'

Philip raises his hand like the Pope: 'Don't forget, people, theatre changes lives. Enjoy yourselves out there tonight, but above all, be brave. OK, I'll see you all at the party.' (Muted applause.) 'Right, thank you, Piers, they're all yours.'

The Actor

As you may have observed, I am probably on the cusp of being a cynic. Despite this, there is always something exciting about an opening night, even for me. It doesn't matter if it's the first performance of *See How They Run* in the village hall or the new Pinter on Broadway, there's a ludicrous optimism here that I've yet to encounter in any other walk of life – except perhaps the Church. Of course, by the second performance the knives are usually out and 'That's the best you've ever done it, love' has suddenly turned into 'Are you *really* going to do it like that?' or 'Would you mind not breathing over my laugh lines?' But for the moment, let's just enjoy the atmosphere. While Piers is taking the company through one of his interminable warm-ups, why don't we pop backstage for a snoop?

Blu-tacked to the pass door is a notice which reads:

'INSTEAD OF FIRST NIGHT CARDS I SHALL BE MAKING A DONATION TO AIDS CHARITIES. HAVE A GREAT SHOW. LOVE PHILIP XXXX'

Despite the casting of a female Rosencrantz and Guildenstern, the gentlemen far outnumber the ladies, and the girls' dressing room is a converted broom cupboard that smells of disinfectant. Someone has placed a large bunch of white roses in the old enamel sink. I sneak a peek at the card: 'Anna, you make me wish I was a real boy – love Michael.' The writing's so awful you could almost imagine he'd scribbled it himself.

'What are you doing here?'

I smile too effusively, like a first-time adulterer. 'Nikki. The pleasure is all mine.'

Ms Hardbody doesn't attempt to contradict me. 'I thought you'd be with Michael. You always bloody are.'

'I try to do my best for the young gentleman.'

'Of course you do, Timothy, you're all heart.'

Now that I'm 99 per cent certain she's never going to sleep with me, I feel at liberty to be more honest with her. 'It's working with you, Nikki. You bring out the philanthropist in me.'

'Oh, Jesus!' says Nikki, reading Anna's card. 'Have you seen this? Ueurghh, what a horrible thought.'

'By the way, Nikki, when are we going to talk about my voice-over?'

She pulls out her cigarettes. 'What?'

'We need to talk about it sooner or later. I imagine you'll want my input before you finalize the script.'

Nikki inhales nervously and blows smoke in my face. 'Let's just get *Hamlet* over with first, shall we? You have no idea what tonight means to me.'

'Oh, I think I have,' I say, eyebrow raised for my imaginary audience, twenty years' experience in all areas of the profession – apart from feature films and voice-overs – loading those five little words with the maximum amount of irony.

'Is something the matter with your face, Timothy? Talking of which, have you seen what Valerie Owen is wearing?'

'Oh, right, Valerie's here. How is she?'

'Batty as ever,' says Nikki delightedly. 'It takes weeks in the editing suite to make someone look as bonkers as that, but she does all the work for you. I've got this fab idea to get her dancing with Michael at the party.'

'Do you think that's really . . . ?'

'Oh, come on, she deserves it. When she's not boring my tits off with how wonderful Jesus is, she's freezing my fucking fanny over with her ballroom-dancing shit.'

Sometimes I think I'm too soft-hearted for show business. I should have been a pimp or a Nazi war criminal. 'The other day you called her an inspiration for women everywhere.'

'Yes,' says Nikki, drowning her cigarette butt in the sink, 'an inspiration not to become a fucking God-botherer with the dress sense of an ant. Anyway, what are you doing hanging around the women's dressing room? I thought you were gay.'

Before I have time to protest my heterosexuality (and by the way, I've had no occasion to do so since my little misunderstanding with the choreographer of *Beauty and the Beast*) something crashes into me from behind, and the sound of a mildish profanity is followed by the clatter of humanity on patterned lino. 'For God's sake,' I roar, deepening my voice for Nikki's benefit, 'you clumsy oaf, can't you look where you're . . . ? Oh . . . right . . . sorry about that.'

Nikki hands him his white stick and leather satchel. 'You dropped these.'

Apart from the stick, my assailant is totally clad and accessorized in black. 'Hi, I'm Steve. I'm with the BBC Disabilities Unit.'

'Good for you, Steve,' I say, trying to atone for my

earlier faux pas. 'Bit of an outing, is it? Pity they couldn't take you to a decent show.'

'I'm the director,' he says, 'we're doing a piece on the young lad playing Hamlet. Unfortunately, I seem to have lost my crew.'

Nikki grabs his arm and steers him towards the door. 'Let's go and find them, shall we? Then maybe you'd like to meet Michael. He's an amazing guy, you'll love him. Did you get the press pack by the way?'

'Before you go, Nikki,' I say, not quite able to let it pass. 'About what you said earlier, I'm not, OK? Not that it would matter if I was – I mean some of my closest . . . acquaintances are . . . you know – but *I'm* not. I just wanted to make it clear.'

'Not what?' says Nikki.

'Not gay,' I reply.

'Methinks the gentleman doth protest too much. What do you think, Steve?'

I want to say 'How the hell would he know?' but I manage to stifle it with a strategic coughing fit.

'See you at the party then, Timothy,' says Nikki, leading away her latest victim. 'Enjoy the show.'

'Oh, don't worry,' I say, 'I intend to.'

Philip Sidney has caused quite a rumpus in student theatre circles by moving away from the traditional Auschwitz setting and placing the whole thing in a maximum-security prison. On the way in, a couple of camp choral scholars in warders' uniforms frisk us for weapons.

The designer has obviously gone for the minimalist

approach. Hanging from the ceiling is a red banner with 'Denmark's a Prison' graffitied on it, and in the middle of the space (naturally we're talking theatre in the round) are six large building blocks with letters on them. Throughout the evening, the actors playing the gravediggers will rearrange them. At the moment they're set up for the first scene on the battlements:

As expected, word has got out that this is not to be your conventional all-singing, all-dancing Prince. There are at least two film crews (not including Blind Pugh and his mob), an assortment of radio presenters and journalists, and I'm sure I recognize that heavily coiffured lady with the lapdog. The media vultures were to be expected, of course, but it's heartening to see that the general populace has not lost its appetite for a freak show. Consequently, it's standing room only. Even Michael's tutor, the same tutor who issued a solemn warning against 'bardolatry', is sitting in the front row fussing over his trophy PhD student wife.

'Ooh-ooh, Timothy,' sings Valerie Owen, waving her programme at me from the outer circle. 'How are you, dear?'

'Fine, thanks, Mrs Owen,' I mumble. 'How are you?'

'Couldn't be better, Timothy, couldn't be better.' And I'm forced to agree. As Nikki Hardbody pointed out, purple is not necessarily a colour which one associates with cutting-edge fashion, but Valerie wears it well. In fact, she's almost unrecognizable from the washed-out woman I first met three months ago. Her figure has a pleasing roundness to it, and with her hair swept back like that you get the full effect of her delicate cheekbones and wistful eyes. She's even wearing make-up. It's not quite the full ugly duckling, but it's at least as impressive as one of those horrendous makeover shows.

'We still on for that drink, Valerie?'

'Course we are, dear,' she says, as the lights begin to fade. 'You know, I'm really looking forward to this. I'm as proud as punch.'

Just for a moment I feel a twinge of something akin to guilt. Who am I to deny Valerie her moment in the sun? But the desire for self-preservation is stronger, and anyhow it's too late now, I couldn't stop it if I wanted to.

So, as the actors file on in their green arrowed uniforms, and the strains of 'Working on the Chain Gang' fill the Methodist Hall, I pop a fast-acting Flatuleeze lozenge into my mouth and settle down for a treat.

The Quadriplegic

'*Who's there?*'

'*Nay, answer me. Stand and unfold yourself.*'

Anna tiptoes up to me, behind the battlements, and kisses the back of my head. 'You're going to be brilliant, babe,' she whispers. 'Get out there and knock 'em dead.'

She looks totally amazing in her school uniform. No wonder they wanted all those pictures of her draped over my spaz-chariot like a model at the motor show. 'I'll do my best.'

'Not nervous are you, babe?'

'Me? Course not.' But you know something? Just for a nanosecond, I have this horrible feeling that I'm actually starting to care. A layer of moisture appears on my forehead, and considering I'm supposed to be paralysed, that churning in my stomach feels suspiciously like butterflies. 'Could you get me a glass of water, please?'

'Course I can, babe, I'll be right back.'

I've never felt under pressure to be entertaining before. Most people expect a guy like me to be pissed off 24/7, which is why when I *do* make a joke they act like they're the studio audience for a crap American sitcom. I know they're going to come out with all the usual 'remarkable courage' bullshit, but I happen to think I can be good at this. Not Special Olympics, halfway-for-ladies, well-done-for-trying good; but totally fucking awesome, Premier League, at-last-I-know-what-Shakespeare-was-getting-at brilliant.

'*But look, the morn in russet mantle clad*
Walks o'er the dew of yon high eastward hill.'

Shit, *shit*, SHIT. What's my first line? And where's Anna with that water? As I prepare for my entrance, I find myself attempting something I haven't tried since I stopped believing in Father Christmas. It's not always as effective as it's cracked up to be – as anyone who's ever died of an incurable disease will tell you – but right now, words are all I've got: 'Oh, God, please let me get through this. Please make me good tonight. Amen.'

The Actor

The audience treats the battlement scenes like a warm-up band. It's obvious what they've come to see. Is there such a thing as 'car crash' theatre? The only person who appears to be paying any attention is the *Hammer Horror* refugee in the front row. Philip sits entranced, ostentatiously scribbling notes and probably wishing that he had an enormous hat with 'I am the director' on it. It's a shame because Piers has really improved: having such an undeniably camp Horatio gives the production a subtext that Shakespeare probably never intended, but he has stopped emphasizing every word and he doesn't shuffle his feet any more.

Projecting the ghost onto the battlements sounded like a good idea at the time. Unfortunately it looks like a tacky wedding video, and the satellite dishes in the background are quite at odds with the fifties setting.

'Let's do't, I pray, and I this morning know
Where we shall find him most convenient.'

Pandemonium breaks loose when the court arrives, and in their midst a polo-necked Hamlet who glides on regally and plants himself centre stage. Despite the pre-show announcement, the Methodist Hall erupts in an orgy of flash photography. Somewhere above the hubbub I catch the director of the BBC disabilities unit enquiring, 'What does he look like, what does he look like?' in an anguished stage whisper.

Finally, an expectant hush descends as everybody in the theatre focuses on the boy in the wheelchair and waits for him to speak. The moment he opens his mouth, '*A little more than kin and less than kind*,' the audience lets out a collective gasp. The high-pitched timbre, coupled with the somewhat crude amplification, gives Michael a vocal quality the like of which you have never heard.

He takes the first soliloquy slowly and carefully. I've heard him deliver it better, but the meaning is crystal clear, and within minutes he's got the punters in the palm of his hand. Philip Sidney closes his eyes as if in prayer, and I reflect that if I didn't know what was going to happen next, tonight could have turned out to be a bloody tragedy.

The Quadriplegic

I'm totally loving this. I still think Shakespeare is one seriously overrated dude, but you've got to admit he had a way with words. The soliloquies are best; just me and the audience. For the first time in my life, I feel as if I'm in control. I'm the matador for once, not the bloody bull; it's me leading them, not some idiot in a white coat sticking tubes into me or Pastor Reg telling me how grateful I should feel. OK, they might have all come here for a good laugh, but just you watch how I send them away crying.

'To be or not to be, that is the question . . .'

Yeah, I've thought about it, suicide, I mean. Who hasn't? In fact, there's probably a good few concerned citizens out there who'd volunteer to do the deed for me. Some nights I think it might be best all round if I went to sleep and never woke up again.

'The heartache and the thousand natural shocks that flesh is heir to . . .'

But tonight's not one of them. I squint out into a sea of faces, and there at the back I pick out my mum's. See that smile? No wonder Jesus wants her for a sunbeam. Forget the quadriplegic; what's the best present you can get for the quadriplegic's mum? You know what, this is probably it: public recognition that she was right all along, and her beloved son really is special – not spacky-cretin special either, the real deal. Well, they say the audience never lies. Look at that lot; even De Niro can't keep his eyes off me.

'*Soft you now, the fair Ophelia . . .*'

The scenes with Ophelia are a real kick in the face. When Anna steps out from behind the blocks A R R A S she looks so beautiful I think I'm going to cry. Hamlet must be a total headcase to dump a bird like that.

'*Are you honest?*'

'*My lord.*'

'*Are you fair?*'

When we're on stage, it feels so real – the boyfriend/ girlfriend stuff. I mean, I believe in us as a couple, you know? That's why it does my head in, because, when we're in my rooms listening to fucking Mozart and saying how much we love each other every twenty-five seconds, I have my doubts. I want to believe in it, I really do, but like that all-loving, all-powerful God who was supposed to make me walk again, sometimes it all seems too good to be true. '*Get thee to a nunnery . . .*'

Thank Christ we're coming to the interval at last. Philip's 'master stroke' of doing the whole play within a play as a

Punch and Judy show was a crap idea in the first place, and having the gravediggers dressed as life-sized marionettes was just plain fucking stupid. When Polonius finally wanders offstage, there are only twelve lines of blank verse between me and the sanctuary of the dressing room: '*By and by is easily said. Leave me, friends.*'

Wait a minute. Something's wrong here. I puff into my controller so that I can move into the spotlight for my final soliloquy, and nothing happens. Shit. What's wrong with this thing? I suck and blow like the star of a porno movie, but my spaz-chariot stays rooted to the spot.

Two hundred and fifty thrill seekers hold their breath and fix their eyes on the asthmatic Prince as I struggle to find my light. I stare back at them. Not for the first time in my life, I am well and truly paralysed.

It's De Niro who brings me to my senses. By the look of that twisted smile I'd say he's enjoying himself. It's exactly what I need to get me focused again: '*Tis now the very witching time of night . . .*'

But just as I'm thinking that things can't get any worse, they do. The microphone is dead too, and my voice comes out as a girlie whisper. From where I'm sitting, '*not* to be' is by far the most attractive option.

The Actor

Oh, dearie me. I fear we have a technical problem. Hamlet, it seems, is in urgent need of the theatrical RAC. No, forget 'seems', he's well and truly up a gum tree without a paddle.

What a bummer. Though he puffs and blows like a woman in labour, his chair remains obstinately stationary. And did I mention that his microphone has cut out too? That's the trouble with all this new-fangled technology; there's no substitute for good old-fashioned voice projection. He continues with the soliloquy – old trooper that he is – but all you can hear is a distant squeak and the unmistakable whiff of desperation.

I'm no boffin, but I'd hazard a guess that someone has neglected to recharge his wheelchair battery properly. I suppose this sort of thing happens from time to time. But for it to happen at such an inopportune moment – what are the chances of that?

With admirable presence of mind, Philip Sidney jumps from his seat and cries, 'Lights, lights ho.' He grabs the Prince's wheelchair, and for the first time in four hundred years, Hamlet makes his exit performing a wheelie. There's an embarrassing pause in which the audience starts to whisper, before stage management finally take the hint and bring up the house lights. All in all, I can't remember a more satisfying evening in the theatre.

The Quadriplegic

Back in the dressing room, Philip looks in urgent need of the first available virgin for a blood transfusion. 'What happened out there?'

The rest of the cast has gathered in the corridor. Even though I shout, I can't compete with the anxious whispering and Rosencrantz and Guildenstern's girlish laughter. 'It's my chair; someone's been pissing around with it.'

'But you're in that thing 24/7, surely you would have noticed.'

'What else could it be?'

'Jesus Christ,' says Philip, leaning back against the wall and slowly descending to the floor, 'I've got a guy from the RSC out there. What the fuck are we going to do?' He takes his head in his hands, rocks rhythmically like a Rabbi and repeats his mantra: 'Fuck, fuck, fuck, fuck . . .'

The door bursts open, but unfortunately for Philip, it's not the first available virgin. 'What's going on?' says Nikki. 'You didn't do that at the dress rehearsal.'

'It's his fucking wheelchair,' groans Philip. 'It's fucked.'

'Then what are you going to do about it?' says Nikki. 'The show must go on, of course.'

(Hamlet without the Prince? Yeah, right.)

'How can it?' says Philip. 'Without that chair, he's a complete waste of space.'

'Do you think I don't know that?' says Nikki. 'What is the matter with you people?'

The door opens again, and a salad-dodging slaphead, with an ear-to-ear smile, emerges. 'Do we have a problem, Houston?'

'Leave it out, Timothy,' says Philip, climbing to his feet at last. 'Look, you're his fucking carer; what are we going to do?'

'Well,' grins De Niro, 'I suppose you'll just have to get out there and apologize to your public. I know I only went to a red-brick university, but I did warn you there could be problems.'

Philip kicks the costume rail; the gravediggers' clown outfits fall onto the floor. 'Bastard!'

'Little poser for you, Philip,' continues De Niro. 'Can you tell me the last time a production of *Hamlet* had to be abandoned midstream?'

Philip stares at him in disbelief. 'What?'

'Actually, it's happened several times over the years. There was a power cut on Shaftesbury Avenue during the winter of discontent. Then of course there was that famous occasion in Stratford when Michael Pennington had to—'

'Shut the fuck up, you idiot,' screams Nikki. 'We've got a crisis on our hands. If we can't get him back on that stage, I'm going to lose the best climax to a documentary since Father Keith turned out to be a paedophile.'

Piers skips into the dressing room, followed by Anna who lets out a yelp of pain the moment she sees me. 'Are you all right, babe?' She kisses me repeatedly on the head. 'I was so worried about you. Do you want a drink or something? Does your bag need changing?'

'Do you mind?' says Philip. 'We're really in the shit here.'

'That's what I'm trying to tell you, if you'd just listen,' says Piers. 'I think I may have solved the problem.'

As a man we turn towards him and ejaculate: 'How?'

Piers seems to find this very gratifying. 'After the warm-up, I ran into an old chum of mine from Christ Church. I know you said we should stay in character, Philip, but we were actually very close once, and you know how nervous

I get. Anyway, it turns out Gavin's on the May Ball committee. Did you know they'd booked George Melly this year?'

Philip is chomping at his knuckles. 'For fuck's sake, Piers, get to the point.'

'Don't you dare talk to him like that,' says Anna, stepping between them and hitching up her gymslip. 'At least he's trying to do something. Carry on, Piers, we're all listening.'

'Yes, all right,' says Piers, looking slightly wounded. 'Well, Gavin happened to mention that they'd invested in a spanking new sound system. I've asked him to toddle back to the House for a radio mike so that we can rig him up for the second half.'

'Piers, I could kiss you,' says Nikki, bearing down on him like a demented groupie.

'It was all Gavin's idea,' says Piers, hastily. 'He's DJing at the party, so you can thank him yourself.'

'That's fine as far as it goes,' says Philip, 'but how's Michael going to move around? Don't forget we've got the swordfight coming up. He says his chair's completely fucked.'

'I've thought of that too,' says Piers, beginning to sound a little smug. 'All you need is someone who knows the play to push him around. They can be a sort of personal attendant – like Seyton in the Scottish Play.'

Philip has worked his way up to his fingernails. 'Well, *I* can't do it. I've got notes to make.'

'You wouldn't have to,' says Piers. 'Well, it's obvious, isn't it? There's only one person who *could* do it. He's been to most of the rehearsals, he knows what it's like to tread the boards, and most important of all, he's got a great relationship with Michael.'

I don't know who Piers is talking about, but from the way the colour has drained from his cheeks, I'd say De Niro has a pretty good idea. 'Oh no, no, absolutely not. I'm sorry to disappoint you, gentlemen, but I would rather spend Christmas with Andrew Lloyd Webber.'

Nikki Hardbody drags him to one side and whispers something I can't quite make out.

The Actor

There's a desperation in Nikki's voice that isn't in the least bit attractive. 'Timothy, I'm begging you here. Do it for me, why don't you?'

She can point her bazookas at me until the cows come home, I'm not budging. 'Sorry, Nikki, no can do.'

'Are you sure about that?'

'It's a matter of principle, you wouldn't understand.' (It was a line I had in a play once; I knew it would come in handy some day.)

'That's very laudable . . . *Tim* . . . but I thought you wanted to get into voice-overs. Is it really worth throwing away the chance of a lifetime for a silly little principle?'

'You wouldn't . . . you couldn't?'

Her teeth gleam like a crocodile's. 'Couldn't I? I don't seem to recall you signing any contract.'

'But you promised.'

'Listen, *mate*,' she hisses, 'if you don't get up on that fucking stage, I'm going to call Martin Jarvis's voice-over agent right now. That'd be a shame, don't you think? Because if you get on there and save the day, it could be the best career move you ever made. I'm talking book deals, I'm talking personal appearances, I'm talking pantomime – *Comic Relief* even. Do you see where I'm coming from?'

Next time you go to the theatre, spare a thought for the poor buggers who come on at the beginning of the curtain call and have to stand around for hours, with game-show-hostess smiles, dissembling enthusiasm like plucky prostitutes.

The audience screams its approval: 'Bravo, bravo!' I stare back in silent disgust, just as the director instructed. Suddenly, the festive season chez Lloyd Webber sounds rather an attractive prospect.

If only those flash guns were the real McCoy. Anything would be better than soaking up this humiliating applause. With a speed which wouldn't disgrace those blokes with the huge arm muscles that get to start first in the London Marathon, I push Hamlet out of the limelight and I don't stop running until we're safely back in the dressing room.

Neither of us speaks. We're both transfixed by the distant whirlwind which slowly gathers pace until it bursts through the door.

The Quadriplegic

Philip is first, salivating like Tom and Maggie, the drool dripping down his carefully manicured goatee. 'Respect, Mike, that was so fucking beautiful I nearly cried.'

Nikki and her camera are next. How like a fawning publican she looks. 'Michael, that was fab, I don't know how to thank you.'

She's followed by virtually the entire cast, all in a state of mild hysteria. Someone pops open a bottle of champagne, and Piers slips into his crap Dame Edna: 'G'day, darlings.'

'Back in a sec,' says Nikki, spotting someone more important on the other side of the room. 'Don't forget the producer of *Stars in Their Eyes* wants to meet you.'

De Niro meanwhile has drifted into a corner. 'Cheers, Tim,' shouts Philip, 'you got us out of a hole.' But the man who saved the day doesn't even look up.

Oh, crap. That purple thing pushing its way through the crowd towards me is my mum. 'That was lovely, dear. And the black jumper looked really smashing. Now I know what to get you for Christmas!'

'Thanks, Mum. Glad you could make it.'

'And wasn't it wonderful of Timothy, stepping into the breach like that?'

Without my microphone, making conversation is bloody impossible. 'Where's Anna?'

'I don't know, dear,' says Mum, 'she's probably making herself look beautiful for the party – not that she needs to, of course.'

'We're supposed to be going to the party together.'

Mum bends down and kisses me on the cheek. Unlike most self-respecting adolescents I can't pull away. 'Sorry, dear, I just need to have a quick chat with that nice young man from *Newsround*. You don't mind, do you?'

'No, Mum, you go for it.'

Just as I'm wondering who's going to push me to the party, a fruity voice stops me in my tracks: '*Michael*, I can't tell you what a pleasure it is to meet you. You were super tonight, by the way.' A plump, middle-aged woman, expensively dressed, programme in one hand, lapdog in the other, is standing in front of me, gushing. 'Tikki Montague – Montague Casting. Look, I know you've got a party to go to, so I won't keep you, darling, but I've given the gorgeous Anna my card. Next time you're in town, perhaps you'd like to pop in for a chat. I'm casting a First World War feature in January and I'm sure the director will want to meet you. Ciao.'

When she turns to leave, something very strange happens. De Niro jumps to his feet and pursues her to the door, wringing his hands and smiling like a cretin.

'Tikki . . . *Tikki* . . . *TIKKI!*'

15

Toys of Desperation

The Quadriplegic

Philip's nose stud glistens in the moonlight. The JCR by the lake is already throbbing with the sound of music as he struggles to push my spaz-chariot along the soggy wood-chip path. Trust Nikki Hardbody to book the only venue in college that the star of the show can't get to.

'Fuck this for a game of soldiers,' says Philip, collapsing onto one of the benches donated by friends of the college, 'I need a rest.'

'Where's Anna?'

'Can't hear you, mate.'

'*Where's Anna?*'

He takes out his tobacco pouch and begins rolling a joint. 'She went off with a guy from the *Daily Mirror*. But you needn't worry,' he says, aiming a kick at a passing duck, 'your little girlfriend's saving herself for Mr Right.'

Yes, go on, laugh, you public-school tosser. You

wouldn't know what love was if it jumped up and bit you on the bollocks. 'Can we go inside now, please?'

'Psycho was right,' says Philip, blowing out a stream of sickly-sweet smoke, 'this is really good shit. Here, try some.'

'No! Look, it's cold out here, let's go inside.'

He squats in front of me, like a Masai warrior. 'Chill, bro, it's time you and me had a little chat.'

And there was I thinking he'd offered to push me to the party out of the goodness of his heart: 'What about?'

'The woman from the RSC loved it tonight. She thinks I'm really talented.'

I nod ironically, like one of those dogs that post-modernists have in the back of their Ford Escorts.

'Wasn't it great, though? Like the best orgasm you ever had, but a hundred times better.'

I nod again. I'm well good at nodding; especially the ironic kind.

'Michael, I'm going to make you an offer you can't refuse.' He jumps up and saws the air with his joint. 'If you and me are going to top *Hamlet*, we need to come up with something really amazing. I've been thinking about it all night, and I've finally found the part you were born to play. Go on, have a guess.'

'Romeo?'

'Yeah, nice one. Now have a proper guess.'

If Piers hadn't already been such a hit in *The Elephant Man* we wouldn't be having this conversation. 'Go on, surprise me.'

'Shylock, of course. I don't know why I didn't think of it before.'

I shake my head in sheer fucking dismay; I'm good at that too.

'Yeah, yeah, I know it sounds mental, but I'm sure I can make it work. Do you know the lines?'

'Well, yes, but . . .'

'It's brilliant. Shylock in a wheelchair – a perfect metaphor for the archetypal outsider.'

There are about a trillion reasons why this is the worst idea since God planted the Tree of Knowledge in the Garden of Eden, but the first thing that springs to mind is, 'How would I be able to take my pound of flesh?'

'The same way we did the swordfights,' says Philip. 'Come on, Mike, what do you say? I think you'd make a terrific Jew.'

'I'm not doing it.'

Philip lowers his head so that his ear is right in front of my mouth. 'Sorry, mate, can't hear ya.'

'I said I'm not doing it.'

He puts his hand on my shoulder and attempts a caring-profession smile. 'Look, I know it sounds daunting, Mike, but you wouldn't be on your own. You know how hard I work for my actors. With your dedication and my talent we can't go wrong.'

'No,' I say, shaking my head without a trace of irony, 'I'm sorry, I can't do it.'

A look of panic fills his eyes. 'I *knew* this would happen. OUDS want you for *The Duchess of Malfi*. I'm right, aren't I?'

'No, I just . . .'

He stumbles back to the bench, tosses his joint to the ducks and waves his finger at me like Piers does when he's acting. 'You ungrateful bastard. I took a chance on you, and this is how you repay me. Do you think anyone else would have cast a fucking mentalist?'

I'm the only one who does the crip jokes around here. It's about time I told Philip Sidney a few home truths. 'I'm not doing it because you're a talentless dickhead. I'm not doing it because you couldn't direct a fucking funeral. I'm not doing it because I won't have you using me any more.'

'Oh, I get it,' he says, 'you've been talking to that so-called girlfriend of yours. Listen, matey, if anyone's been using you, *she* has.'

'You're just jealous because she dumped you.'

'Oh, Michael, Michael, Michael, don't tell me that frigid little todger-dodger has got to you too?'

'What do you mean?' I say, really wishing I could stick my fingers in my ears.

'Typical edge-of-the-bed virgin, that's what she is. Any bloody excuse to keep your wankshaft out of her fur-burger. With me it was . . . well, never mind, but with *you*,' he throws open his arms like that picture of Jesus Mum's got in the kitchen, 'it's the best bloody excuse of all. You couldn't shag her if you wanted to.'

I hear the distant cackle of Rosencrantz and Guilden-stern. 'It's not true. We love each other.'

'Yeah, whatever,' he says, grabbing the handles of my spaz-chariot. 'But just you remember, Michael, actors are ten a penny. Why don't you ask the pathetic bastard who's been pushing you around all night?'

The Actor

After my embarrassing performance in the dressing room, the last thing I need is a first-night party; especially for such a palpable hit. Many's the God-awful show-business soirée I've spent up the arse (metaphorically, you understand) of some leading supporting actor who's known in the business as a marvellous raconteur – or to be more accurate, completely boring bastard. I was all for limping back to my rooms, but Nikki Hardbody somehow persuaded me that *Wheelchair of Fire* would be incomplete without a couple of shots of yours truly putting away a few peanuts and mingling expertly. Who am I to argue? And anyway, I promised Valerie Owen we'd meet up after she'd done her interview with Radio Oxford.

This is my idea of hell: a hall full of half-cut teenagers, more dry ice than a provincial pantomime, and a huge white screen palpitating with a migraine-inducing light show. If it wasn't for the fact that I've managed to commandeer a perfectly drinkable bottle of Rioja, it's quite possible I would have spent this evening mugging up on the scenic route to Beachy Head; although perhaps I've become so accustomed to wallowing in other people's success that now I'm immune to it. So instead of venting ire on the iniquities of my life in art, I content myself with getting really angry about this ghastly, repetitive 'music'. I don't know what's worse; the incessant bass line, or the shameless plagiarism of familiar riffs from eighties rock classics. Popular music should be about self-pity and frustration, not jigging mindlessly to an electronic fart.

'Awright, bro, how ya doing?' A young man in an old-fashioned tracksuit holds his hand in the air like a traffic cop, inviting me to slap it. I know that politicians have got this obsession about getting disadvantaged kids into Oxbridge, but disadvantaged usually means coming from a one-horse family or only going skiing twice a year, and this lad looks like a bona-fide oik. He's got more rings than Joan Collins (how in God's name can he possibly articulate with that thing through his tongue?) and 'psyco' tattooed across his knuckles. I have a feeling I would be ill-advised to point out the spelling mistake. 'Great show, man.'

No doubt he's another well-wisher wanting to tell me how great Michael was. 'I'm sorry, I don't think I've had the pleasure.'

'I'm Psycho, Phil's big brother.'

'Oh, right,' I say, vaguely remembering that the chap who empties the wheelie bins is called Phil or Bill or something similar. 'Glad you enjoyed it, er, Psycho.'

'You was brilliant, man,' he says, flexing his knuckles ominously. 'I could feel your pain, innit? It was like you was banged up for something you never done.'

'Well, that's awfully kind of you, Psycho. My agent, Bunny Michelmore at Bunny Michelmore Management, will be very pleased to hear it.'

He stares at me for a moment, as if I'd just asked him to explain the theory of relativity. 'You sorted, mate?'

'Do you know, I think I have pulled myself together a bit. I don't mind admitting I was pretty desolate back there, but your kind remarks have cheered me up no end.'

Psycho stares at me again, and then steps backwards into the smoky shadows. 'Catch yer later.'

It's a good thing that my state of mind has improved a little; otherwise what happens next could have been the final straw. Even Piers's floppy-haired chum, who's been DJing or whatever they call it now, turns it down a couple of notches when they appear in the doorway. Someone strikes up a chorus of 'For he's a jolly good fellow' and although, I'm pleased to note, it dies out almost immediately, the applause which accompanies it lasts long enough for Philip to push Michael the entire length of the JCR. He parks him next to the Pringles (well, what did you expect, quail's eggs?) and hushes the crowd with an imperious hand gesture:

'A lot of important people have said some very flattering things about me. That's always nice, of course. But I just want to say, it's not all about Philip Sidney, is it? I couldn't have done it without you guys. And there's one person in particular who's been absolutely magnificent throughout this whole, crazy journey.' Everyone cheers. I take a swig of Rioja and brace myself for the inevitable eulogy of the Wheelchair Prince. 'So here's to Dave and his fantastic stage-management team. Cheers, Dave, we owe you one.'

Dave sheepishly raises his can of lager, and Philip makes a swift getaway to a smattering of bemused applause. Stranded by the nibbles, Michael looks like the proverbial spare prick at a wedding, until a steady trickle of admirers make their way over to congratulate him: Piers drags himself away from his DJ chum for five seconds, the girl who played Rosencrantz (or was it Guildenstern?) kisses Michael on the forehead, and Polonius has a game stab at making small talk. But gradually they tire of him and go off in search of more earthly pursuits.

Looking across at the abandoned figure in the wheelchair, I can't help reflecting that, even though he's just given the sort of performance I could only dream about, from where I'm sitting his life looks almost as horrendous as my own.

The Quadriplegic

I could kill for a salt-and-vinegar Pringle. What kind of a sicko parks a quadriplegic next to the snacks? I can't even make a quick getaway. I've got to sit here like a lemon until Anna turns up.

Even though Piers's mate Gavin is the worst DJ in Oxford, some of them have started dancing; throwing themselves about and all the usual random stuff. The girl who played Guildenstern (or was it Rosencrantz?) is passing around a two-litre bottle of Evian, Polonius is waving a twenty-pound note at the bloke in the tracksuit, and Philip has disappeared into the Gents with one of the make-up ladies. That lot are in the middle of a best-years-of-your-life moment, and I can't even get some cheap wine in a plastic cup. Only De Niro, crouched in the corner like a paedophile at a convention of tabloid journalists, looks as pissed off as I feel.

'Guess who?'

I know instantly, from the chocolatey smell, that the hands belong to Anna. 'Where have you been?'

'Sorry, babe, the *Daily Mirror* guy insisted on buying me a drink. Wanted to know if I was up for a bit of tasteful nudity.'

'Do you mind if we go now?'

'Can't hear you, babe.'

'I said, can we go now, please?'

I don't know why Anna's still got her school uniform on. She looks like a refugee from one of those pervy discos. 'Aren't you going to say goodbye to your mother? I think she and Nikki might have something planned.'

'What are we waiting for then? Let's get out of here.'

'Too late, I'm afraid,' says Anna, turning my wheelchair to face the door. 'Look.'

Mum bounds towards me with a smile the size of a B-list chat-show guest. 'Hello, dear, enjoying your party?'

'Yes, thanks, Mum.'

Nikki Hardbody is at her side; turning herself inside out to get a good shot of Mum's ankles. 'Hi, you two. How's British television's favourite couple-to-be?'

'We were just leaving actually,' says Anna. 'Mike's really tired, aren't you, babe?'

'Course he is,' says Nikki. 'There's just one little thing I want to get in the can before we wrap.'

Mum fiddles anxiously with her wedding ring. 'If Michael's not up to it, maybe we should call it a day.'

'It's cool,' says Nikki, 'won't take two minutes.'

'Well, if you're sure then,' says Mum.

Nikki gives the DJ the thumbs-up and his hopeless hip-hop lite thuds to an abrupt halt. 'I don't want to choreograph anything,' says Nikki. 'It's just a bit of fun, that's all. But I think it would be really nice if we could get the two women in your life on the dance floor with you.'

Just for a moment, I have the crazy idea that the whole thing has been one of those take-the-piss-out-of-the-public programmes. Then I realize, to my disappointment, that they'd never dare do it to a crip. 'You've got to be joking.'

'It's a bit tacky, yeah,' says Nikki, 'but everyone loves *Grease*, and your mother's always telling me how much she enjoys her dancing lessons.' Camera primed, she focuses on my horror-struck face. 'OK, you guys, go for it!'

Nikki hands Mum a lighted cigarette; she takes a couple of non-smoker's puffs before grinding it into the JCR floor with the toe of her Mary-Janes.

'Mum?' I say, trying to disappear up my own arse.

'Well, hello there, stud,' she says in a crap American accent.

Before I can shout, 'NO FUCKING WAY,' the first bar of 'You're The One That I Want' spews out of the sound system, and Anna pushes me onto the dance floor.

Mum warbles the verse and everyone joins in with the chorus. Surely only a complete moron could fail to realize that this is the *last* thing that I want.

'Stop it, stop it,' I scream, but the whole pack of them are too busy singing along, and whooping every time Anna spins me around, to take any notice.

Mum hitches up her skirt and skips towards me, finger wagging, like a geriatric Olivia Newton-John. If I didn't feel like puking before, I certainly do now. Nikki's nipples can't conceal their excitement as Piers and the rest of the cast break into a frenzied hand-jive.

I close my eyes and pray for the big finish. 'Please, please, just leave me alone . . .'

They cluster around me, whispering. I feel like I'm back in intensive care.

'Michael, what's the matter with you, babe? You OK?'

'Oh, cripes,' says Piers, gesturing to his DJ chum to get the music going again, 'I think the poor fellow's crying.'

'I knew we should have asked him first,' says Mum. 'Whatever was I thinking of?'

'Don't worry about it,' says Nikki, not looking up from her viewfinder, 'this kind of thing happens all the time. Some people find it very hard to say goodbye to the cameras.'

'Oh, look,' drawls a familiar voice, 'it's John Travolta and Olivia Newton-John.'

'Shut up, Philip,' says Anna. 'Why don't you piss off back to the gutter where you came from?'

Philip grins, and gropes the giggling Guildenstern. 'Yes, I think I might just do that. At least it's not full of tight-arsed virgins.'

'Now, now,' says Mum, still trying to get her breath back, 'there's no need for that kind of language.'

'Just listen to the proud mother,' says Philip. 'Don't you think you've embarrassed the poor bugger enough?'

Mum bristles menopausally. 'I don't know what you're talking about. And anyway, it was only a bit of fun. Tell him, Nikki.'

Nikki is too busy finding the right camera angle.

'Grotesque, I'd call it,' says Philip. 'Isn't it bad enough being a dur brain without your own mother drawing attention to it?'

Mum pulls a tissue from her bosom. 'I'm sorry, Michael, I didn't mean to . . . I was so happy for you tonight. I don't think I've felt like that since . . . since . . . All I wanted was to . . .' She stumbles out of the JCR like a geriatric Cinderella. Nikki captures her exit before panning back to Anna.

'You bastard, Philip,' says Anna. 'Now look what you've done.'

'Just telling it like it is, babe,' says Philip. 'You should try it some time.' He turns to Guildenstern. 'You won't believe this, Georgia, but Little Miss Metal Knickers and Superman here are in love.'

'It's true,' says Anna. 'Michael's twice the man you'll ever be. All you can think about is your pathetic little cock.'

'Well, at least it's in perfect working order,' says Philip, 'unlike your boyfriend's. Oh, but I forget, that's the way you like them, isn't it, babe?'

Anna tries to look dignified, but it's not easy in full school uniform. 'God, you make me sick.'

'Shall I tell you what makes *me* sick?' says Philip. 'The way you smother him. Just seeing you together makes my flesh crawl. It's gross. And as for you, Michael, I thought you had more self-respect. She's using you, can't you see that? With my help, you could have been one of the best Shylocks of your generation, and you're going to throw it all away because that old swamp-donkey is too witless to get herself a decent psychiatrist.'

'Come on, Michael,' says Anna, grabbing my wheel-chair and doing an abrupt U-turn. 'We're leaving.'

We're halfway to the door before Nikki calls out, 'OK, everybody, it's a wrap,' and only halfway to my rooms before I realize with painful clarity exactly what has to be done.

The Actor

'Wait until you see that after the edit,' says Nikki Hard-body, 'TV heaven.'

I'm still recovering from the bizarre floor show. If it wasn't all there in high-definition video, I'd be ditching this Rioja and swearing a vow of abstinence. 'Surely you can't make it look any worse?'

'That's what they said about Father Keith's funeral.'

'But poor old Valerie will look ridiculous. Couldn't you just edit her out?'

'No can do, I'm afraid,' she sighs. 'It's a public-interest thing, simple as that.' After a hard night's filming, Nikki looks like a contestant in a wet T-shirt competition. I can't help daydreaming of what might have been. 'Right, I'm off to pick up a few GVs of the college, and then my work here is done.'

'Will you contact my agent about the voice-over, or do you want to call me direct?'

'What? Oh, yes, right. Maybe I'd better go through your agent. What was her name again?'

And suddenly I think of Valerie Owen's face; that look of abject misery as she fled the dance floor. 'Oh, look it up in *Spotlight*, why don't you? There's someone I need to talk to.'

Outside the JCR, it's like an episode of *Casualty*: eager young medical students perform detailed gynaecological examinations, and goose-pimpled girls in cocktail dresses throw up onto the grass. I tread softly; grateful that I have the moon to guide me through a minefield of writhing flesh and vomit. Taking another swig of Rioja, I try to conceal my jealousy in a fug of *Daily Mail*-reader indignation.

Valerie Owen is sitting on a bench by the lake. She doesn't see me at first. It gives me time to dredge up a suitably banal opening gambit from one of the plays I've been in. 'Mind if I join you?'

'You can if you like, Timothy, but I won't be much company, I'm afraid.'

Just as I'm about to sit down, I spot a blob of bird poo. But now is not the time for squeamishness. 'Are you all right, Valerie?'

'It's not me I'm worried about.'

'Here, take my jacket, you must be freezing.'

'Thank you,' she says, 'it'll hide this silly dress. What on earth was I thinking of?'

'It suits you,' I say, not sure whether I mean it or whether it's just a reflex action from when I was married.

'Did you see the way Michael looked at me? I made a complete fool of myself.'

'It wasn't that bad,' I say, this time quoting directly from *The Married Man's Survival Manual*. 'I don't suppose it'll even make it onto the screen.'

'I hadn't thought of that.'

Speaking as someone who would probably try and squeeze into a Japanese tourist's holiday videos, I find this hard to believe. 'We'll cross that bridge if we come to it – what do you think?'

'I wish I'd never agreed to her stupid documentary in the first place. I knew Michael would hate it. I just wanted everyone to see what a wonderful person he is, how someone so terribly . . . disabled could lead such a . . . normal life.'

'And I'm sure they will.' (Perhaps I'm a better actor than I thought.)

'No,' she says, 'your young director fellow was absolutely right. I'd been praying so hard about it that I only saw what I wanted to see. I thought Oxford would be the making of him. He was fitting in so well.'

I nod, a little too enthusiastically. 'Yes, yes, that's right.'

She smiles and pats my knee. 'You're very kind, Timothy, but I think we both know that's not true. How on earth could someone like Michael ever really fit in? Let's be honest,' she giggles nervously, 'he's never going to be Fred Astaire.'

'That's not necessarily a bad thing. And anyway, why would he want to be when he's just given one of the finest performances I've ever seen?'

'You really think so?'

'Oh, yes,' I say, forcing the bottle of Rioja between my gritted teeth, 'he was . . . magnificent, far better than I could ever have been.'

'I'm sure you're a lovely actor.'

'You should be my agent.'

'You're a good man, Timothy. You've done so much for Michael.'

'I'm not so sure about that.'

'You've only known him for five minutes, and you've been a tower of strength. How could his own mother be so selfish?'

'That is *not* true, Valerie. I don't think I've ever met a more generous person than you, I mean that.'

She pulls my jacket tighter round her shoulders and stares out into the middle of the lake. 'And what if I told you that these last few months have been the happiest times I've known since . . . since . . . ?'

A tear the size of a small marble trickles past her nose. I reach for my handkerchief and then remember that I stopped carrying one after She of Whom I Never Speak told me they were a 'dirty old man thing'. 'Here, try some of this.'

'I don't think so.'

'Go on,' I say, pressing the bottle into her hand. 'It'll put hairs on your chest.'

'Oh, all right then, just a drop.' She drinks like an amateur; sipping cautiously, recoiling the moment the liquid reaches her lips. 'Well, Timothy, aren't you going to tell me what a terrible person I am?'

'Why on earth would I do that?'

This time she takes a proper gulp. 'It was really difficult at first, far worse than when my Terry left. I didn't think I'd ever get used to not having him around. The house seemed so empty without him. I didn't know what to do with myself.'

'That's understandable. Looking after Michael's a full-time job.'

'I started noticing that I wasn't exhausted the whole time. It was amazing really. All the little things I'd always wanted to do – sit down in front of the telly for five minutes, have a nice long bath instead of a quick shower, get my hair done – suddenly I could do them.'

An *idée fixe* from *Be Your Own Psychotherapist in One Weekend* pops into my head. 'There's nothing wrong with a bit of "me" time.'

'There is when it turns you into a selfish old woman. I swore to myself that Michael would always come first.' She hands me back my bottle of Rioja. 'It's the dancing, you see. Before I started, there was never a moment when I wasn't thinking about him – even in my sleep. I mean, I'm not very good or anything, but when I get up on that dance floor, the music just takes over, and nothing else seems to matter. That's terrible, isn't it?'

I can hardly speak. It's exactly how I felt when I started acting. Shine a few lights on me, throw in a couple of lines of iffy dialogue, and I was as happy as Larry. 'No, no, I don't think it's terrible at all. It's good that you have something you feel passionately about. There's nothing wrong with that.'

The moonlight filters through the treetops, catching the ripples on the water like a cinematographer's wet dream. 'Lovely, isn't it, Timothy?'

'That's the trouble with this place. It's so ridiculously beautiful, it makes everything one does seem so squalid.'

'I'm sure *you've* got nothing to be ashamed of.'

Even *I* have to laugh at that one. 'I've got precious little to be proud about – except if you count wasting my life in the most spectacular way imaginable.'

And now Valerie is laughing too. 'Oh, Timothy, listen to yourself. Wasted your life? What a lot of nonsense. Your life is just beginning. It's never too late, you know. Look at me. Why don't you get yourself an interesting hobby?'

'I can't dance, if that's what you mean. My agent – Bunny Michelmore at Bunny Michelmore Management – used to send me up for musicals until she saw me in *Beauty and the Beast*.'

'Come here,' she says, taking my hand and leading me onto the grass in front of the lake. 'And you can put that bottle down, you won't be needing it.'

'I'm not sure I like the sound of this.'

'*Anyone* can dance, Timothy. That's what Mr Horn-brook says.'

'My ex-wife has her own little theory about that.'

'Now, put your right hand on my shoulder blade, fingers straight – yes, that's right – and I'll just rest my hand on your upper arm like so. How's that?'

All those excruciating dance auditions have left me somewhat traumatized. 'Fine, I think.'

She encloses my other hand in a sort of freemason's

handshake, curling her thumb around mine and linking wrists. 'You're not frightened of me, are you, Timothy?'

'No, of course not.'

'Then what are you doing over there? Come on, don't be shy. We're supposed to be dancing, not taking Holy Communion.' She presses her hips into mine. Blood hurtles towards my face and groin. 'There, that's nice, isn't it?'

'Yes, yes, it's very . . .' It's been so long since I felt the warmth of a woman's body that I'm at a bit of a loss.

'The important thing is that the gentleman always leads, you mustn't forget that, Tim.'

'Maybe that's where I've been going wrong.'

'It's quite simple. You step forward . . . then to the side . . . aaand together. Let's try that, shall we?'

She pulls me gently towards her. I lurch forward like a learner driver. 'Sorry about that.'

'It's fine,' she says, withdrawing her foot. 'All it takes is a bit of practice. Come on, you can do this, I know you can.'

I'm not sure how long it takes, because I lose all track of time, but X minutes later, we're captivating the ducks with a rudimentary waltz. We don't look much like that couple in *The Sound of Music* – more like a physiotherapist and her plucky amputee – but all the same I feel really chuffed with myself.

'By Jove, I think he's got it,' she says. 'Well done, Timothy, that's really good.'

Do you ever look at the shape of someone's lips and think about what they'd be like to kiss? The dizzier I get, the more I want to find out. 'Where are you staying tonight, Valerie?'

'The Randolph Hotel, very swish. Nikki's paying, isn't that nice of her?'

'Yes, yes, she's good like that.' Although we've ground to a halt, Valerie and I are still joined at the hip. Convention demands that I pull away; the moonlight commands me not to. 'I could . . . I could walk you back if you like.'

'That would be lovely,' she says, her cheeks colouring slightly. 'Maybe you could come up for that drink I promised you.'

Now the ducks are cheering us on. 'So what are we waiting for?'

It's Valerie who breaks the hold. 'Don't you think I ought to say goodnight to Michael first?'

Sometimes everything falls into place. It's a combination of homespun wisdom and a couple of things I picked up from *Be Your Own Psychotherapist in One Weekend*, and it comes so spontaneously that I think I actually believe it. 'No, Valerie, I don't think you should say goodbye to Michael. I think what Michael needs right now is his own space. You are a *very* good mother, the best. But the thing is, Valerie, whether you're disabled or not, there comes a time when you have to break away from your parents. I think the most sensible thing you can do right now is to show Mike that – although you'll always be there for him – you have got a life of your own.'

I seem to have touched a nerve. 'Do you know, Timothy, you're absolutely right.' Thank you. That's made a little dilemma of mine so much clearer.' She takes my arm. 'Come on, let's go.'

It's a sure-fire sign that my life has taken a turn for the better: as we pass the Oxford Playhouse, I notice that a chap I worked with in a profit-share in Clapham is halfway up the billing of a TV names revival of an early Ayckbourn; despite the fact that he was a terrible actor – and a crashing bore to boot – I hardly bother to spit.

I don't suppose even a computer-dating service would have identified me and Valerie as the perfect match, but there are fewer years between us than I would care to admit, and she has a quality quite unique amongst the women of my acquaintance: she makes me feel good about myself.

'You know, Timothy,' she says, squeezing my arm, 'I'm so glad you said what you did. There's something I've been praying about, and I think you might just have shown me the answer.'

I try not to sound like the cat that got the cream: 'Pleased to be of service.'

We come to a halt outside the hotel. I have the most glorious intimation that she's going to kiss me. 'You see, Bill – that's Mr Hornbrook, my dancing teacher – he's asked me to have dinner with him.' She smiles coyly. 'Like a sort of date, I suppose. Anyway, I keep putting him off because I'm afraid of what Michael might say. But maybe you're right, maybe I need to show him I have a life of my own. What do *you* think, Timothy? What should I do?'

'Oh, I see. Well, I think that . . .'

Oh, come on, you didn't think I was serious, did you? I mean, I'm not denying that she's fairly attractive, for an older woman, but do you really think I'm that desperate? And anyway, look at her little face; if I don't tell her what she wants to hear, it would break her heart. 'I think Mr Hornbrook is a very lucky man.'

'You mean . . . ?'

'Absolutely. Go for it, Valerie, you deserve it.'

'Well, I don't suppose it would do any harm,' she says, practically breaking into another dance routine. 'Look at me, I'm shaking.'

Which is strange, because I'm not feeling so good myself. 'I'd better be making tracks. Cheerio, Valerie. See you again next term perhaps.'

'Aren't you coming up for that drink?'

'I don't think so. I'm a little bit tired. I wasn't expecting to be up onstage tonight – excitement must have got to me.'

'Yes, you really saved the day. Thank you for everything.' She puts her hand on my shoulder and kisses me on the cheek. 'Say goodnight to Michael for me.'

The Virgin

Why's he so quiet? And why does he insist on sitting in the dark? I can't stand it when he's like this. Trust his soppy mother to freak him out. And we were having such a lovely evening. Why did she have to ruin it all with that sick-making dance? He stares out of the window, like a movie psychopath, barely grunting when I ask if he wants a drink or a nice head massage.

'Would you mind turning that off, please, Anna?'

At least he's talking to me now. 'I thought you liked Mozart, babe.'

'Not really.'

Without my music, I feel so jumpy. 'I could put on a bit of Hindemith if you like, or how about some Saint-Saëns? You said you thought the Organ Symphony was amazing.'

'It's OK, I suppose. But if you really want to know, I'm a country-and-western fan.'

'You're not, are you?'

There's a hardness in his voice I hadn't noticed before. 'Of course not, but I could be for all you know.'

'That's not fair. How am I supposed to work out what you like if you won't tell me? I'm not a mind reader, you know.'

Out in the quad, the rugger buggers are singing that disgusting song: '*It's green, it's long, it looks just like my dong, CUCUMBER.*'

'That's all we bloody need,' he says, sounding almost as suicidal as when he did '*To be or not to be*'. 'Listen to them. In ten years' time, they'll meet up at the college reunion, and after a couple of drinks, they'll do several hundred encores and still be finding it funny. Where in God's name will I be?'

'That's easy, babe. You'll be with me, of course.' It's something I've been dying to talk about for ages; this is the perfect opportunity. 'I've been thinking about our future

242

together. I know it won't be easy, but we can do it, I know we can.'

He looks right past me and shakes his head. I feel a sharp, stabbing pain in the pit of my stomach. 'I'm not sure that would be a very good idea, Anna. I don't think . . .'

'This isn't about that silly dance, is it?' I fake a girlish laugh that comes out more like a twitter of pain. 'Look, I told you, that was nothing to do with me. It was all Nikki's idea. I tried to tell them how much you'd hate it, but they wouldn't listen. And your mum was really up for it.'

'This isn't about the dance.'

'Then what is it about? Please, babe, you've got to be straight with me.' I kneel in front of his wheelchair, looking up at him through a veil of tears. 'I thought you said you loved me. You do love me, don't you, Michael?'

He closes his eyes tight shut. He does that sometimes. I suppose it's his equivalent of rolling up into a tiny ball. 'Yes, yes, I think I do.'

Why's there a 'think' in there all of a sudden? 'That's just what I needed to hear.'

'It's not that simple. You know it isn't.'

'We love each other – what's so complicated about that?'

'I'm a fucking quadriplegic, Anna. Do I have to spell it out for you?'

He hasn't heard a thing I've just said. 'You think I don't know that? I'll do what it takes, Michael, whatever it takes for us to be together. I know it'll be tough, I'm not stupid, but I can look after you, you know I can.'

It's the first time I've seen him cry real tears. I thought that was a physical impossibility, but if this is a miracle, it's absolutely wasted on me.

'I don't want looking after. I've already got one mother, Anna. The last thing I need is a younger model.'

'I am nothing like your mother! That is a horrible thing to say.'

'I didn't mean it like that. Philip told me that—'

'That bastard, I thought we weren't going to talk about him.'

'Philip said—'

I sink my nail extensions into the side of my head. 'Oh, yeah, "Philip said". And why would anyone take any notice of *him* after all the lies he's told? You do know he's not a baronet, don't you? He didn't even go to Winchester.'

'He never told me he did.'

All I want to do is dry his tears and give him a big hug. 'Look, I can see you're tired, babe. Why don't I make you a hot drink and put you to bed? We don't have to do this right now.'

'No, no, I want to.'

I summon up the falsest smile in Oxford and prepare for the worst. 'So go on then, what *did* Philip say?'

His face is paler than Granny Devonshire's on her death bed. He licks his lips and coughs up a gobbet of phlegm. 'He said . . . he said you were only going out with me because you knew we'd never be able to have sex.'

'*It's green, it's stout, it's what this life's about, CUCUMBER, CUCUMBER.*'

'Unbelievable, isn't it? Just because I wouldn't sleep with him, he thinks there must be something wrong with me.'

'You mean it's not true then?' says Michael, starting to sound like that wheelchair barrister guy that Mummy was so gaga about.

'Course not.'

'You mean you would if we could?'

'There's nothing I'd like more in the world,' I say, trying to picture what making love to Michael would actually entail.

'But why me, for God's sake? There are millions of guys out there. Why choose one with a plastic tube coming out of his dick?'

'That's easy, Mike, because we're soulmates.'

'Cell mates, more like it.'

'Why can't I get through to you? We're made for each other. You make me laugh, you know exactly what to say when I'm down in the dumps, and you're a fantastic listener. What more could a girl want?'

'Yeah, well, maybe that's not what *I* want.'

'You're talking in riddles, Michael.'

'Ask any man what he'd prefer, and you'll get the same answer. Do you want a woman to love you for your sense of humour and your listening skills, or because every time she sees you, she wants to rip off her knickers and make love for three hours?'

'Yes, well, that's just not possible, is it?' I say, smoothing down this nasty nylon skirt. 'I'd like to but, well . . . we can't.'

'Kiss me then.'

'I'm always kissing you, babe.'

'I'm not talking about the sort of peck on the cheek that Snow White gives Dopey before she pisses off with the first available Prince. I mean, kiss me properly.'

'All right then.'

Taking his head in my hands, flicking away a blob of dribble with my thumb, I lean forward and place my lips on his. I sneak a final peek at his china-doll features, close my eyes and wait for him to stick his tongue in my mouth.

But nothing happens. We stay, lips lightly touching, for what seems an eternity until, as if by some strange telepathy, we open mouths simultaneously and our tongues meet in no man's land. Part of me's expecting a tentacle to grab my tits or something, and all the time I'm saying to myself, *You don't have to do this, you can walk away whenever you want*. Only I don't want to walk away. He tastes of salt-and-vinegar Pringles, and his breathing sounds like a tubercular tramp, but he's a phenomenal kisser. Where Philip tried to suck the life out of me, Michael is sweet and gentle and nervous and never once forgets that it's a duet not a flashy solo. It's just about the perfect kiss, and I want it to last for ever. But it's Michael who pulls away first.

'Don't stop . . . please!'

'I think you'd better go, Anna.'

'What are you talking about? That was lovely.'

'I know.'

'I don't understand. That's good, isn't it?'

'Please, just go.'

'What do you mean?'

'I mean, I don't think we should see each other any more.'

My mouth falls open. I let out a silent scream as it suddenly dawns on me exactly what he's saying. 'You mean, you're . . . dumping me?'

He nods and stares down at his kiddies' trainers.

This time my bitter laugh is for real. '*You're* dumping *me*? I don't believe this. You said I was the best thing that ever happened to you.'

'You are.'

'And you're just going to throw it all away?' (Why's he crying again? I'm the one who's being dumped.)

'It's wrong, Anna. I can't do this any more, it's not fair. You should have a proper boyfriend, not someone like me.'

'I don't want a "proper" boyfriend. *You're* the one that I want.'

'Well, I don't want you.'

'I can't believe how selfish you're being. I thought you were different, Michael. It turns out you're just like every other bloke.'

And just like every other bloke, he doesn't even know what he's done wrong. 'Hang on a minute, Anna. We can still be friends, can't we? What difference does it make?'

'You know what, why don't you just fuck off, yeah? I don't want to talk to you any more. In fact, I don't ever want to see you again.'

The Actor

By the time I get back to college, I'm beginning to think that things have probably worked out for the best. Valerie Owen is an admirable woman in many respects, but could I honestly cope with Michael as a stepson? Come to that, I don't suppose he'd crawl over hot coals to have me as his wicked stepfather.

Valerie's right about one thing, though: I do need to get myself some new interests. Masturbation's a young man's game, and what with the twenty-first century dawning, it's probably time I experimented with Internet pornography or some other form of self-improvement. One thing's for certain: I'm feeling a lot more sanguine than the tasty piece of jailbait who bursts from our rooms.

'What's the matter, Anna, lovers' tiff?'

'Leave me alone.'

'I didn't manage to catch up with you at the party, but I thought your performance this evening was beautifully felt – congratulations.'

Unlike every other actress of my acquaintance, she doesn't stick around to hear more. 'Oh, sod off.'

I check my flies and enter. These days, there's always a Mozart piano quartet or an early twentieth-century choral work playing in the background. It's such an improvement on the ghastly, thuddy stuff that nearly drove me to assisted suicide (his, not mine) when we first moved in. But tonight, what hits me first is the sound of silence. 'Michael, Michael, where are you?'

I step into the sepulchral gloom, secretly hoping that

Anna has put him to bed, thus sparing me the torture of having to browse through the catalogue of tonight's disasters with one of its principal protagonists. 'Is everything all right in here?'

I reach for the light switch and try to locate the origin of the high-pitched whimpering sound that cuts across the silence like a surgeon's knife. And I'm just about to contemplate the worst-case scenario when I realize that it's not coming from a mortally wounded rodent, but from the wheelchair by the window and its young occupant who appears to be sobbing his heart out.

'Michael, what's the trouble, old chap?' I draw closer so that I can see his face. 'Sorry I'm a bit late, only I got held up with . . .'

For once, I can honestly claim to be dumbstruck. It's such a disturbing image that for one terrible moment it feels as though I've stumbled into a rehearsal at the Royal Court. I've never seen someone in a wheelchair crying before. There's no earthly reason why Michael's tears should be any more disconcerting than the next man's. So why do I find myself reaching solicitously for the box of Kleenex, why am I thinking that as symbols go, a weeping man in a wheelchair is a pretty fair representation of the whole of humanity? 'What's the matter, Michael? What are you so upset about? Come on, why don't you tell me all about it?'

Five minutes later, I'm none the wiser. Michael appears to be in a state of shock. I'm reminded of that Agatha Christie season in Frinton, when the old soak playing the inspector dried on me, and I was forced to improvise for what seemed like decades. 'Your mother says goodnight, by the way.'

He looks so helpless, sitting there with that haunted expression and the last remains of an Elvis quiff, that I almost want to shake him by the hand, pat him on the back or some such. 'Nice perf by the way. I'm sure we'll make a verse speaker of you yet.' Up until just now, I had him down as just about the least vulnerable person I've ever met.

'*It's hard as rock, it looks just like my cock, CUCUM-BER, CUCUMBER.*'

'You'd think they'd be cold with no trousers on, wouldn't you?' I'm not unaccustomed to talking to myself, but it's still hard not to take this personally. 'Oh, come on, Michael, it can't be that bad.'

(It speaks! Thank the Lord for that.) 'Anna and me have split up.'

To be honest, I'm surprised their little *folie à deux* has lasted this long. However, in the light of Simon Butter-worth's comments when I told him that SOWINS had asked for a divorce, I won't be so insensitive as to point this out. 'Really, that is, er . . . how unfortunate. Still, these things happen to the best of us, you know. Tell me, how did she dump you? Not the old "can we still be friends" routine? I always think the most appropriate riposte to that old chestnut is, 'Yes, absolutely, so long as we can go on having casual sex together.' I mean, call me old-fashioned but—'

'It was me that ended it.'

'*What* did you say?'

'I was the one who ended it.'

That's what I thought he said. Even more amazingly, I have a strong suspicion that he's actually telling the truth. 'But why? I had the impression you were rather keen on the girl.'

'I was,' he whispers. 'What a tosser, eh?'

'Well, I wouldn't say that exactly.'

'Crips shouldn't have girlfriends. We should sit at the back with the rest of the spazzers, and wet our knickers every time some C-list celebrity wants us in their publicity shots.'

'That's show business for you, I suppose,' I say, trying to look on the bright side. 'And anyway, why worry about that when you've just given a very presentable Hamlet?'

This doesn't appear to console him. 'Who am I trying to kid? People like me never get to play the Prince, we're always the spacko little brother in the loony bin that Hugh Grant visits, every other weekend, to make him look more fuckable.'

'Sounds like a decent supporting role to me. I'd be lucky to get cast as the non-speaking psychiatrist who ogles his beautiful foreign girlfriend.'

'What's all this about beautiful girlfriends? Not talking about me, are you, boys?'

As soon as I hear Nikki Hardbody's voice, a reflex action compels me to hurl myself at Michael's wheelchair. 'What are you doing here?'

After recent events, she's the last person I expected to see. 'I came to say goodbye to you guys.'

Her camera doesn't appear to be loaded. I drop my

guard a little. 'I thought we'd already said our fond farewells.'

When he's handing out desirability, why does God always get it so wrong? 'It's Michael I really wanted to see. I just didn't want to hurt your feelings.'

'That's awfully decent of you,' I say, wishing that someone would invent a proper punctuation mark to denote extreme sarcasm. 'Thank you for your kind consideration.'

Nikki wraps herself around Michael's wheelchair like an importunate boa constrictor. 'I'll be down at Beachy Head for the next three weeks, shooting *Teenage Suicides*, but the launch party for *Wheelchair of Fire* is going to be amazing. Did I tell you Steven Hawking is really interested?'

'There isn't going to be a *Wheelchair of Fire*,' says Michael.

'Sorry, Michael, I don't think I heard you right. You'll have to speak up a bit.'

'I said, there isn't going to be a *Wheelchair of Fire*.'

Nikki plants a kiss on his quiff. 'Just you let me worry about that, Mike. I know you think a documentary about a quadriplegic will be like watching paint dry, but trust me, *Wheelchair* is so, so much more than that.'

A grotesque image of mother and son cavorting on the dance floor sets me nodding ruefully.

'Especially if you've reconsidered using that little gadget I bought you,' says Nikki hopefully. 'Ah, well, never mind, I'm sure you'll be an inspiration all the same. And if the great British public aren't up for a bit of inspiration, there's always a heart-warming love story for them to get their teeth into. And if they're complete fucking cynics, they'll just watch it for the incredible supporting cast. You wouldn't believe some of the stuff I got from your mother. Why, even chummo here,' (that's me, I'll warrant) 'is a bit of a character in his own sad way.'

'You don't understand,' says Michael. 'There's not going to be any *Wheelchair of Fire* because I don't want any part of it.'

Nikki lets out a cautious giggle. 'That's what I like about you, Mike – you haven't lost your sense of humour.'

Michael doesn't look like he's joking. 'I mean it, Nikki. I won't have you using me. And I won't have you making a fool of my mum either. So why don't you stuff your documentary up your cute little arse, and get the fuck out of my face?'

Nikki is also having difficulty seeing the funny side. 'I'd like to, of course,' she says in the soft and reasonable tones of the hired assassin, 'but that's why I always get my subjects to sign consent forms first. It can save an awful lot of unpleasantness.'

'I've changed my mind,' says Michael. 'My life is degrading enough without broadcasting it to the nation.'

'Yes, well, this is my life too,' says Nikki, 'and I can't afford to have it ruined by a bashful teenager.' Suddenly she reminds me of the DHSS official who first consigned me to this hellhole. 'You see, you and your mother did sign those consent forms, Michael, so I'm afraid you have no choice.'

I'm surprised as anyone that the next voice I hear is my own. 'Sorry to be a bore and all that, Nikki, but *I* didn't sign anything. Equity are rather particular about that sort of thing, I'm afraid.'

Her mocking laughter sounds like a cat trying to exorcise a hairball. 'And what a loss that would be. Still, it's up to you, Tim. If you don't want to be in it, I'll just have to edit you out – easy peasy.'

'One would have thought so. However, I think you'll find I feature rather heavily. In fact, I do believe I'm in virtually every shot.'

Nikki looks momentarily flummoxed. A few seconds later her face relaxes into a triumphant grin. 'I think you're forgetting something, Timothy. If there's no documentary, then there's no voice-over. I thought that was an area you were rather keen to get into.'

Twenty years of humiliation processes in front of me; a long line of theatrical managements and producers, critics and casting directors, anyone to do with the National Theatre, that woman from *The Bill*, each one of them finding a slightly different way of conveying the same message: 'Fuck off and die, Timothy.' *Wheelchair of Fire* could change all that. Nikki hovers above me in her helicopter; the rope ladder of dignity dangling just above my head. All I have to do is jump.

'Do you know,' I say, not even pausing to question my sanity, 'I'm really not that bothered about it. You'd better give Martin Jarvis a ring.'

Nikki has no doubts about my mental state. 'What, are you crazy? I mean, take a look at yourself, Timothy. I don't want to be unkind or anything, but you really are one of the saddest losers I've ever come across. This is a once-in-a-lifetime opportunity. You're not really going to throw it all away out of some ridiculous sense of misplaced loyalty?'

'I'm with Michael, actually. As you so rightly point out, my life is also degrading enough without broadcasting it to the nation.'

'Well, I didn't mean . . .' Nikki looks like a cornered animal; an instinct for self-preservation leading her to yet lower depths of desperation. 'Actually, you're quite attractive in a strange sort of way.' She walks towards me, hips swinging. I try to divert my gaze from her mesmerizing mammaries. 'In fact, I thought we could get together some time. How about tonight? Do you see what I'm saying, Tim?'

'Sorry, Nikki, you're not really my type. What price dignity, eh, Michael?'

For once, the actor and the quadriplegic are in complete agreement. 'You're not wrong there, Tim.'

'Think you're so clever, don't you?' says Nikki. 'Well, it might be funny to you, pissing all over someone's hard-earned career, but actually, it's just pathetic.' She stabs her index finger at us and backs towards the exit. 'And don't give me all that bullshit about dignity. Every man has his price – I should know, I work in television.'

It's late, and probably highly inadvisable with my middle-aged prostate, but it seems to me that there's only one appropriate way to celebrate her departure. 'Tell you what, Michael, I've got something rather special in my room. How do you fancy a coffee?'

*

At £16.54 per 250 grams the Jamaican Blue Mountain is a rather expensive olive branch. Fortunately, Michael seems to savour it as much as I do.

'Cheers, Timothy. You know something? For a sad loser, you make an excellent coffee.'

Epilogue
Autumn 2008

The Virgin

It must be a London thing. A couple of times a year, I feel so guilty about not getting my state-recommended dose of culture that I toddle off to the Tate Modern to stock up on arty postcards, or brace myself for lunchtime Lieder at Wigmore Hall.

Last week, I was coming out of a matinee at the National Theatre when I stumbled into a chance meeting right out of one of those nineteenth-century novels a certain Oxford acquaintance of mine was so snotty about. Given that I hadn't set foot anywhere near a stage since that too too shaming performance of *Hamlet* and that, ordinarily, wild horses wouldn't have dragged me within a hundred miles of a play about pimps and drug dealers (thank you very much!), it really was the mother of all coincidences.

Drizzle was the order of the day, as it so often is on the

South Bank. I stared into the grey, choppy waters and wondered whether I should have found little presents for the children. I was on the point of making a mercy dash to the gift shop for something slyly improving, when a roar of communal laughter averted a Pavlovian lunge for my credit card.

A crowd had gathered on the walkway. At first I thought it must be another tiresome demonstration. When I realized it was just the audience for a rather feeble-looking pair of buskers, I decided to have a look-see. I don't normally do crowds, but something I'd read in a book I picked up at the South Ken Cancer Shop had made me a tiny bit braver than usual. My husband thought that *Be Your Own Psychotherapist in One Weekend* was a splendid joke – which is why I stopped reading it in bed. But I was still working my way through the 'Rules for Life' and if it hadn't been for number twelve *('Try to go beyond your current "mindset" by exploring parts of yourself that you are reluctant to expose'),* I would almost certainly have given the buskers a miss. So I hovered at the back, not wanting to be drawn into some vile act of audience participation, poised to make my escape should an accomplice with a hat suddenly materialize.

The two performers were fast approaching their climax. The Prime Minister was bent over a unicycle, exposing his plastic, comedy bottom. The crowd whooped deliriously as the President of the United States buggered him with a stars-and-stripes dildo. Quite frankly, it was actually rather sick making. As my husband is always saying, 'Political satire's a piece of piss when you don't have to come up with a single bloody policy.'

I suppose I'm a bit of a sucker for waifs and strays. I can't think of any other reason I would have stuck around to watch the pair of them getting changed. I didn't recognize him at first. It was only after he'd squeezed his comedy bottom into a canvas holdall and taken out his tobacco that I realized who he was. His hairline had retreated a couple of centimetres, but age had not withered his finely chiselled features, and he still smoked like a 1950s movie star.

I thought it would be kinder not to make myself known; by the age of twenty-nine he ought to have been running the National Theatre, not being buggered in the streets outside. And anyway, I wasn't sure if he'd forgiven me. He'd been quite convinced that I was responsible for Michael's withdrawal from *Hamlet*, and when that ghastly woman's documentary failed to materialize he stopped speaking to me altogether.

In the end, it was Philip who made the first move. 'Anna? It is you, isn't it? Didn't recognize you with your hair like that.'

I couldn't remember the last time I'd done anything new with my hair. 'Philip, hi . . . nice to see you . . . shame about the weather.'

'Hey, Klaus,' he called to his acting companion, 'over here, there's someone I want you to meet.' He was a lot more affable than the last time I'd bumped into him, on Magdalen Bridge, when he'd accused me of 'trying to ruin' his 'fucking life'. 'This is Anna. We were at Oxford together.'

Klaus wasn't half so scary without his strapadicktomy. 'Pleased to meet you, Anna.'

'Tell you what,' said Philip, 'got time for a quick coffee? You don't mind, do you, mate?'

Klaus shook his head and wandered back to his juggling balls.

'Sorry, Philip, I really should be getting back.'

'Yes, yes, of course,' he said. 'You must be a very busy lady.'

The moment he popped his fist into his mouth, I had to relent. 'Well, maybe a quick one then – for old times' sake.'

Philip insisted on the National Film Theatre café. He was engrossed in a continuous loop of a black-and-white Hungarian masterpiece when I arrived at the table with his coffee.

'It's nice in here,' I said, trying to ignore the terrible china and the organic-muffin-infested beards.

'The coffee's not up to much,' he said, 'but they show some interesting movies now and then.' He emptied four sachets of demerara into his cappuccino and I tried to think of a subtle way of bringing the conversation round to *Hamlet*.

'You remember that rather sad character who looked after Michael for a bit? The one who always said he was an actor? We saw him on telly the other night. You'll never guess what he was doing.'

Philip shrugged. I noticed an angry scar where his nose stud should have been.

'It was ever so funny. He was in that ad for piles cream.

You always said he was a pain in the arse!' My fake laughter was not as infectious as I'd hoped it might be.

Philip attacked his froth with a teaspoon. 'I suppose he's only doing what he has to do. It's a tough world out there.'

'Yes, I suppose it is,' I said, half wondering if he still carried his silver cigarette case. 'Listen, Philip, I never did get to say sorry about *Hamlet*.'

'There's no need,' he said. 'I was a prat. I didn't know who the hell I was back then. You did me a favour. It should be me who's apologizing.'

I couldn't help smiling; nine years ago Philip's admission would have made the front page of the *Oxford Gazette*. 'I guess I had a few issues of my own!'

'I hear you two have got kids now,' he said. 'That's amazing.'

I didn't say that we'd been forced to adopt. 'Two boys, Theo and Jack.'

It was Philip who brought it up; I wasn't going to mention it. 'Michael seems to be doing very well for himself.'

'Yes,' I said, trying not to sound too triumphant, 'I'm really pleased for him.' There was no need to go into detail. Like the world and his wife, Philip was bound to have come across Michael's blog. (*Postcards from the Veg* is a wry look at the often hilarious life of a disabled guy in the twenty-first century.) And I was quite sure he'd have read the rave reviews for his one-man show *A Wank at Oxford*. He might not have known about the Five Live phone-in yet, or the fact that I had it on very good authority that Mike was about to be created the new Tsar for the disabled, but I didn't say anything because it might have looked like bragging. 'Don't listen to all that nonsense about how much he hates being "Britain's favourite celebrity cripple". He loves it, I know he does.'

'What did you think of the show?' said Philip, after a long pause.

'You know me,' I said. 'I'm not terribly knowledgeable about crack whores.'

'Not that crap,' he said, waving at my programme, '*the* show, Klaus and me. Great, wasn't it?'

'To tell you the truth, I only caught the, er . . . finale, but it looked very interesting.'

'Like I said, you did me a favour, babe. Building-based projects are so last century. 9/11 changed everything. I wouldn't touch the RSC now if they got down on their bended fucking knees and begged me to.'

'Really?'

'We call it Theatre Bombing,' he said, eyes flaring like they used to. 'My idea, *zeitgeisty* or what? One minute we're on the South Bank, next minute we might turn up in the Arndale Centre Manchester or the Metro. Believe me, Anna, it's the only way to win hearts and minds.'

'Yes, right, if you say so.'

'I always knew I was a great director. I didn't realize I was a brilliant actor too.'

I could hear my gin and tonic summoning me all the way from Chiswick. 'Gosh, is that the time? Sorry, Philip, got to dash, I'm afraid.' I know it was naughty of me, but after all that gumph about 'hearts and minds', a little parting shot was impossible to resist: 'Will we be seeing you at Michael's movie premiere?'

'No,' he said, the light in his eyes clicking off abruptly, 'I've got far more important fish to fry.'

'Yes, well, catch you in the Arndale Centre perhaps.'

When I looked back, he was chewing thoughtfully on his knuckles.